DRĒMA DRUDGE

Southern-Fried Woolf

A Novel

First published by Wit & Whimsy 2023

This novel is entirely a work of fiction. The names, characters and incidents portrayed in it are the work of the author's imagination. Any resemblance to actual persons, living or dead, events or localities is entirely coincidental.

Drēma Drudge asserts the moral right to be identified as the author of this work.

Library of Congress Cataloging-in-Publication Data. Drudge, Drema. Southern-Fried Woolf. I. Title Library of Congress Control Number: 2022923097

First edition

ISBN: 979-8-9870315-1-3

This book was professionally typeset on Reedsy. Find out more at reedsy.com

For Barry Drudge, husband and life partner extraordinaire... let me use your words: "What would I be, without you..." (Lyrics copyright 1992 Barry Drudge)

Contents

Foreword   ii

Preface   iv

Acknowledgement   vii

Chapter 1   1

Chapter 2   29

Chapter 3   36

Chapter 4   55

Chapter 5   60

Chapter 6   87

Chapter 7   96

Chapter 8   110

Chapter 9   140

Chapter 10   150

Chapter 11   162

Chapter 12   176

Chapter 13   187

Chapter 14   220

About the Author   274

Foreword

Preface

The book by Virginia Woolf that I most want to read is one that, alas, I cannot, because it does not exist in final form. She conceived of a bold experiment, a novel-essay, that she wanted to call *The Pargiters*. It would have been just what it sounds like: the alternating of fiction and fact in one book concerning women's rights (or lack thereof) and their intimate lives.

No one knows for certain why she abandoned the attempt, but it couldn't have come naturally to such an accomplished novelist, switching between the two in the same book. And it's not as if she didn't have her say about women's rights: all of her writing is full of challenges to society's viewpoint and expectations regarding women. Ultimately, however, she folded the novel portion of her novel-essay efforts into the 1880 chapter of *The Years* without finishing her initially conceived project.

This novel of mine is intended, first of all, as an homage. This is my love letter to Woolf's writing. It's also an invitation to those unfamiliar with Woolf to learn a bit about her. I am no Woolf scholar, though I deeply admire her writing, fiction and otherwise. There is such beauty, such depth of thinking and feeling, to her work. Such precision. I love her daring style, how she attempted so many forms of literature. I learn every time I open one of her novels. I learn about not only writing, but about what it is to be human.

Woolf's novels are not immediately accessible, at least they weren't to this reader, who grew up primarily on Reader's Digest Condensed Books and Harlequin romances, on the exciting boxes of eclectic books my father brought home from auctions. I didn't encounter Woolf until college, and it took discipline to settle down with her essays. Then I read *Orlando*, that strange and wonderful novel, and I didn't know what to make of it or Woolf, though I knew the writing was gorgeous and that it spoke beyond the obvious, something I craved.

It wasn't until I read *Lighthouse* that I quit being too intimidated of Woolf's writing to read deeply. I re-read the novel numerous times, and even now I return to it for poetic prose and wisdom. It's as much mine now as anyone's, something that can (and should) be said of all of the arts. That's one of the reasons I married Woolf with country music in my novel.

Whether before or after you read *Southern-Fried Woolf*, I invite, nay, implore you to read Virginia Woolf's *To the Lighthouse*. And while you can read my novel and fully understand it without reading *Lighthouse*, these books speak directly to one another, an open case of intertextuality.

Why the title of my novel, *Southern-Fried Woolf*? First of all, yes, I am worried that people might think I can't spell "wolf" when they see my novel's title. But I wanted to combine two very unlike things, creating a fusion of literature, if you will. Since my husband is a musician and we lived in Nashville for five years, I thought Woolf and country music would be very different sensibilities to rub together. That excited me. It's a way of honoring two very different sides of myself, too.

And I really wanted to write about country music. The richness of storytelling in the genre speaks to me, and having been brought up in the South for part of my life, it has been with me since childhood. I'm especially interested in songwriting. Dolly Parton, Loretta Lynn, Johnny Cash, on and on. Classic country forever!

While I don't pretend that what I have written reaches Woolf's original intent in writing a novel/essay (mine is very much a novel with a light essay component), it does match mine, and I am thankful to have, as painter Lily Briscoe does in *To the Lighthouse*, "had my vision." Thank you for joining me on my journey.

Drēma Drudge

Acknowledgement

Love and thanks to:

—To Barry, my chosen life partner, spouse, father to my kiddos, the man who makes me cry with laughter and weep at his thoughtful gestures. Who hears "I have an idea" and doesn't run from my crazy schemes. Who reminds me it's perfectly fine to do absolutely nothing some days, but who is the first one there if I need help. My heart is always full when I look at you. I love you.

—As ever, my and Barry's beloved children, Mia and Zack. I am so proud of you, every day. Your father and I know better than others your journeys. Watching you navigate life's highs and lows has been/is inspirational, and I will always believe in you. My heart expands three sizes when I think of you two.

— My family and family-in-love, all! XOXO!

— The Pages & Platforms Team: Sue Campbell, Anne Hawley, Rachelle Ramirez, and Ruth Shepard. The hugest hugs to you all! What a fun team!

— Ashley B. Davis, a writing friend, a gift who led the way in self-pubbing. So many thanks!

— All of our MFA Payday guests and listeners. It's such a delight to host the podcast. We're ever learning.

Though I didn't repeat all of the names of those I acknowledged in my first book, you remain an integral part of my writing, past and future, and I will be forever grateful.

Chapter 1

2018

I push my whining phone across the bed with my toes until it dangles over the edge like an imperiled onscreen Marvel superhero. Not that it stops ringing. I admire my freshly polished toenails, (sunset chrome, very cool), but force my fingers to return to the home keys while my thoughts hunt for a similar perch. I sweep my hair off my shoulder with determination; my graduate thesis I have nicknamed Beastis is due too soon to allow interruptions of any kind, I sternly warn myself. I thwart the creeping dusk with the twist of a lamp switch to extend the day, and I once again position my fingers. This time, I actually move them:

In what has been seen by some as her most autobiographical work, Virginia Woolf weaves into her novel, To the Lighthouse, a "femininely" knitted and "masculinely" knotted marriage of covert and subtle madness, though not one without warmth and love. She challenges the reader with a paradox: She makes sacred the domestic arena while revealing madness by the domestic activities themselves, thus showing us the "twisted (and twisting) finger" of one of the main characters, Mrs. Ramsay....

1

...and of herself," I type while frowning at my insistent phone, while wondering how much shit I'll get for using the word madness, and especially in relation to Woolf. I highlight it to consider it carefully in light of previous and present scholarship, to decide if it even makes sense to use it.

Hell, madness is a word literature has pretty much co-opted for centuries. Then again, it's also one that can be seen as making light of mental illness. That's a topic for my feminist mother, "madness" in women in literature.

The marimba stops, then almost immediately resumes, bones on metal, and finally it registers that the noise is my husband's ringtone.

I groan and lean across the time-softened quilt for my phone. My shifting sends a cascade of mini-chocolate bar wrappers onto the floor as I rescue the phone just as it vibrates over the edge.

Wait, could this call mean Michael actually *wants* to speak to me, even though he has Queen Velvet around? Hope grows the flimsiest bones and then sags back to the ground, the garbage cartilage it was to begin with. Hope, the enemy of peace. Sponsored by Tanqueray and tonic, my thesis writing beverage of choice.

Staying home this leg of the tour was so I could work on my monstrously overdue thesis (not to mention the screaming-towards-us Ride 'Em Benefit), not tell the band which bus cabinet the TP is hiding in. Some days I feel half road manager (which I am), half toddler wrangler (which I have repeatedly shouted that I am not).

After months of research, of Pinterest boards full of quotes and sources, of online JSTOR searches so extensive and particular if the search engine had been human it would

2

have chortled, after false starts and over fifty proposed thesis statements, after asking myself (and my mother) again and again what I want to say so my advisor won't have to sort my thoughts for me like a drawer of mismatched socks, I finally have a long, admittedly conjoined, couple of sentences with as many branches and as much punctuation as I think I can get by with, though it *still* doesn't embrace all I want to explore about Woolf and domesticity, about anything and everything Woolf, and most especially, about all things *Lighthouse*.

A well-crafted thesis statement launches the logic and thus the essay, so it is imperative to get that right, or so says my mother. This might be the one, *the* thesis statement. It feels close.

I sit up and hit the talk button on my phone harder than necessary.

"Hey, Briscoe," Ben says, his voice billy goat deep but gentle as a kid's. It can't be good news if the huggable one is calling, and from Michael's phone.

It isn't.

Michael, I am informed, has fallen off the stage during a show and sprained his arm; Ben claims an Ace bandage and a sling will take care of it.

"Hand Michael the phone." With a musician, any arm or hand injury is potentially worrisome. Ben says that the doctor is still finishing up with Michael.

"Fine. I'll book myself a flight." I open Kayak, click on the "flights" tab, and plug in "Alabama."

"No, it's just a minor sprain," Ben says.

My fingers freeze at the edge of panic in his voice which seems more at the thought of me flying to them than about Michael's welfare. My suspicion rises, and "not again" knots in

3

me. I wonder if I'll finally get the Tiffany's sapphire necklace to complete the ring and bracelet set if I'm right. Or maybe I'll ask for earrings this time.

"I'll have him call you in the morning, after his pain killer has worn off."

In the background, Michael shouts at someone to leave him alone.

My involuntary ab crunch vaults me into a sitting position and knocks my MacBook onto the floor.

"Ben, hand him the phone."

"Hang on," Ben says. A door slams, and I hear a muffled announcement made by the hospital's public address system blares – some doctor needing to report to some room.

I pick up my computer, shake it gently, relieved nothing shakes back.

"Ben? Benny?"

Finally I get a response. "He'd had a few, said he'd open for himself when V. had to leave unexpectedly."

"Idiot."

At the best of times, Michael is not inhibited. I count it a mercy he fell off the stage before he could remove his pants. Not that he ever has, but you never know, if it might get him attention.

"He must have had more than a few," I say, belatedly scrolling through social media, which tells me plenty about the incident, except why Velvet fled the tour. It slowly sinks in.

"V. left? Why wasn't I notified?"

If I'd known I was going to be called upon to be rational, I would have started drinking earlier and less leisurely.

Michael's tumble explains my phone pinging like it was possessed about an hour ago. I had convinced myself to

4

ignore the messages because I assumed they were related to the show, how great Michael was, etc. Where exactly has Patrick, Personal Assistant and Keeper of All Things Social Media, been, though, to tell me what was going on?

I click on one of the videos so courteously provided by my followers and watch Michael's not-so-glamorous fall. As he lands on his arm, my eyelids slam, and my stomach clenches.

On the video, fans come forward to help, security pushes through. The person recording moves unsteadily closer to Michael, who rolls over and groans. The clip ends. I play it again, pausing it right as Michael's face turns towards the camera. Oh, god. He closes his eyes as if he's been defeated by David and his slingshot.

But why *hasn't* Patrick alerted me? Heads. Will. You know.

"If it's only his arm, tell him to call me, no matter how late. Nothing wrong with his mouth, is there?" I say to Ben as I text Patrick, who is only in town because he drove me back to Nashville so we could prep for the benefit as the rest of the crew headed to one last concert before coming home long enough for Michael to cohost the event with me.

I turn my laptop back on. It still works, a minor miracle performed by the surely minor angel assigned to me because *I'm* not the star of my marriage. I need a lanyard with a badge reading "Support Staff" to wear all the freaking time.

Ben breathes into the phone, which is about as excitable as he gets. That's usually comforting.

"I've asked Joy to have brunch with you tomorrow."

"Why?" I hope my tone doesn't reveal my dislike of his wife. She works in the health care industry in some high-level capacity, and mercifully, I don't have to interact with her much.

"Just...please, Briscoe. I don't want you to be alone right now."

I hang up without promising to have brunch with his irritating wife, and I watch the video again, guessing new answers to a couple of questions.

Like why it was suddenly okay for me to leave the tour for a few days when Michael has always insisted on having me in his pocket, or at least immediately accessible for troubleshooting for those times when Patrick isn't tough enough. It explains why Michael now cares about my schooling when he regularly laughs at my mother's academic fetish that I have contracted. He literally howls every time one of us says "Woolf."

This same man told me to "Go, go, go" when I confided how worried I was about being able to meet the deadline for submitting my overdue thesis and prepping for the benefit. (I should have come home sooner, but I was afraid to leave him alone. Rightly so, wouldn't you say?)

I shoot Michael a text: *Call me* before remembering Ben has Michael's phone. No answer. For a few seconds I contemplate calling V., or even Robert, V.'s husband. But you don't make calls when you don't want to know the answer to what you *have* to ask if you do call.

The possibility that *my* husband of a decade has been with that moth-eaten Southern Belle who dresses in head-to-toe Manuel or its ilk...not a rhinestone within the lower 48 safe from her. (No shade to Manuel's gorgeous work, obviously.)

Michael's atrocious taste usually amuses me, but I hadn't thought his sexual and romantic inclinations so banal, so textbook tacky country. Even if he is a hat act with an insatiable need to be adored. Typical performer personality.

Not entirely true. Therefore, not entirely false.

6

A quick call to Janice, Michael's publicist, to fill her in (but she's already seen the news) and tell her I'll send her a release to approve as soon as I can. I hang up without saying goodbye, without explaining why I feel the need to write it myself.

My fingers type five different scenarios as quickly as possible to release to the press. The last one: "Because he's a selfish prick who doesn't know what he has, and he's had a musical crush on V. since he was a teen." That one seems truest, not that Janice would ever let me send that one out. I email her the mildest one and await her tweaking.

I go find more tonic water and lime, ice, and most importantly, more Tanqueray.

After pacing our bedroom, I strip the bed and toss everything into the corner to avoid even the idea of Michael's scent. I spread the antique quilt back atop the naked bed and hop onto it, wondering how many stories the quilt has borne witness to. My and Michael's is just one more. Someday, it will belong to the past, too. (It smells of the past, not of Michael, I am relieved to discover.)

The inevitability of death has never frightened me. Opposite, really.

I turn off the lamp and watch the darkness finish conquering the sky out my window before turning it back on and running for the bathroom, my hands over my mouth.

With damp eyes and fresh breath, I get back to work. They don't call it the ivory tower for nothing. In the event that I *have* had a breakthrough, I email my mother my current thesis statement and text her to check her inbox, wishing my words to convey what I won't allow myself to mention. She lives alone on a mountainside, so I think I know what her advice would be about my marriage.

7

Sucking on a piece of ice, all that remains in my glass, I fire off more useless texts to the band, then hunker back over the laptop.

Mother responds. Let the clouds part; let the sun shine – she approves of my thesis statement. Actually, she says "This works."

It's enough. I drill at the thesis, erecting guideposts, a frame. I've come to enjoy this intellectual stimulation that is the antithesis of writing country songs.

Before you get your cut-offs in a twist, I don't mean that disparagingly. Country music is meant for the emotions, and I love it for that. I need it. God, how I do. Intellectualism has no place in *it*. But academia is a marvelous place to hide.

I don my manager hat and, not ignoring my phone now, soothe venue owners and friends, promising answers as soon as I have them; I wisely leave social media for Patrick, wherever he is. Not answering my texts and calls, that's for sure.

The brawny aroma of gin and the citric tang of lime fill my nose and mouth as I make myself another drink.

As I fight down nausea again, half-seen images from the road come to mind, things I wouldn't allow myself to comprehend before. They didn't have to throw it in my face. I left them alone, didn't even confront them before I left; what more did they want? I wasn't even sure it was happening. When I asked Patrick, he avoided the conversation so adroitly that in retrospect I know he either knew or had his suspicions.

Bottomless lust. Humans clutching onto one another as if anything could stop the inevitable.

I think of inventing a reason to wake our housekeeper, Bernita, but what would I say?

I glance at the title of my essay once again.

Knitting and Knotting: The Paradox of Domesticity in *To the Lighthouse*

Heart aching, I begin with the quote that started me thinking from the get-go. That twisted finger seemed no throw-away item when I noticed it.

"What was the spirit in her, the essential thing, by which, had you found a crumpled glove in the corner of a sofa, you would have known it, from its twisted finger, hers indisputably?...she opened bedroom windows. She shut doors. (So she tried to start the tune of Mrs. Ramsay in her head)" <u>To the Lighthouse</u> (26).

I add the definition of *twisted* from the OED, Oxford English Dictionary, the dictionary's dictionary, so that I don't appear to be cherry picking. I mean you always are when it comes to essays, because there's no other way to do it, but you're not supposed to *seem* like it.

I check on when *twisted* was first used to mean unbalanced to be sure I'm on the right track. I am. You don't, Mother has drilled into me, want to give the committee any excuse to reject your work. They will find enough holes anyway, no matter how carefully you write, she says.

There's also the combining nature of twisted, as in braiding; I make a note.

My mother suggested early on that I add my personal thoughts on Woolf's novel to my essay to warm up the committee. She spat out at the time that this is a recent academic "concession to readability and accessibility." She disapproves of those who think academic jargon is BS. (That would be me and anyone, say, under 35.)

Accessibility. That's what I love about country music. It's

utterly relatable, even for those who refuse to acknowledge that it is. It's take-off-your-Spanx and stay awhile. It's "feel every last pain or drink a beer or two and forget anything hurts. Your choice."

I first read To the Lighthouse *all in one sitting.*

Which, as you will learn, isn't entirely true. It *is* true of the first time I read it as an adult. *Its sentences and point-of-view shifts thrilled me with their complexity, with the novel's mundane subject raised to the level of worthy of Woolf's scrutiny. Which made me dislike my own life a little less and find it deserving of examination, too.*

The next day, I read the novel again. In all, I read it six times before I felt comfortable talking about it; the novel's intricacy and cleverness demand and reward more than a single reading. What drew me most was Woolf's complicated stance on domesticity. It confused me. Why were there such moments of discontent and near madness in the book related to the topics of marriage and parenthood, paralleled with moments of tenderness in the Ramsays' own marriage? Why elevate domesticity to an art at times, but then make it seem mindless and unfulfilling?

And underneath those socially acceptable questions (because literature), my heart asking, am I no better than a fool?

For the academics in the balcony, and to maintain my sanity while I wait for my jester, here:

The paradox manifests, unexpectedly, in the structure and style of To the Lighthouse. *It plays itself out in the choice of specific words and is reflected in the larger overview of the novel. Both in its details and its framework, the novel dynamically expresses the self-contradictions of Mrs. Ramsay (and Woolf herself) when it comes to the role of nurturer, caretaker, wife, and domestic angel. The "angel in the house" was a Victorian ideal, a wife who was*

10

submissive and devoted to her husband and household in all things. She was self-sacrificing and pious.

The Ramsays' astute son, James, comments upon the ambiguity of life: "For nothing was simply one thing" (95). This phrase keys us into Woolf's design. If we forget to apply this to the entire novel, however satisfying that upper layer might be, we miss its rich, meaty core.

To make her point, Woolf uses symbols, as writers do: a boot is not just footwear on Mr. Ramsay – it symbolizes his discontent and desire – it represents the journeys he would like to make with those shoes. By having James tell us outright that everything is more than one thing, Woolf invites us to reexamine her writing for symbols, a practice not unfamiliar to readers of Woolf, or, indeed, to literature as a whole.

In part, the ambiguity of domesticity in To the Lighthouse is bound up in Woolf's choice of multifaceted words. One I focus on is the word "twisted," as seen in the opening quote, a word that can be negative (as in a snarl) or positive (uniting).

Woolf chooses a young woman who wants to be a painter, Lily Briscoe, a house guest determined to have her "vision" upon canvas, to "see" the Ramsays' marriage as art for us.

Mrs. Ramsay insists that Lily must marry, as if all young women must, but Lily does not wish to marry. Throughout the novel, Lily repeatedly gazes at the Ramsays' marriage, at the complex relationship, at her own longing to be a painter, rather than a wife, examining them with her paintbrush. She cannot bring herself to desire such a union or be part of an institution she views with ambivalence at best.

To lend to the argument that Lily is studying marriage, (as is Woolf), in the abstract, rather than individuals, neither of the Ramsays is given first names in the novel, something this reader finds disconcerting and dehumanizing for the characters, however much she understands the author's aim. Here, perhaps more than anywhere, we see remnants of Woolf's original ambition that became part of her novel The Years *– to write a novel essay, something that will be revisited later.*

It says even more about Woolf's relationship with her own mother and her own leanings towards art rather than motherhood if Mrs. Ramsay symbolizes Woolf's mother, and it's safe to say she does. Woolf's family vacationed at a place similar to this when Woolf was a child, which also nods to the autobiographical.

****

Since Michael won't contact me, regardless of what Ben says, I'll go to him. I send Patrick a text telling him I have to take off and that he should hire temps if he needs extra help prepping for Ride 'Em. Not that he does – his checklists have checklists. We're nearly ready. As much as I hate to desert him, I can't think about tablecloths just now.

I pack and jump into my car, but a vehicle swoops into the drive before I can leave it. Patrick hops out and literally stands in front of the car in his red Iron Man pajamas with outstretched hands while I tell him to move and curse him until he motions for me to get out.

After I bless him out for not being on top of The Story, and only half hear his lame-ass excuse (something about an argument with his boyfriend, the extended version), I stand with my arms crossed while he tries to explain why it makes no sense for me to go, especially since he needs my help. (*He* is the one helping *me*, but whatever.)

"Let Michael sleep it off. Ben swears he's bringing him home as soon as the doctor okay's it. They just want to be sure he doesn't have a concussion."

"A concussion? Nobody said anything about a concussion."

"No, he doesn't for sure *have* one; it's routine to keep patients overnight to be sure they're okay."

"I know that. Everyone knows that. But are you sure they don't think he has one?"

I lean against my car door, the faintly vanilla scent coming from the partially opened car window competing with my ire. Insects chorus, asking me if I really want to go to Alabama.

Not so much. And does Michael *deserve* to have me rush to his side just because he decided to be Public Idiot #1?

I take the opportunity to razz Patrick mercilessly about the pj's, naturally, before sending him for Round 2 with his guy.

"Listen, I know you're Iron Man and all, but trying using your words and not your gadgets on him, 'k?"

He put his hand to his forehead and staggered. "RDJ..."

We both adore Robert Downey Junior, incipient wrinkles and all. Who doesn't love a wiseass?

Patrick doesn't apologize, but he looks hangdog enough that I kiss him on the cheek, and he says I should have that brunch with Joy. Except I haven't told him about the invite. So yeah, a part of me knows to get ready, get ready, get ready like that preacher on TV says. But the part of me that wants to be face down in cake at least three hours a day already knows.

Considering, my preparations involve ordering a cake. Happy Fake Birthday to every damn acre of my expanding posterior end.

****

Sleep denied, the next morning I groan around the house, shove the remains of the cake down the trash disposal, and chase it with water, then ready myself for brunch with Joy. I care about Benny, dammit, so of course I'll go, regardless of my light cake-and-gin hangover.

Eventually, I'm dressed and made up (red Grecian-style blouse, dark wash jeans). My hair is brushed and clipped up. I pull on heeled white sandals to give me a tiny hint of height aided by the rise of hair at the front of my head.

I can't get out of our gates: news vans and reporters with mics and cameras block the driveway of our mini mansion on Moran Road. I wave and yell out the window for them to let me through. They know better than to be on private property.

I duck my head and stomp the gas with what must be a wicked grin.

The reporters run towards my vehicle for a statement. I go. I continue unimpeded when my foot nudges the gas pedal, so I assume I've successfully cleared them with no to minimal loss of life. I suppose the news will tell me soon enough of anything to the contrary. Musicians have great lawyers, so whatever. (Jesus, I can feel your judgment. So maybe I peeked over the dash at the last minute and my path was clear. Way to ruin my story.)

Brunch, as expected, is agendaed. This is Nashville. No one gets together just to eat, although get-togethers always include food. Which those of us under a certain age and above a certain status studiously avoid.

Why is it the more money you make, the less food you're supposed to eat?

I have had my pre-brunch shop, feeling the hollowness of too many bags in my trunk, but preferring that to more cake. Maybe. At least for now. It's hard to avoid the shops at Green Hills, especially when I'm in a mood because denying myself just serves to remind me of all the times my father and I did without.

At the chic Green Hills restaurant, Etc., Joy covers my hand with hers and says how "sorry" she was to hear the news.

Our food arrives, apple and kale salad for me, the roasted beet salad for her, grilled sour dough on the side for us both that neither of us will touch.

Joy insists on us clinking our wine glasses together as the colorful plates are arranged before us, and my "smile" surely qualifies as little more than a grimace.

After the server leaves us with a promise to return to refill our water glasses, I reclaim my hand and assure Joy that Michael will fine in no time, noting how she pretends to hide her triumphant smile with a too-late head duck: Haven't I heard? She is sorry to be the "bearer of bad news," but Ben let "slip," (her hand now crossing her chest) — Michael is having an affair with Velvet (or, as we all call her, V. Appropriate nickname, wouldn't you say?). According to Joy, when V. told Michael she couldn't stand the guilt and was leaving the tour, Michael got drunk. Quickly. Then, the fall.

You're afraid your "Oh, that rumor again" doesn't sound convincing, so you stay for another half hour, finger the stray strand of hair hanging out from the front of her so-last-decade ponytail-through-ballcap style, ask if she's ever thought of getting highlights. Order another glass of wine. You're so convincing she asks for your stylist's number, which you promise to text her. You won't.

When she heads to the bathroom you gulp from her wine glass, gargle, and spit the liquid back into it. Then you pull out a Xany, dangle it over her drink, and reconsider. At least she told you. You swallow the pill yourself, something you ever only take when you're under mega stress. You realize you are referring to yourself in second person in your head, probably

15

so you don't implode. You will encourage her to "drink up" when she returns. You will not finish yours. Because driving.

You'd have to be naïve to have not entertained at least the possibility this seasonal infidelity of Michael's could come around again, and of course, you strongly suspected it had. But with *V.?* Too bad you're not writing as much as you used to, because country songwriting benefits from a constant chaffing of the sorrow bone.

While you wait for Joy to return (ironic name), you open your purse and contemplate swallowing another pill. You refrain. In this marriage, one of you has to have some self-control, no matter how slim a margin. You try not to think about that sluggish kitchen drain this morning after its meal of stale cake.

I expend any remnant of restraint saying goodbye to Joy. I deny her news again even as I pull her in for a hug, slide her colorful Hermes scarf from her neck, and shove it into my pocket.

As I leave the lil' brunch of horrors, I thrust my Mercedes into drive with my right hand while extending the middle finger of my left in an unmistakable gesture of contempt at the rando jackass in front of me with the raised phone. When a video of your husband falling off the stage is trending, there's no way someone's lifted cell phone is taking a selfie.

The punk with the phone jumps out of harm's way, no doubt getting video of my squealing tires, too. So? Why should *I* care about my public image when my husband doesn't care about his? (Sane Briscoe says *Don't do this. Potential negative viral video opportunity alert.* Sane Briscoe isn't driving. She also wasn't doing the point-and-buy at Absolution and Z Gallerie before brunch with Joy. Had to almost sit on my trunk to shut

16

it.)

When I dig into my pocket for a tissue, I come up with Joy's scarf instead. I gag at the pea soup smell, start to toss it out, but pause and put the swathe of multi-colored silk on the seat beside me. Bernita might like it.

There are many things I ought to regret, like being the dummy who left my husband alone with that puma, V.; taking the scarf, I do not. Follow the bouncing ball: Joy gets her money from Ben, who gets his money from Michael. Michael's money is partly mine. Ergo, *my* scarf to take.

But there's this: what do you have to *do* to smell of pea soup?

Michael's cell is still off, I discover, when I attempt calling while tearing through the miles, pausing at red lights, pushing the yellows, leading the greens, barely seeing the split-rail fences, the brochure-like backdrop of horses and the spurts of blue chicory flowers; the white, undulating blossoms of the sourwood trees that would calm me any other day.

The cradle of mountains feels more like a coffin today. I want to drive somewhere that I can see for miles, with flat land not concealing the future that is momentarily beyond me.

My grip on my phone would be attempted murder if I were holding anything living.

"Michael, I'm jacked up on white wine and gossip and if that pony-tailed, ball-cap-wearing Joy is right about you and V. (I tighten my lips, twist my head repeatedly), you'd better call me back. You'd better call me either way." I pause, then add, "How's the arm feeling?" I punch "end" with my thumb and toss the phone onto the black leather seat beside me.

Not that I have any doubts about the veracity of what Joy claimed.

17

At least I won't suffer the indignity of people thinking he traded me in for a cliché of a younger woman. I'm almost 29 to V's what, darkening months of 45?

If I were ever tempted to have an affair, I would warn Michael. It's the decent thing to do. I'd give him the chance to provide what he wasn't, if he would. Just like he could have given me a chance. Except, in this case, what can you give a man equal to the contact high of the presence of the overly lacquered (hair, nails, shoes) reigning queen of country music from the royal family of the same? Normal, married love must seem like a dead, plucked, bird by comparison.

I speed around a curve, regretfully successfully.

My hand drops from the steering wheel to cup my left breast. High, firm, full size D. Pretty much legendary. I know my physical strengths and weaknesses in great detail – Michael's fans aren't afraid to tell him and *me* that he could do better, regardless of how hot Patrick reassures me I am.

Am I really inventorying myself? My third, trending to fourth, wave feminism is in serious danger of lapsing. Not like anyone knows what fourth wave exactly means yet (like anything, you often don't know what something is until after it's over), but I would prefer to advance it. This is not doing it.

My nose is fine, whatever, unremarkable. Loretta Lynn cheekbones, tapered chin. My heavy brown hair could be listed in both the asset and liability columns, capable of being either unruly or straight. Gray eyes. Overall, a pleasant enough picture.

Ah, but as a feminist, I am not trying to be anyone's picture (Read the seminal essay by Laura Mulvey called "Visual Pleasure and Narrative Cinema." Also known as the "male gaze" discussion. Fine, lazys: it says the camera, via men, who wield the camera, objectifies women, in film and elsewhere, for men's pleasure. As a feminist, women are supposed to not care if men want to look at them while still wanting to look at themselves. A tough line even for a fourth waver, even if I have been married a decade. Who doesn't like being admired? Which means striving to conform to both attractiveness norms and standards while pretending to give no fucks. Confusion inherent. Contradiction-infused theory – feminism, not Mulvey per se. End parenthetical. Include written device at the end of this sentence for sticklers who might see it as a mistake otherwise.)

An aftershock of Michael's betrayal hits in all its magnitude, and I can't breathe until I remind myself that I'm not some tuberculin Victorian rose dying of rejection.

As a result of my rescuing our marriage (and his reputation) from his ridiculous, ill-considered early fan fuckings, I now wear a tight size 8. I was a size 4 before his first indiscretion, a hard-won victory brought about by treating carbs as poison and the gym as my church. Still, not even close to the size 0 Velvet wears (I sneaked a peek at a jacket label of hers once, and I am 5'4" versus V's what, 5'8', curses upon her and all her skinny-gened, vocally blessed, taller ancestors), so maybe the betrayal *is* partially about what, in calmer moments, I prefer to think of as my bonus-sized body.

I beat the dash until something rattles, then pet the poor thing like it's a pony.

As Michael's road manager, my job is to contact the media, scout venues, and manage stuff. I'm not supposed to have to oversee my husband's tragically delicious dick.

You know he is head over for V., but with fandom bordering on obsession, professional adoration, you *think/thought*. You

19

remind yourself that V. is a decade older than Michael, which makes her fifteen years older than you. So not exactly a deb. Something to cling to. Something to further despair about.

Why *should* I have been on guard? Everyone knows women years are automatically doubled in terms of desirability or not. Even feminists know as hard as women secretly pray to Our Lady Botox, that's the perception.

What I hadn't factored in for this newsbreak of an affair but should have is the powerful aphrodisiac fame is on both sides.

I unlock my phone and try calling Michael's crew instead, sequentially in the order I think they might be frightened enough of me to answer. They are, it would seem, to a man, too frightened to answer. As they should be.

For a moment, I consider calling my mother, but she's not exactly my go-to in times of trouble.

While we wait, then (biting on fingernails, catching up on the digital plague, the inquiring emails/notifications that have overtaken my phone) some necessary backstory.

****

My mother left my father and me for a decommissioned forest fire tower in West Virginia, when I was 12. We all thought it would only be until her grant ran out, until she had finished the book on Virginia Woolf's abandoned essay-novel that my mother had been working on for a decade. Turned out her leave of absence extended not just from the University of Nashville, but from us, her daughter and husband, too. Who knew that her funding would be renewed instead of her commitment to her family?

Still, I loved visiting her. As small as my mother's cabin in the shadow of the tower was, she must have had 300 books ranging along the walls on worn oak planks resting on piles of

20

flat rocks, the combo serving as shelves. No need to lock the place, because who would climb half a mile up Blair Mountain after nothing but her books, papers, and clothes?

On my visits to Mother's, I was drawn to her Woolf books. Since I was named after Lily Briscoe (though I'm Briscoe, no Lily), a character in *To the Lighthouse*, I asked my mother to read the novel to me. She sometimes read Woolf's short stories and essays aloud, but never *Lighthouse*. Which felt like being allowed to smell dinner without getting one bite. It left me with the impression that there was something illicit about the novel, making me determined to read it.

I waited for my mother's daily compulsion to take hold, for her to get dressed and start muttering to herself, as was her wont. One afternoon, when she threw her camo army jacket around her shoulders and left without a word, I seized the opportunity.

I never knew if she'd be gone ten minutes or ten hours, because she always marched out in what can best be described as a fugue state, carrying a tablet and pen. Funny how she never forgot those items but never asked me along and never even said where she was going. Usually, it didn't matter, because I always had a book du jour, or Virgil I (her dog) and I would keep one another company, if she hadn't taken him with her.

More afternoons than not, I was content to sweep the room with the sparsely bristled broom, remake the bed so I could touch the threadbare quilt with its log cabin design, and sit by the empty wood stove with a book, pretending it was cold out.

This insert-day-of-the-week (because summer), the small air conditioner groaned in the cabin like it was tired of August already. As soon as the door shut behind my mother, I dragged one of the two next-stop-kindling chairs in the house to the shelf and took down the novel from which my name came, sat on the bed, touching the book's cover as if it could reveal the mystery inside. My mother had shown it to me on numerous occasions, told me that Virginia's sister, Vanessa, had drawn the original cover, which seemed to mean something to her.

The edition my mother owned reproduced the abstract pen-and-ink-drawing with its thick lines that could have represented a tree instead of the intended lighthouse, or, to my eye, what resembled a forest fire tower. How fitting, I'd later think, that the design was as incomprehensible to me as the novel itself.

I flipped through the pages and noted the sweeps of my mother's sharply curved handwriting, like Appalachian train tracks. My fingers traced her ink and the spots where the paper was indented by the passion of her pen. Her notes per page almost rivaled the amount of Woolf's words there.

In one spot, my mother's marks inched alarmingly across the print.

I shut the book and tossed it back onto the shelf. It fell, as if preferring to be in my hands; I picked it up and slid it back between *Orlando* and *The Years*.

What a magic trick Woolf pulled off, inspiring people to co-create alongside her in her book, putting their own thoughts in writing beside hers even though she's gone, a potential conversation in every copy.

My mother made every book in her collection hers with a pen and her tripled dog-earing. Once upon a time her cabin was crowded with boxes upon boxes of essays and articles, a small building's worth of paper and bent books out back was moved to a storage shed in Logan because one of her Department of Natural Resources friends who still habitually checks on the tower (and thus my mom) claimed it was a fire hazard, and her out there on a mountain littered with pine trees and unraked carpets of leaves in every direction.

I can just picture my mother frantically hauling water from the hand pump to save her research, if there had been a fire.

Since birth, I have been surrounded by the detritus of both of my parents; the scent of her aging layers of paper, foxed books teaching me that more than humans age; the fading covers of my father's vinyl albums representing his tremendous, unseen, contribution to the music scene, the yellowing sleeves inside adding to my education with their inevitable, progressive decay. When I asked my mother once what an intriguing mound of paper in the dining room was, she shrugged her narrow shoulders and said they were students' papers to grade and Woolf-related research as if they were one and the same to her.

Above all, Woolf's books held court in our house. Until Mother left, a prime shelf in the bookshelf held the novels, surrounded by various biographies of her and scholarly works.

I was in high school before I realized Woolf wasn't her own subject like Science. When my guidance counselor asked what I might want to major in when I went to college I said, "Woolf."

"You mean literature?"

That afternoon I called my mother and told her she had made me unfit for human society. When I explained, she laughed before warning me not to major in literature.

"Dad told me not to major in music."

"He's right."

"I must have the weirdest parents in the whole world," I said.

"Undoubtedly. Hey, can you send me a box of Goo Goo clusters?"

In the background, Virgil howled, and Mother tutted him quiet in an unfamiliar sweet tone.

On the day I had my Come to Woolf moment in my mother's cabin, I ended up pulling *Lighthouse* back off the shelf, tried reading it. Impressions came to mind, but I couldn't follow the plot, if there was one. It was like being in water, not sure which direction I was headed, but enjoying the sensation.

The opening words were about a boy with scissors and what was it, a page from a catalog? A battle between parents about whether to comfort the boy or immediately force the inevitability of reality on him: it was going to rain the next day, and the trip he hoped to make to the lighthouse was out of the question. An immense family with a flock of guests in a small, moldering vacation cottage. A motley group that for some reason put me in mind of the mix of people my father and I, then, served Thanksgiving dinner to at the Rescue Mission every year.

I didn't understand the plot. It seemed like Woolf was someone learning the language who doesn't yet know how to put sentences together, how stories are told. I felt the urge to help her along, to ask her to settle down enough to choose a person's story to tell. One person, not a whole group at once or flitting like a bird from shoulder to shoulder. Then again, something about her method seems generous, like a schoolteacher calling in turn on one student after another, leaving no one out.

Ultimately, her writing urged me to read the novel again, became a code to break. Genius. Each time I reentered it when I was older, I found something new to admire, to study, and I realized I was the one lacking, not her style. But that came later.

The day of my first reading, I had read most of "The Window" section of *To the Lighthouse,* the first part, before my mother came quietly into the darkening cabin with Virgil, causing the remaining light in the room to shift into the crevices between the logs.

She sat on the edge of the cot beside me, the canvas sagging beneath us.

I closed the book guiltily and reached for the stale remains of my breakfast, bread that hadn't quite become toast in my impatience to read, smeared with what I had thought was blackberry jam but turned out to be clove-laden apple butter, a wet, devil-dark taste.

Virgil stood on his hind legs and leapt for the hunks of bread I tossed him.

"Well?" my mother asked.

"It's…it's…" I sobbed, though even then I knew my mother expected a more coherent answer.

As she leaned over to touch my face, I noticed that her hands were stained brown, and I fought the urge to remind her that she shouldn't have picked up with bare hands the walnuts she'd cracked. I hoped her hands would stain me, so I would have something tangible to remember her by when my visit ended.

My mother's sun-dried face softened. "Nothing about Woolf is easy. If it were, I would have moved on years ago."

Implied: my father and I are not complicated. Like country music is not. We're plain spoken. Maybe not as clever as Woolf. And that is *our* failing. That is the defect that causes her to reject us the way she rejected her parents' fortune. Nothing uncomplicated, nothing that could ease life's passage with its comfortable simplicity and warmth, is worthy of her attention.

I didn't have those words, not then, but the impression stayed with me.

She rinsed her hands in the sink, dried them on the red and white plaid towel, leaving streaks of brown. She chased the light back out from between the logs by switching on a lamp. Then she crossed to the shelf. Hands on her hips, she reached decisively for a substantial, blue-covered paperback.

"Try this," she said, handing me the book. "It's Woolf's first novel, *The Voyage Out*. I think you'll enjoy it. Especially the debate about writing versus music."

"But you named me after Lily. I want to understand *this* book."

Affection brought on by direct contact with Woolf made my mother's face a lit house at night. I desperately wanted to provoke that expression myself.

She sat beside me again.

"The best way to understand it is to read it several times in a row. Each time write down every question you have about it. Then go back until you've answered all you can. Let me know what remaining questions you have."

"You'll answer them for me then?"

She grinned, the skin about her eyes bunching. "I don't know that anyone could. The good news is that there are no 'wrong' answers. There are right ones, but no wrong. Don't listen to anyone who tells you differently," she said, frowning. "And never forget: there are no answers without questions."

I weighed the book in my hands, felt the softened cover.

"Why haven't you made me read *Voyage* before if it's so easy?"

My mother's mouth opened wide with ready laughter.

"If you force someone to read something, they'll hate it, guaranteed." Her knees met, and she pulled them to her chest and crossed her arms around them, as if she were about to do a somersault. "And I didn't say it is easy."

We sank into the moment until my stomach rumbled, which she heard without giving the slightest indication that it was her problem.

It wasn't.

"Why don't I make dinner?" I offered.

"None for me," she said, getting up and emptying the zinc washtub of pillows, liberating it of its secondary function as a reading nook. She snatched up the water bucket and headed for the pump, admitting the scent of pine as she opened the door.

When she returned, she sat at the place I had set for her at the log-fashioned picnic table, eating the Thrive chicken noodle soup and the improvised Reuben sandwich made from canned corned beef, and after finishing her pickle spear, forked one off my plate. I surrendered my second pickle with a smile before getting up to boil a pot of water to wash the few dirty dishes. Once done, I refilled the pots and put them back on the stove for her bath water.

After her bath, we read in our respective cots far into the evening, me traversing one word of *Voyage* after another, until our books fell from our hands when our eyes closed. I understood the book better than *Lighthouse*, but I can't say I enjoyed it nearly as much.

My father fetched me home the next morning, just in time for me to start a new school year, and I waved at my mother from his dusty Ford truck, calling back for her to bring *Voyage* with her when she returned. It would have been unthinkable to take it myself. It would be like assuming I had a right to a piece of her.

When I learned she wasn't coming home for Christmas that year, I visited a secondhand bookshop in Hillsboro Village and located a copy of *The Voyage Out*, wrapped it, and put it under the tree for myself. I read Rachel to the other shore and · discovered a crossover couple, the Dalloways, in the novel that made me want to read another of Woolf's books: *Mrs. Dalloway*. By then, I liked Woolf more. Or maybe I was just accustomed to her fiction.

Mother belatedly sent me a journal and a set of fountain pens for the holiday. The bottle of ink in the package leaked all over and into the journal. At my father's insistence, I wrote her a thank-you note.

Chapter 2

My phone rings as I slip out of my heeled sandals, an acceptable transitional day shoe here – not a stiletto, but not an ungraceful flat. Also Nashville acceptable: boots, platforms, wedges. Translation: anything but flats.

I have settled onto our bed with my laptop, hoping to write more.

"Jessie?" I answer, not that I want to talk to anyone except the fallen one.

"Is he okay?"

I sigh. Until now, Jessie, a late teen, has seemed particularly promising.

If Michael's ascendance can be attributed to my efforts (and it can), I am a born kingmaker.

Thanks to Drake Williams, the head of Sweet Thunder Records, the label I interned with when I was in school, I have an eye for spotting and developing talent, not to mention my own respectable (if neglected) songwriting career. Nowadays, I work almost exclusively with Michael, managing, but I can't keep myself from evaluating a person's abilities, can't keep myself from stoking banked-over or unrealized dreams for others and trying to blow life into them when I run across someone at a songwriting event, at open mic nights. Occasionally, someone will give Michael a demo and I listen to it because he tosses them into his bag without another thought. Especially if they're by women, I'll listen. Because women get so much less exposure, even now.

Nashville is a secretly ambitious city, that ambition belied by its laid-back reputation and appearance. You only have to look at the congested construction to see that it keeps growing past its bounds, wants to go places. Look at the rejected historic buildings on music row and elsewhere that are being flattened, despite protestations.

The city needs more of everything to accommodate the influx of hopefuls: housing, roads, employment.

Michael and I have taken people needing mentoring on the bus with us, have worked them in as opening acts when possible. Have found them positions in studios freelancing if they prefer not to tour. Have financed demos.

If I can help give anyone in love with the music business what my father didn't receive, then I will.

Jess sounds like she's crying.

"He'll be fine," I say, rolling my eyes. Does she have herself a little crush? Who doesn't? He's a fireball. Crushes I totally understand, and can handle. "He just took a tumble."

"Good."

Her breathing tells me there's more, and I should know by now that there is always more, life just keeps dumping buckets of more over your head, and if not on you then in your vicinity and trust me, it's never rose petals in those buckets.

"Anything else I can do for you?"

"I don't know if this is a good time, but you said I should call if…if…"

The younger ones are so needy that I hand them off to Patrick to refer to resources, but every now and then I attempt, against my better judgement, to take one on.

"If what, sweetheart?" I flinch after I call her that. It's so condescending, and she's not that much younger than me.

"I was offered a songwriting contract," she says with a wary tone.

"With whom?" This could mean anything from a legit contract to something essentially worthless to something sinister.

"Hattrick Music."

"Which agent?" Not Al; not Al.

"Al."

My phone beeps. Ben.

"First of all, congrats. And here's what you do. You tell him you'll take the offer, and that I'll be present for the signing. I'll be sure to get you switched to Julie as your contact person, and you are never, and I mean ever, to allow yourself to be alone with him or in that building without a can of pepper spray, got it?"

The beeping persists.

"You think it's going to be all right?"

"If you promise me you won't sign anything until I can be there, then yeah, as much as I can promise anything. Try to stall until next week; that would be easier for me. Let me know."

"Briscoe, thank you."

I switch over, but Ben is already gone. No message.

Someone should drop Al off the Natchez Trace Parkway Bridge. He is a capable agent, and many songwriters and artists have him to thank for their success, but his personal morals are nonexistent. I keep a mental list of people to steer newbies away from, and he is number one on it. But I never tell the talent in advance because that would only cause problems for me if it got back to those I had talked ill of, so I save it for when necessary. For when discretion is a given for the new talent to keep their careers.

When Ben doesn't answer my return call, I call Jessie back. There had been something about her voice…

"Tell me what he did."

Mercifully, Al had "only" stroked her hair and told her he would "enjoy working with" her.

"You sure that's all?" It's more than enough. I have the urge to pay him a visit this afternoon.

He might have patted her lower back – well, ass, she admits.

Three more texts come in. A couple of email notifications. None from Michael's crew. People still wanting to know if he is going to show up, or if we are rescheduling. Just a part of my job. "And the way he said it, I know if I sign the contract, he'll want even more."

"Just do what I say, and it will be fine. There's plenty of time once you're known in the business to point a finger at him."

I wish I could tell her to do it now, but the rash of bad boy behavior revelations hasn't hit Nashville in quite the same way it has other places yet, not that there's nothing to reveal. A Southern city, for all its charm and positives, let's be honest, is a little behind the curve when it comes to feminism and calling powerful men out.

One call rolls into the next. Condolences, inquiries, more tentative rearranging of the tour schedule, friends, acquaintances with their endless curiosity.

"Patrick! Some backup, please," I call before remembering I

sent him to run the errands I now can't for the benefit.

I can't get the flowers myself right now and how dare Woolf or anyone expect me to. Everyone is perfectly capable of picking out flowers. No one talks about as limiting as sexism is to women, it limits all sexes. It weakens us all.

And P.S. the flowers are being delivered.

Sorrow saws just below my ribs, but I run it off with a Coke Zero Sugar, barely resisting adding a shot of Jack. People might say small comforts, are just that, but they would be wrong. Looking back, what made every day bearable? Rituals of the modest kind.

Those have never been enough for Michael. I don't know what the man wants, what it will take to make him happy and content, but sadly, it's not Coke Zero Sugar. Apparently, it's not me, either.

I jump on Amazon and send a defense kit with a whistle and pepper spray to Jess. It doesn't feel like enough. Someone needs to write a secret, anonymous handbook, a guide to navigating Nashville while woman. That someone will not be me – I've got a thesis due, and I'd like to work again, so no.

All of this does very well to distract.

Looking through my notes, I spot the word indisputably. Such a weighted word, meaning, of course, unquestionable, undeniable. Wait, where have I seen it before?

I pull up the e-book of *Lighthouse* and search. It's only there twice, both times about clothing. Ooh!

Glove and *boot*. I'm so excited that I text my discovery to my mother, while simultaneously hoping she will leave me alone to explore the idea on my own.

Woolf also uses symbols to represent the ambiguous nature of domesticity in the novel. Mr. and Mrs. Ramsay have articles of clothing which represent their domestic arts as well as their "madness." Mrs. Ramsay is depicted by a glove, something that covers the hands she knits with, while Mr. Ramsay is linked with his boots, whose laces he knots and which, of course, cover his feet. Which suggests, for Mrs. Ramsay, having the upper hand, but for Mr. Ramsay, the image of a heavy boot brings to mind something being squashed beneath a heavy heel. Woolf goes back and forth, leading us to wonder who exactly has the power in this relationship. Perhaps she intends to suggest that, as in many marriages, both alternate wielding it.

Now I add in what I'm fairly certain will earn me publication because this is some next-level shit. I expound upon my earlier findings.

The twisted-fingered glove of Mrs. Ramsay and Mr. Ramsay's boots are underscored by the word "indisputably," used by Woolf only twice in the novel, about Mrs. Ramsay's glove, and now, Mr. Ramsay's boots.

Remarkable boots they were too, Lily thought, looking down at them: sculptured; colossal; like everything that Mr. Ramsay wore, from his frayed tie to his half-buttoned waistcoat, his own **indisputably**. *She could see them walking to his room of their own accord, expressive in his absence of pathos, surliness, ill-temper, charm. [Emphasis added] (59)*

Euphoria hits me as I read the word *twisted* once again! My fingers race to make connections. My mind hooks and loops, backtracks, and ties.

"Indisputably" gives weight to these passages. Woolf means for us to see that these objects are the husband and wife, the Ramsays. (The positioning of the glove in a corner of an imaginary sofa begins Lily's attempt to define Mrs. Ramsay outside of her painting.) A

34

sofa holds more than one person. While Mrs. Ramsay is willingly sitting in this theoretical position that opens a space for company, the glove shoved in the corner suggests Mrs. Ramsay is hiding something. She is represented by one glove, in contrast to Mr. Ramsay's pair of boots. There is the public Mrs. Ramsay with the soothing manners, and the private.

Mr. Ramsay's boots are plural, a pair; he is whole. She is half. He expresses affection and even negative emotions freely. She cannot; her affection for others comes out in the domestic arena, in the things she does every day in caring for them.

Hidden things. Public things. Literature and the country music scene have much in common. I may be half her age and without children, but I sympathize with the Mrs. because smiling in public is excruciating when you're not feeling it.

Something about the paragraphs feels unfinished. I mull.

A text comes in, one that demands answering. I shut down my computer and close the lid. Again.

Chapter 3

T+12 hours and No. Show. No. Call.

Barely waiting for Michael's voicemail greeting on this my umpteenth call, I spew a creative country combo of curse words he won't bother listening to before I get into my car. Who checks voicemail anymore?

I never thought I'd be reduced to doing an internet search to find out my husband's health status. Dr. Google told me when I checked that he was released after a "minor accident" resulting in a sprained arm, like Ben said. If he's been released, where is he?

My phone rings. I redundantly swerved off to the side of curvy Vaughn Road, taking advantage of the wide, paved berm at this pass.

Mouth locked and loaded, I punch the green button, only to hear the tobacco-smoke-thickened voice of Robert on the other end.

"Hey, Briscoe. Has Rhonda called you yet?"

Rhonda Stafford, half reporter, half pit bull?

I inhale so deeply I need to exhale before I can speak. "Not yet. You give a statement?"

"Of course: Velvet's uncle fell ill and needed her immediately. He's her closest remaining family... It's true, all except his being sick. But as I told Rhonda, since neither you nor Velvet were around to keep an eye on the 'boys,' the drinking before the show got out of hand."

"Why the hell didn't V. mention her uncle as an excuse to the press to start with? And why are you making statements that mention Michael?"

"I gather her decision to leave was made quickly. I didn't know about it until she'd already gotten on a plane headed back here. As far as I can tell, Michael's declaration that he would open for himself was the only public announcement made. Trust me, I've spoken with her about her unprofessionalism. And I had to say something, didn't I?"

"I recently found out the whole story, so." I draw out "whole." Quiet.

"I haven't managed to get Michael on the phone yet." Another slice of silence.

Somehow Rhonda knows more, he says finally, than the other news outlets. Claims to have something "solid."

"Then I guess I'd better call her. You know we need to coordinate stories here, right?"

He chuckles. "I get where you're coming from, but I'm gonna cover my girl's ass as fast as I can, any way I can, every time."

He doesn't need to add that I'd do, am doing, the same for Michael.

"Right, but don't you think it would have been better for both if..."

"Of course. I'm sorry. Like I said, I had to act fast."

As swiftly as a blink, I ask: "How are *you*?"

There's no answer but a deep, sympathetic "Take care," words I can't bring myself to reply to without losing it; we hang up simultaneously.

37

I lean out of my car and vomit, this time unaided and unintentionally. Which might help my studded Rock Star jeans (worn ironically, of course) fit a little better, though I don't want to lose the breasts I display in tight tanks most of the time because I have badass arms and a tan, the tan honestly more like my freckles joining together, but is at least darker than my normally pale skin.

I eye the side of my car to be sure it is clean, then rest my head on it before flinching away from the blazing metal. I find a piece of Trident at the bottom of my purse and gratefully shove it into my mouth while rubbing the side of my face.

There will be plenty of time for anger later. Plenty of time to curl up in bed with a bottle and good ol' classic country tearjerkers. Plenty of time to plot the dramatics if I have any energy left. Right now, it is a matter of protecting those assets that will soon be half mine. If I hire the right lawyer, more than half.

I agree in theory with my mother that filthy lucre is just that, but I sure do like its trimmings.

I spit my gum in the direction of a field of white sweet clover before asking Siri to call Rhonda. Siri obliges.

"Rhonda? How ya doin', hon? It's Briscoe." Being fake still burns my mouth.

"Hey there, girl. I was about to call you."

I hold the phone away from Rhonda's commercially advantageous twang. Since I have been known to exaggerate my own in the right circumstances, I can't exactly blame the woman, but it makes my blood pressure rise.

Notice that even though we are both grow-ass women, in Nashville we are "girls," a battle I'll never win, no matter how many times I complain when someone uses it for women.

The only thing that makes it halfway bearable is the equal opportunity infantilizing of men to "boys." Not the same thing though, is it?

"How's Doggie?" I ask. Rhonda's black Lab, Scout, I learn, is now two years old, and loves running with her.

"We should go for a run at Warner Park sometime," I say, knowing the celeb-frequented area will appeal to her. (Although truth be told, with those hilly trails, it would be less running and more walking, at least on my part. But I'll take that spectacular view any day.)

Calling Rhonda suggests, I realize too late, that I take her inquiry seriously. Rookie mistake.

"Like I told Robert, I'm about to run a story. How 'bout a statement, preferably during a sit down?" she asks.

Robert didn't give her a sit down; why should I?

"I'd love to, but there's the benefit..."

"I was thinking we could talk at it, since I have a source. I want to give you the chance to tell me your side of the story."

Who? Who, who would dare talk? I will find them and slow roast them over an open flame. It has to be either someone who hates me or hates Michael. Or someone who wants the money and/or attention. Yeah, that brings a couple of contenders to mind who wouldn't mind violating their NDA's.

After Rhonda asks a few more probing questions she knows I won't answer but that her "professional integrity" requires, questions that make me uncomfortable because they reek of insider info, I offer to meet her at the Pancake Pantry. The benefit will not be the place for the kind of talk we'll need to have, and time is not my friend.

Spin is always easier in person because you can see if the other party is buying it. You can stage your expression. It also tends to make people less combative on both sides, because you exchange humanity, however briefly. It means fitting her in when I have zero time and even less inclination to do so, but it has to be done.

"Thank you," Rhonda says, the "ew" sound dragging out for three syllables. "I'll see you tomorrow."

I silently pretend to gag myself and end the call.

A song comes on the radio (having the radio on is more memory lane and market study than entertainment, though of course it's that, too) with a hook that Michael swore the band of record stole from him at a cookout. He makes me turn it out whenever it comes on because they didn't even acknowledge him on the album.

Next up there's the cashier-turned-singer, Andrea, who I discovered belting Patsy Cline tunes during one of my late-night Target runs. Her boss told her to shut up or shut down her lane and go home. I gave the cashier my card and told her to call me. She did at six a.m. the next morning, saying she had quit her job. That wouldn't have exactly been my recommendation, but hey, that's believing in yourself.

I managed to get her some studio work and then a Christmas gig at Opryland Hotel.She has three towheaded children who, she said when I went to see her perform, were about to have the best holiday ever. Her ethereal angels joined the other children circled about her while she sang, and dang if I could quit crying.

It was one of those pearly holiday moments that you wish you'd had as a child, but you didn't ever, in part because your mother refused to let you believe in Santa because that was commercialized nonsense. But you did get gifts, and you only ended up ruining one friend's Christmas before realizing this insider info about the bearded saint was not something you should freely share. Because your friend cried and asked her mother the truth, who made you go home before the cookies were finished baking.

I turn the radio off when Andrea's song ends and cruise in rare and blessed silence with nothing but regular bursts of hurt and the intense desire to purge to keep me company as I drive towards Fairview. For a few minutes at a time I forget, and I actually miss Michael until I remember that apparently I'm no more to him than his scruffy bus slippers.

My tiny, rustic writing cabin, an itty-bitty hideaway that I don't get to as much as I'd like, is the ideal spot for some writing while I wait. I bought it before Fairview built up, so I paid nothing for it. I wanted a place of my own, a refuge outside of the city proper, for songwriting. The graduation bonus Drake gave me paid for three quarters of it.

I discovered the cabin on Highway 100 near that greeting card factory on one of my drives. It's easy to miss if you don't know to watch for the curve it's on. This was before you-know-who built his house out there and drove up the property prices.

Once I'm inside my cabin, I note with approval that there's not much more than a sofa with a pullout bed, a table and chairs, a pile of notebooks on the table, and a small kitchen with a folding door to conceal it. I keep it stocked with a couple of bottles of wine and some shelf-stable goods. Soup, mostly.

Having switched on the small window air conditioner unit, I stand in front of it while my laptop starts. Something stubborn in me likes that I can keep it together enough to write even now. Something else whispers that it's likely the only thing that lets me keep it together.

The cabin is sturdy, even if it is old. The logs are treated, so no termites, though they smell like the old version of the Loveless Café, a deep woods scent. The bathroom manages to hold a pedestal sink, toilet, and small shower, no bath. I could live here again if I had to. That's what I tell myself whenever I'm afraid of our lives burning down.

The match is lit.

Lord knows there's nowhere else affordable enough to live in or around Nashville nowadays. Even apartments are outrageous. As I said, Fairview is building up, steadily — now they even have a Walmart, I overheard someone brag a few years ago at a gas station there in the small city.

Michael and I actually did live in this cabin in our early marriage, though not for too long. I miss the days of no possessions except each other. Yes, I heard what I just said.

I shoot a series of texts to Patrick, distasteful commands that must be accomplished if I'm to get Rhonda off my ass. I wait for him to report back that we're good to go, and I ask him to hire extra help if he needs it. I hate piling my crud onto his shoulders, but I can't do it all, not now. I just can't. And mama buys great thank-you gifts, so there's that.

I return to my writing, finding a hint of unexpected venom in my analysis. Novels are a master class in human behavior, both actual behavior and what they wish they or others could or would do.

Mrs. Ramsay's nearly magical art of knitting allows her to comfort her daughter and son with separate stories of the same truth. Someone has sent her son, James, a boar's skull that is inexplicably hung on the wall, and it frightens his sister, Cam, when she tries to sleep. Mrs. Ramsay wraps her shawl around it

42

several times, whispering to Cam that it's no longer a skull but a bird's nest, a mountain. Thus, death is transformed into something desirable.

Is the skull also a foreshadowing of Mrs. Ramsay's (spoiler alert) coming sudden death? She tells James the skull is still there underneath (ugly reality), and she covers him with her stories. Later, feeling for her shawl, she realizes it is gone; she's left it behind. She has knit herself to the concept of death, wound part of herself about it, though it's only upon reflection, after the revelation of her sudden demise, that we make the connection.

Mrs. Ramsay also covers artwork with her knitting to overlay her own viewpoint onto the family, and there's something rotten about that: she uses a green shawl to drape a picture frame that will turn mossy from the excessive moisture whether covered or not. She covers and uncovers it repeatedly, almost as if she's trying to reinterpret the fluctuating story of her family, and her own story, through the "art" of knitting:

Knitting her reddish-brown hairy stocking, with her head outlined absurdly by the gilt frame, the green shawl which she had tossed over the edge of the frame, and the authenticated masterpiece by Michelangelo, Mrs. Ramsay smoothed out what had been harsh in her manner a moment before, raised his head, and kissed her little boy on the forehead. "Let us find another picture to cut out," she said. (12)

She simply tells another story.

And don't ask me what the hell that sentence about the "authenticated masterpiece" means. If it means there's an original Michelangelo sketch there, then who would be foolish enough to leave it to molder in a vacation home? If it's not, what *does* it mean? Essays have no doubt been written about this, but that is not my line of inquiry, and I don't have time for that much digging. If you figure it out, let me know.

Standing, I bend to one side and then the other. The cabin shrinks. A friend said something to me once about Michael that I used in a song: "He's done nothing to deserve you." (Ambiguity noted.) But Michael was the authenticated masterpiece left to molder, or he would have, if *someone* hadn't taken him in hand.

In the miniscule closet just off the living room, I find my father's first acoustic guitar, which became *my* first, a blue Ovation Applause. I stare at the coffee can of his ashes on the bureau and play my songs at it, telling him my woes, something I would never have done if he were alive.

The can reproaches me, and I promise once again that I'll set him free. Soon. Once he's gone, who will I have?

A service cleans and airs the place monthly, but otherwise, I pick up after myself whenever I use the cabin. Cinnamon apple wafts around the room from an air freshener plugged into an outlet and though I like it, I want something lighter to suit the season.

Sometimes Michael and I let newcomers to Nashville stay here, those we mentor for a few months, just until they get established or, the more likely scenario, run back to wherever it was they came from. Who could blame them? It's a great town, but it's hard to survive here financially, emotionally, and despite Hallmark movies and documentaries to the contrary, it's tough to get into the music business if you don't count open mic nights.

If you're in the healthcare business, though, welcome to town! You'll do great.

My E string is wildly out of tune, so I turn the peg and ping the string, turn and ping, until my ear tells me it's close if not dead on.

I pull a tablet out of a kitchen drawer, find a pen, and turn to a clean page. When I look down, all I've written is "Picnic, lightning" over and over.

When Michael and I were dating, we'd often come here to write because it's quiet, but not too far from the city. We'd sometimes run just up the road to the little local diner with its cheap burgers and the sort of colorful décor you might find at your grandma's house, tables covered in mismatched vinyl cloths with chairs that don't seem to mind which table they congregate at, just like the town's seniors who sit in the chairs most of the morning getting endless coffee refills.

Michael and I would usually get takeout when we went there. After eating back at the cabin, we'd sit on either end of my floral, velour-covered couch with the sagging springs, guitars in hand. First, we'd play a couple of songs by other people to warm up. Johnny Cash, The Judds. Some Sugarland, Lady A., Loretta Lynn, and Jason Aldean, whoever came to mind.

Then he'd play something he'd written I'd never heard before, and he'd lean towards me, and I'd say whatever words showed up and as soon as they settled into some kind of order, I'd write them down. We always recorded the sessions just in case, which anyone without a perfect memory would be wise to do. That's just standard operating procedure for songwriting.

With Michael, though:

First, the ring of a string, a cavalcade of notes. The air filling with the auditory equivalent of fireflies: *snap, snap*. He, a live wire, *don't touch*, until disconnected from the source.

Sometimes I think I fell for Michael primarily because of how he makes an acoustic *bleed*. Acoustic guitars are hollow, melancholy, felled trees until musicians resurrect them. We immortalize the trees.

Isn't that immortalization what we all want for ourselves?

As much as I love to hear a sweet Tele groan, if country music is the music of the feeling soul, then acoustic guitars are the soul of country music. Others would say it's the steel guitar or more obviously mournful instruments. Maybe even the guitar's brash, outspoken (but friendly) cousin, the banjo. For my money, acoustic guitars are the better-adjusted family member: sometimes joyful, sometimes sad, but always self-aware.

During our early cabin sessions, eventually the train of melodies would slow, Michael's playing softening like a satisfied penis. Making music has always been our truest form of intimacy.

After we'd been dating a few months, Michael showed up at my cabin during a spring rain saying he wanted to write about how invigorating the weather was. As if that wasn't cliché enough for me to see through, he put his guitar down without wiping the moisture off the case; he patted his back pocket incessantly, further giving his motive away.

So I took him by the hand and pulled him out in the rain, behind the cabin, the deluge soaking us within minutes as he asked what I was doing. I showed him by stripping off my shirt, and then my bra, peeling away my leggings and underclothes and letting the rain run over me.

"What are you doing?"

Tugging at his shirt until his chest was as naked as mine, I put my hands in his back pockets and swayed our hips in slow

46

circles. Then I pulled him to me and covered his lips with mine. He pushed away, knelt, and put his hand behind him.

"Looking for this?" I held out the red box.

I got down on a knee, too, refusing wordlessly when he urged me to stand, and he opened the box as I held onto it. He slid the small-stoned ring onto my finger. It's the one I still wear today. By choice.

My kiss said the yes. Neither of us mentioned that Drake had spoken with us about getting married. So what that it wasn't an entirely organic union?

I, for one, didn't (still don't) require a fairy tale.

We ran back indoors, and I rubbed the rain from our bodies with my Muppets towel. We didn't waste the tingling.

After, he dressed in my orange Titan sweats and a Hank Sr. tee that stretched beyond repair on him. He picked up his guitar and strummed a song he said he'd meant to play before proposing, one he wrote just for the occasion. He would have let the song propose; I should have let it.

He only made one recording of the song and he gave me the only copy. We play it every anniversary.

This cabin, or should I say the world, is too full of Michael right now. I put the guitar away and get back into my car, returning to the cabin briefly when I realize I haven't cleaned my strings. Sure, you can buy new strings, but my father raised me better than that. (For heaven's sake, you think I ought to say "reared?" Proper is as proper does.)

Before Michael, I used to love driving the rural side of Nashville, from where busy Davidson County relaxes into posh Williamson County. When stressed, I would take myself into a corner of nature and a song would come to me.

I pass stands of densely leafed hardwoods: maple, oak, elm,

and ash. I glimpse the Cumberland River and a tributary, the Harpeth River (though I don't know where one ends and the other starts), too far out still to see the steel bones of buildings rising as shopping centers clone themselves at five-mile intervals. No sooner is one downtown area rehabbed than the next is started in on, with accompanying, expensive, apartments. A new-to-town starter set.

I fear for what remains of the trees. Because of my father's love of them, I planted an ash tree behind my cabin to commemorate him the year he died of brain cancer, eight years ago now.

Michael and I plan to eventually spread my father's ashes among the coneflowers he loved so much, the ones Dad introduced me to when I was a kid, when I can bear to. Dad used to take me to his two favorite parks, Long Hunter or Cedars of Lebanon, where we'd carefully tread on the hollow-sounding limestone at the cedar glades and he'd talk about the series of caverns under the stone, and that this area, home to many plants and critters we couldn't see, needed to be honored and preserved even better than it was.

He often sang the same sermon about country music, just as passionately.

Whenever we visited a park, Dad would point to witch's butter, a slippery-looking bacterium that seemed more octopus than not, to the fame flower, a rarely blossoming succulent that we only succeeded in seeing in bloom twice. There was also the unexpected cactus in this zone, the only one, he told me proudly, native to Tennessee, the Eastern Prickly Pear, or "Devil's Tongue." Seeing it, you'd think you were in a desert.

My father had worked at Cedars while he was in college for a time with the woman who rediscovered the Tennessee

48

coneflower that was thought to be extinct. I wonder how it felt for her to stumble upon this flower and see that despite reports to the contrary, it lived.

"It was the first plant put on the Federal Endangered Species List," he bragged, even though he knew I could say it along with him by now. Every year we visited the coneflowers. He said it was a symbol that what was thought dead could be just hiding "real good." And that you have to nurture precious things. Then he tousled my hair.

Between my parents' love of nature, I'm practically a tree.

If only I were right now. I drive a little faster than necessary, even for me.

Near Franklin, I scramble to find my ringing phone. It's Sweet Thunder Records. Jolene, the receptionist, informs me that I have a command two p.m. meeting with "Mr. Williams." Drake.

Jolene should be Satan's receptionist. She's so bubbly no one would be scared to go to hell. And that's exactly where I'll be heading this afternoon. Until I saw Drake's flaming eyes for the first time, I hadn't realized hell's portal blazed blue. He's okay if he's not angry with you, but he's a man accustomed to getting his way and will do whatever it takes to get it.

As I change lanes, the mirror mocks the frizz ball that I convinced myself would do earlier. If I must do the bow and scrape, I'll do it with meticulously groomed hair.

Reggie agrees to squeeze me in after I stress I will pay *whatever* he wants, underscoring this by declaring this more of an emergency than my found-my-first-gray crisis of 2015 when I begged him to come in at two a.m. and color my hair. He did, though. Of course he did. We were leaving later that morning on tour, and I don't trust just anyone with my hair.

Next, I call our sainted housekeeper, Bernita, to ask if any of the reporters outside have dared come to the door. She says no.

"And have you heard from Mr. Chambers?"

"Mr. Chambers no call."

"Thanks."

Sometimes I forget that Bernita isn't Hispanic. Nothing but hillbilly, as far as I know. I put an ad in the paper saying that at least a little English was required for the housekeeping position, and Bernita answered it with whatever you'd call the language she pretends to speak. I guess she thought that I *wanted* her to speak something other than English. I tried explaining when I hired her that I only meant it would be acceptable if someone didn't speak it much, but for the past five years I've been treated to some facsimile of a foreign language from a housekeeper who still goes for weekly spray tans. I've tried straightening her out, but I almost think Bernita likes pretending. I barely notice it anymore.

"What you want for supper?"

"I'll pick something up." I'm not hungry.

As soon as I get off the phone, I take a deep breath and call Patrick. First, I ask for an update on Operation Rhonda. He says it's almost settled.

"Good. And send Mr. Williams a five-pound tin of Deep South pralines from Leon's, stat. Don't let them tell you they don't deliver. Deliver it yourself if they can't send it within the hour," I command, not waiting for an answer before hanging up.

Past the shock of betrayal now, my brain is computing, quickly. Patrick *had* to have known the truth about Michael and V. and he didn't tell me. What is the world coming to

50

when you can't even *hire* loyalty?

The candy is Drake's favorite. I know his favorite wine, cologne, and scotch, too. To be safe, I am also familiar with his favorite horses to back and his favorite hotel suite at Opryland where he "interviews" prospective talent. The women, anyway. As problematic as he might be, having no label would be worse. Besides, he has always treated me with respect. I suspect that has more to do with his relationship with my father than anything else.

Mind, not every music exec is like Drake, but Drake is one of the old guard from the time of Vinyl, The Original.

****

Shear Obsession perches on a cement platform in Green Hills and is shaped like a country church. Parking around back. It's painted Grecian white. A sign the height of a McDonald's arch spells out its name. Instead of an arch, though, it is in the shape of a huge pair of partially open scissors.

I keep my sunglasses on as I enter and walk right past the receptionist of the week, sit in a dryer chair near Reggie's station while he finishes with his client. He nods and murmurs that he'll be right with me as he carefully clips bangs for a woman who is too old for them. When I blanch, he rolls his eyes and mouths "I know."

Slowly my eyes adjust to the pink, white, and black interior, its walls festooned with scriptures. I believe in just the right amount of God for surviving and thriving in the South. I haven't spent too much time worrying about what I do or don't believe in, because how does my believing in something make it true or untrue?

I take off my sunglasses, and head after head ducks. Magazines mesmerize. Cell phones require immediate attention.

Chances are, one of them will feel brave and approach me if I don't do the stare down. Especially with the breaking news.

I open the Pinterest app on my phone to read my Woolf quotes for inspiration for my essay. Quickly, I give up and play a word game instead.

Mercifully, mere minutes into my visit, a shampoo girl dashes over and whisks me away to a sink. Reggie leaves his VIP (she's from medical money; I've seen her at galas – she's not glamorous, but she's important) to say hello too close to my face as I lie prone in the chair, me in the oh-so-flattering cape, hair wet, my head back as if I'm fixin' to get my throat slit.

"You doin' okay?" he asks, his double meaning apparent.

"I'll survive."

He pats my arm with his warm hand and disappears like a ship on the horizon.

No more than five minutes after my hair is bundled into a towel, I'm in Reggie's chair. I pretend I don't hear his previous client complain about being handed off to the stylist at the end of the room.

As Reggie dries my hair, something he typically relegates, I think about what to say to Drake. Then I remember I owe Rhonda a statement; too bad it won't be enough, but I text Janice, who says she is almost finished and will run it by me before sending it to the usuals. Yes, Rhonda is on the list, she confirms. I talk to fastidious Janice as little as possible. But she's a necessity. Usually, I make Patrick communicate with her.

The latte from *Honey Bee* that Reggie hands me just after I sit down gives me much needed caffeination. I lean forward and decimate half of the accompanying flaky croissant from

Provence like it has done me personal harm.

"Michael gonna be ok?" Reggie whispers.

"Any butter?"

Reggie snaps his fingers, like in a movie, and one of the shampoo boys come over.

"Please get some butter for Miss Briscoe."

The "miss" is de rigueur in the south, even though I've told him half a dozen times to drop it and call me just Briscoe.

The frazzled employee's eyes dart between the multiple things he has going, and I say he doesn't have to bother with the butter, but Reggie insists. It's me; of course he insists.

"Scottie has the card," Reggie says. "He should have never brought you a croissant without butter."

"The card" is a computer file that tells the salon's employees what its clients like. Until a few years ago, it was an index card literally kept in a box with the formula for your preferred hair color, according to Reggie, the styles you've tried, and your birth date, of course. Which they honor yearly with a vibrant mixed bouquet from Rebel Hill, florist to the stars. I always enjoy the flowers for a day or two every year, and then I give them to Bernita. She grumbles as if I'm putting her out by handing them over, but I catch her sniffing them all day long when I do, so I know she doesn't hate them.

"He's fine. Embarrassed, bruised, wearing a sling, but otherwise fine." I dreamed last night that he was playing onstage, and his left arm fell off. I rushed up and taped it back on, but I knew it would never be the same.

"Good," Reggie says as he flicks the teal comb, whirls around as if to grab a can of hairspray, but apparently picks up the remote instead as the TV switches audibly to another channel so fast I can't catch what he's censored though I can hear the disappointed noises made by the other women. So, Michael?

He moves his large, dark hands quickly through my hair. In the mirror I watch him eyeing it with his wide brown eyes as he spreads it over my shoulders. I suspect he has a lot he'd like to ask about Michael, but he never does. Reggie and I are not exactly friends, yet he's more than an acquaintance.

When a bright-eyed young man thrusts a gold-rimmed saucer with three pats of butter in the shape of a rose on it at me, Reggie pauses patiently while I dig a five out of my wallet to tip the boy.

A text with the final publicity statement comes from Janice; I quickly approve it. It attempts to make light of the incident. He's mostly fine but embarrassed and thanks his fans for the well wishes and flowers

End of news story. Non-story.

There's no need to run the release by Michael: I *am* Michael when it comes to his PR. Even now it's to my advantage not to tarnish his image because the more he's worth, the more I'll get in le divorce.

As I am spun back towards the mirror, Reggie says, "Ta da" and points to my head. I reflexively praise his work as I hands him my credit card, scribbling in an extra 30% over the suggested tip, because I've noticed how he's had to implement crowd control during my appointment.

I endure his air kisses and practically jog out the door. Glancing behind me at the salon from the parking lot, I see a gaggle of women at the window in capes and foil. I gesture to Reggie, who, seeing my frown, picks up a spray bottle, his right hand in the air as he notices them. I turn away before I can see if he actually squirts them. He'd better.

Chapter 4

Michael and I met at a songwriters' night at The Bluebird, back when it was privately owned. The small, unassuming building is something you might pass without noticing if you weren't hunting for it, rather than appearing to be the place where legends have been discovered.

It was already a rare snowy evening in early January when Michael showed up. If there's a flake of snow, no one moves in Nashville. The crowd would have been after-New-Years small anyway, but this night it was reduced to a cook, someone on the sound board, two servers, and five people in the audience, three of them signed up to perform.

I sat up front after my shift, my checkerboard Chucks on my guitar case, my stomach fluttering, knowing my guitar strings were dead, almost rusty with ground-in dirt and finger oil and hoping they would hold up. Having earned only three dollars in tips for the night, I'd attempt when I got home to boil the strings clean instead of replacing them with new ones, a trick I'd learned from my father.

Those were the days when I automatically carried my guitar everywhere I could, its slick body a babe in my arms. The power of music to supersede even severe weather, to block out the long, lonely stretches of time like highway to be sojourned before the destination, not knowing if the destination will be better or worse than the journey itself, is matchless.

The dimly lit, sacred room chanted silently from the front to the rear pews: *nothing allowed but acoustical music here.* The Bluebird's further ban on Pro Tools to fix sweetly off-key moments, of effects to drown sound or brighten it, guarantees only imperfect, intimate moments. Miracles of a moment that dissolve like the cigarette smoke that used to be permitted in the café, the residue of both the music and smoke frescoed onto the walls.

Here, deep in Nashville's roots, in this room, the ingredients of country music: heartfelt emotion, raw sounds, simple chords, repetition, and honesty. Here, the likes of Vince Gill, Lady A, Keith Urban, and even Taylor Swift, were discovered. I never play here to be discovered. I play here because of how intimate it is.

That night, in the very back of the place, in the last pew, sat a swaying bundle of red hair, the man's empty fingers ghosting notes. His pinkened face looked, I would find, always after-orgasm flushed.

At first, I thought maybe he was tweaking when I turned to watch him, but his movement seemed more rhythmical.

Onstage, a girl not more than 13 sang with her mouth barely open to her father's cloying accompaniment. Her voice was nice but only in a best-of-a-small-town way as she avoided the mic. She hit every note dead on like it was broccoli on her plate to be eaten before she could be excused to go do anything else. Her long brown hair covered her features and when I could see her face, I saw that her eyes were tightly closed. I wanted to tell the dad to take her home, let her be a teenager

56

for a couple more years at least. Sometimes voices mature. But his lips moved along with his daughter's.

I watched the girl's father lead her offstage, hand on her back. They moved to the rear of the room, and I finally made eye contact with the girl and smiled. She gave an auto grin. I wanted to pull her into a hug and tell her there is no shame in joining the chess club.

Then a determined strum captured my attention, followed by a host of down-tuned bass notes.

The man who had been in the back of the place now sat onstage; his hair glimmered as he tossed his head backwards like he was doing a shot of air and he sang from a depth I didn't even know existed. His soul was all jagged glass expelled into the dark that would have to find a new name, because when he sang, darkness dissipated.

The muscles of his face contorted as he catapulted syllables from some unidentifiable place in his body. The protracted, terrifying primal scream slowly softened into a vibrato-laden whisper: the pain was still present, but bearable. It was possible to live through it, the notes said, if you sang it away.

The door to my right opened and closed but I barely registered the escape as the father, apparently not wanting his daughter to witness,...what exactly was this? – hustled her out.

The musician's battered Martin had the beginnings of a second hole beat into its face. His thumb and the part of his hand below it must be bruised, the way he attacked his acoustic. Even though his guitar wasn't plugged in, twice the music came from it than should have. With no overhead mic, no less. My eyes couldn't find any other source of amplification. How were his fingers capable of the force that guitar must have taken to be so battered? Surely afterwards his fingers would be bloody?

The man gulped for air, didn't even try to recover before going again.

Then the air grew silent abruptly, but the muscles in his arms remained rigid; he was the song.

No one clapped. No one said or did anything, which seemed fitting.

My shoes carried me out the door after him where I clumsily tried to explain to him and myself what I was feeling with, what were they, words.

Without warning to either of us, my lips attached themselves to his.

After I kissed him, he stood there with his worn Martin dangling from its homemade rope strap across his chest, eyes downcast, hands in his pockets. Though I apologized, I wanted to kiss him again.

"Aren't you going on?" he asked, nodding at my instrument I hadn't realized I had carried out. He wiped at his lips with his shirttail.

The snow fell onto our hair and shoulders.

Still embarrassed I said no, no, of course I wasn't going on, not now. Maybe never.

He loaded his guitar into his green Dodge Caravan with the dented sliding door and laughed the laugh of a musician who knows there's never not another time.

"You haven't been in town long, have you?" I asked.

"A couple of weeks. I found a roommate online, a bassist. He told me to come here the first chance I got."

Yup, Ben.

"He was right."

I called Drake that night, who met with Michael the next day.

Chapter 5

T + 15 hours and *still* no call from the Adulterer of Seville.

After my hair appointment, I hole up back at home. I text Patrick who says there's nothing I can help with just now. (Let's pretend I believe him and that he's not just trying to avoid me.)

Academese was made for these anxiety-laden occasions. The minute you shift into formal language, your emotions check out. I fire my thoughts onto the page, willing this thesis to grow.

Though Mrs. Ramsay's knitting does serve practical ends, she also uses it figuratively. When Mr. Ramsay considers himself a failure, she knits him a new outlook: "Flashing her needles, confident, upright, she created drawing-room and kitchen, set them all aglow; bade him take his ease there, go in and out, enjoy himself. She laughed, she knitted" (16). When he repeats that he is a failure, she flashes her needles again, and this time he believes and can return to his evening routine, refreshed. However, rescuing her husband has emptied Mrs. Ramsay. She only has the strength left to slowly move her finger across the book she is reading to their son. Still, Mrs. Ramsay is happy to have helped her husband: "...there throbbed through her, like a pulse in a spring which has expanded to its full width and now gently ceases to beat, the rapture of successful creation" (17).

I pull a hand down from behind my head and lift my iced tea, flick away the moisture that dribbles off it and onto my chest. I reflexively check my phone and verify that the ringer is cranked open.

I look harder at the working file of my thesis, which I have jokingly named "Southern-Fried Woolf" when I'm not calling it by that nickname born of terror, "Beastis."

My cursor blinks in place on the title page right after my name. Few people recognize that my first name comes from *To the Lighthouse*. When I'm asked about it, I make up different stories every time. One time I'll say it's a family name. The next it's Scandinavian for pie. Once, I claimed it was Hungarian for ravishing as I whipped my hair. If they know where it comes from, I don't have to explain. If they don't know, it's too intimate to share.

In the novel, Mrs. Ramsay knits, and Woolf pairs this with storytelling.

Knitting is a strictly feminine activity in the novel; in several passages, Woolf shows Mrs. Ramsay knitting in a contemplative pose. Vanessa Bell's painting of her sister, Virginia Woolf, knitting in a similar pose in 1912, when Woolf was writing her first novel, The Voyage Out, is telling. The background of gray, repeated in the gray of Woolf's dress, echoed in the mere hint of a face, reveals Bell's understanding of her sister's encroaching mental illness. Woolf makes it clear that Bell knows her better than anyone, so we can take Bell as the authority on her sister.

Bell's broad palette colors Woolf's head, highlighting the knowledge there; sweeps of color emphasize Woolf's pinkish knitting. She "twists" her novel in her mind, perhaps, as she works with her hands

61

on a vibrant creation. Her hunched posture, her sitting in the corner of the chair recalls Mrs. Ramsay's glove found in the corner of a sofa. One part revealed, one part hidden.

Woolf's mental illness doesn't lessen her, not as a person, not as an artist, but since *Lighthouse* is her examination, fictionalization, of her mother, of Woolf's childhood, maybe in it she's trying to figure out if her mental health issues are based on her loss of her mother and the more sinister things that happened to her.

That Woolf literally allowed herself to be painted knitting tells us she found no shame in the activity, yet she makes it clear to the careful reader that Mrs. Ramsay struggles to consistently find her domestic activities important, meaningful. She gives wonderful parties, hosts dozens of guests at their summer home, brings up eight children, and keeps her husband, the famous one, the philosopher, in check, but just. She exhibits a yearning that makes us want to ask what do you want? *if only we thought she would know the answer. But does* Woolf *know?*

Mr. Ramsay has a parallel masculine activity to Mrs. Ramsay's knitting which he delightedly exhibits for Lily: he knots.

"'Now let me see if you can tie a knot,' he said. He pooh-poohed her feeble system. He showed her his own invention. Once you tied it, it never came undone. Three times he knotted her shoe; three times he unknotted it. Thus occupied he seemed to her a figure of infinite pathos. He tied knots. He bought boots" (220).

He can talk for hours about his boots. He delights in showing others how to make knots. In the opening of the novel when Mrs. Ramsay is literally knitting and telling her son he will be able to go to the lighthouse if it is nice out the next day, Mr. Ramsay verbally knots the family situation by saying there is no way they will be able to go, disappointing young James.

62

So knitting = women, knotting = men. This can't be an accident. I shine the language:

Compared to Mrs. Ramsay's knitting, his knotting doesn't immediately seem as constructive, but a family runs on patterns and systems. True, he often knots situations by making guests and family feel his displeasure at petty slights, but the knotting also becomes a means of keeping the family together, especially after Mrs. Ramsay dies. He says of his unique knotting system "Once you tied it, it never came undone" (221). It is something he has come up with himself. He is the knot that keeps the family together. Knots do not come unraveled as quickly as knitting can. He is there even after Mrs. Ramsay exits, keeping the remainder of the family together, something that sounds almost violent and desperate, knotting. He, however, is the one who completes the action of the title, taking his children to the lighthouse.

Woolf said that once she wrote *Lighthouse*, something she did much more rapidly than her other books, she ceased being obsessed with her own dead mother.

There are worse reasons to write.

Mr. Ramsay's figurative knotting lends both negative and positive aspects to the story. He rages and storms about quoting Tennyson. He is capricious. One moment he is fine, the next, angry. When Carmichael, the poet, wants more soup, Mr. Ramsay seethes. But why? A bug in Mr. Ramsay's breakfast prompts him to send the dish sailing out the window. He is convinced of his brilliance, until the next moment, when he believes he is an unmitigated failure. Though it may be a stretch to say the man is mad, he exhibits behaviors that others see as scene making, at the very least.

Though my mother has never complained about anyone wanting a second serving of soup, her mother and father were East Coast, canned soup people. When her parents died in a boating accident (Mother, too, was an only child), she kept the factories running but renamed the soup *Thrive* and turned the business into a charity. Eventually, the company's cans became eco-friendlier pouches which are now frequently shipped to aid in disaster relief.

She kept none of the proceeds and only remains on the board so she can have a hand in what happens to the soup. When I asked, during a period when my father had to work seven days a week whenever he could to pay the bills after she lost her initial funding, how she could bear to give up the soup money, she stared at me. "That only shows you've never had money. I couldn't bear to keep it."

Whenever she and I were at the grocery store when I was a child, I would seek out *Thrive* soup with its nostalgic drawing of what I was told was my grandparents' Hamptons home. Because I never knew them before they passed, it felt like nostalgia by proxy. There was a light on in an upper room on the label, and I asked my mother once if the room had been hers.

"No," she said. She reached out and touched the image on the can, sweeping the trees with her index finger.

"Which room was yours?" I asked, but her hand was already extended towards a bag of oyster crackers.

I now have a standing order for the soup to be shipped to us. I eat a bowl of it occasionally, especially when I'm sick. Whatever we don't finish, when it nears its expiration date, Bernita takes to the food pantry. Rent is so high in Nashville that food insecurity is a given for many families. When I saw a family retrieving food from a dumpster at the Food Lion one evening, I gave them all the cash I had in my wallet (I only had maybe twenty bucks) and took them through the store until they had loaded two carts that I paid for with my credit card. Afterwards, the dad did some yardwork for us until he found a full-time job. They still send us Christmas cards.

I flip through the paperback version of *Lighthouse* that I have pretty much memorized. Mother never mentions that her tower is a stand-in for the lighthouse, yet surely she sees that.

When my mother left my father and me, she permanently shucked her over-articulated manners just as easily as she cast us off. I was shocked the first time she handed me a paper towel in lieu of a cloth napkin at the cabin. When she didn't insist I change for dinner but settled for me washing my hands. Later, she didn't even insist on that.

I toss the book on the table in front of me and pick up my phone. No new messages. But it is time to see Drake.

The beamed foyer of Sweet Thunder Records fills with sunlight as I enter its fieldstone exterior through the door made of crisscrossed logs. Though the air conditioning sweeps welcome coolness towards me on this June day, nervous sweat trickles down my back as if I've entered a hotter domain a whole lot further south.

I say hey to Jolene. She can sing like no one's business, but she swears to Drake, her boss, that she doesn't sing at all, though I've caught her at open mic nights all over the city.

Jolene is all big eyes and mouth, always showing those florescent white teeth, country-cute dark hair, flushing face. By now Drake must know – it's a small town, a smaller business, that Jolene can sing. If he hasn't said anything, then he's not interested. I'd never tell her that, considering what it's rumored she does for him.

Drake and my father knew one another from around town. They didn't develop a friendship so much as a symbiosis; they'd point one another in the right direction on occasion: my father hired himself out (for not more than union scale, I might add) to accompany singers who couldn't play, or if my father played on a demo for someone new to town, he'd pass along the names of the best of the best to Drake, who was always hungry. In return, my father found more gigs than he might have. It wasn't enough to make our family financially solvent, but we survived.

"Been to the open mic at Singalingaling?" I ask Jolene.

"Where's that?" she asks, keeping her voice lower than I've ever heard it. That changes its whole tone and I consider telling her that she should try singing in that register.

I explain to her where the newest west-of-town coffeehouse is, and she says she'll see me there sometime. I pretend to smile as I sink into one of the rustic chairs that is pretty much just hewn from a log. I used to hang out here while my father checked for any work, even short studio gigs after my mother left town. Without her pay from the university, making rent was never a given again.

I fidget with my phone, knowing Drake will decide when he's kept me waiting long enough, trying to terrify me into pre-compliance to whatever he's about to suggest. Because I know that's his game, he's already failed.

"I've been writing, too," Jolene chirps. I smile. Now that might get her somewhere with Drake — he's a songwhore, always seeking a hit for his stable of singers.

Instruments, I secretly call the singers who can't write.

"That's great." It dawns on me she might be asking for me, but probably Michael, to consider writing with her. I play dumb.

Soon after we met and before Drake insisted on it, Michael asked if I wanted to write with him. Everyone co-writes in Nashville. Sometimes it works, sometimes it doesn't. I had already co-written half a dozen times with different people I usually found at open mics or through my father's friends, with various success and little enjoyment. A handful of my songs have done well, recorded by names you'd recognize.

Writing sessions can be tightly timed, regimented get-togethers (always at 10, 2, or 6 o'clock, because everything else in the industry runs on those times) or they can be as intimate as the two (or more) of you just talking about your style. Is there a theme you want to explore? A social issue? A hook you just need help building words around? Sometimes something comes of a session, sometimes not.

If you're smart, you protect your hooks. A great hook can save a lousy song. If fans are singing the chorus, you don't have to worry about the rest. The best songs have strong verses and choruses, though.

And initial the lines you write when you have a cowriter. That can raise the percentage of the song royalties you get. #ProTip

Why wouldn't I say yes to writing with the man with his soul afire? As we wrote, Michael told me he dreamed of performing in stadiums because they would be big enough for his sound.

Performing isn't something I feel the need to do on a regular basis – it's a mechanical method of shopping the songs to others, but for me, once I've written the song, that's all I have to say. I leave it to the performer to serve it. I'm aware that violates the writer/listener circle, but my songs carry what I have to say. Why would you need to hear my voice to get the message?

When Michael and I started writing together, we talked about whether we should date one another, ignoring that I kissed him the night we met. Once I thought it through, I wouldn't agree to go out with him unless he assured me that his asking me out had nothing to do with the fact that I had connected him with Drake. He assured me that his desire to date me had nothing to do with that and everything to do with my pear-shaped ass.

I was all in until he explained that he wanted to keep it casual. He had broken up with a long-time girlfriend when he left Asheville. I'm no prude, but I'm also no booty call, so I said no. For then.

I was young and had just had sex for the first time the summer before with my first boyfriend, an art student I met at the Frist, where he worked in the gift shop.

I broke it off because the guy hated being outdoors. And because his hair was longer than mine, which pissed me off. Whenever we had our sloppy sex, his hair made my face itch.

Michael, however, makes love like he's performing. I almost expect to hear a "thank you and good night," after. I mean, not that his performance isn't spectacular, but I don't feel any closer to him after than before. I've been trying to find the there there; I'm just not sure there is one. Does staying with him make me as superficial as his fans?

Don't answer that.

Art is the sum of its parts. It's not just the wood of the guitar and the steel and nickel of the strings. It's more. Sometimes it's who manages it.

We drifted, early on, into something more without meaning

to. We began assuming we'd be spending time together on weekends without making it official, texting about movies we should go see, or a new restaurant. But we weren't dating, oh no.

Then came the time a guy at a bar asked me out. In front of Michael.

"She's with me," Michael said.

"Am I?"

"Yes," he said, drinking from his beer.

"Actually, I'm with *me*. But I'll date you exclusively if you'll agree to do the same." The guy slunk off, I reckon. I wasn't paying him any mind.

****

My egregiously delayed meeting with Drake goes about as I expect, once he deigns to summon me into his holiest of holies: handshake with the double kiss, sit down, Gorgeous. Thanks for the pralines, had two already. Unacceptable behavior from Michael. Just scandalous. The man doesn't deserve you.

I thank him and move on to a business question.

Drake's hair and eyebrows are cloud white. His skin's pinkish, so his hair is perfect for him, making him more attractive rather than less for the lack of hair color. His body is somehow not soft, though he does have a penchant for candy and can't exercise. I've never seen him wear anything except dress slacks and buttoned-down shirts topped by a blazer of corduroy or denim.

The room's sparse furniture, its desk, fashioned from a vintage barn door, complements the foyer. His laptop has its own desk behind him, like he seldom uses it and keeps it at a distance. From what I know of him, that would be true.

The tour, Drake declares, is officially over. The album

Michael is contracted to write is still due by the end of the summer, to be released in the fall, or Sweet Thunder will have to consider the best course of action. He keeps talking even after I go numb.

I nod and take notes on my iPhone to process later, dabbing at my upper lip when he glances away, trying to give him answers that I don't have.

Those laser blue eyes blaze out of his wrinkled face, one that has known too many cigars and even more secrets.

"What about Rhonda? She seems to think she knows something, Jolene says."

He winces as he reclines in his chair specially padded for his herniated discs. Any other day I might ask him how he's feeling.

"Huh. I just spoke with her this morning." No way am I telling him that we're meeting up.

He brands the air with his cigar. "Speak with her again." He taps the end of his unlit cigar against the desk repeatedly.

Drake attempts to bring himself upright in the chair a couple of times, putting up a hand to stop me when I make to help him.

"I have to take a long-term view of the talent, Briscoe. What might seem like a tempest in a teapot can turn into something ugly and career damaging overnight. I don't need to tell you how conservative our audience is when it comes to fidelity. Which, if you ask me, any infidelity on Michael's part is ridiculous and entirely uncalled for, seeing as how he's married to someone like you."

Flattery and defense of me noted, my softened eyes say. Then I remember Jolene out there, and the rumors I've heard. Drake has been married for as many years as Jolene is old, at least. His wife Edith surely knows, though no one tells her because we're all so sure she does know. And because she's like a dear, sweet dove, favors feathered hats in the palest lilac and soft fur coats. Who could bear to hurt her?

The tin of pralines sits in front of him, and he opens it, picks a sweet and takes a bite, chewing as if it's the only job he has, which tells me how seriously he is taking this scandal, considering he does nothing without extreme forethought. He motions that I should take one. I decline the candy, and immediately reconsider, plucking one from the tin and putting a crumb of it on my tongue.

Why would anyone buy stale, boxed candy when there are fresh miracles made of quality heavy cream and precious pecans mixed with sugar waiting to be bought? This is hope in a box.

****

I met Velvet here at the studio back when I interned for Drake. She refused to shake my hand when I stuck mine out, sliding instead into my vacated seat when I rose to greet her without acknowledging me. She has no idea to this day that I was the one who later uploaded a video to YouTube of her singing off key that session because she, for some reason, (think me) couldn't hear herself in her headphones. She who had never been out of pitch in her life.

Drake reaches into the box in front of him and selects a fresh cigar. He offers me one. I take it, sniff: leaves underfoot in autumn, a rotting banana aroma.

"Have I shown you my newest humidor? Just arrived today. It's lined with Spanish cedar. You get the wrong humidor, you're screwed. Robert sent it over just this morning.

V's Robert. Dammit.

He runs the cigar under his nose. "I think it best if Michael and Velvet remain off the road and work on this next album of Michael's together. That way she can be closer to her uncle. To squash all rumors, let's have her and Michael duet."

I'm on my feet, my face's redness part embarrassment, part rage. I toss the cigar on the desk.

"What are you talking about?" I have never raised my voice to Drake.

He licks the side of his cigar and puts it down. He hasn't smoked in two years, but he always has one in hand.

"Robert suggested the project to me before they even began traveling together and I told him I'd think about it. Let's put it out in the fall instead of Michael's solo album. We'll announce soon, build some buzz. That can be why Michael was upset when he thought Velvet had left – because they were supposed to be working on a project. Just a matter of crossed wires, too many beers."

I sink into my chair, into this alternative reality. "Michael won't agree to this."

Yeah, right. He won't be able to conceal his delight.

He says more, much more. The label needs to capitalize on this brewing "scandal" by announcing that Michael and Velvet will be releasing an album together. As in, writing and recording duets. As in, not wiping away the stain completely but leaving it hanging out there in all its ambiguous glory. A joint album would both "prove" they hadn't been together (because how would they have the guts to record together if they had?), but also leave things open to lucrative insinuation and interpretation (because everyone will think 'who knows?' and isn't listening for "evidence" oneself half the fun?

He says we need to rent a house to stay in for the duration, including V. I protest loudly, but he merely shuffles some papers decisively, sucks on that cigar unlit, and gestures towards the door.

The meeting has left me feeling punched, and I remove the ticket I find on my windshield and shove it into the glovebox without even reading it.

The ice cream shop on my right as I pull out offers instant consolation. I head into the drive thru. At a mental flash of V's corset-like waist, I briefly consider driving away. Though V's face is a bit bony, she doesn't look bad for fifty. Forty-fiveish, same difference. She seems to take no pleasure in food whatsoever. When we are on the road she regularly fasts for "religious reasons," though it would be more socially acceptable nowadays if she simply called it intermittent fasting. I haven't enlightened her.

V's cheekbones get sharper during her restrictions, as well as her tone. We take turns urging her to eat to make her more bearable to be around. Her fasting typically happens near anniversary dates, I've discovered: her parents' birthdays, the day they died, and other, less fathomable to me, dates that I believe are made up just to keep her slim.

"Make it a large," I say as I try not to drown in recalling

I didn't bother telling Drake my thesis is due by the end of September or no degree; he wouldn't have cared. He would only have reminded me that Velvet is a legacy act, that her family's catalog props the company up some years.

I accept the cup from the bored woman at the drive-thru window when she inverts and then rights it. I navigate onto Highway 70 and spoon some chilled crack into my mouth.

"Be sure to confirm the caterer for tomorrow night," I tell Patrick when he answers his phone.

"To the right," Patrick yells off phone.

"We still have to have the benefit regardless. Drake says he will be there."

"Obviously," he said. "Get that tacky thing out of here! This is not a quinceañera," he shouts, tonguing the enye admirably, though with a twang.

I'll bawl him out for that when I see him in person.

My eyes want so badly to close as I speak, but since I'm driving, I content myself with a squint. "So, by the way, Joy told me everything at brunch. You had to have known about the...situation between Michael and V."

"Joy is such a filler face. I mean, is any of her still original?"

"*Did* you know?" We both know he knew, but we have to get past this.

Finally, he says, "If I tell you every rumor I hear, I wouldn't be doing my job. I'm supposed to protect you."

"You're my *assistant*, dammit."

He complains to someone about the chairs again and then, "I work for both of you." This is not the first time we've been around this mountain. Technically he's right, but Michael has so many sycophants around who are more than willing to do his bidding he doesn't require much of Patrick.

And, let's face it, Patrick (until now) has been loyal to me. I thought we were friends.

"I'm the one who hired you." Threat issued.

I locate a lump of brownie with my spoon, scoop it into my mouth and try to talk around it.

Patrick: "We may be in the South but dear God, *what* are you hanging from the fence? Stonewall Jackson does not live here." To me: "Call you back?"

I agree, and after we hang up, I fling the half-full cup out of

74

the car. Imagine my lack of surprise when a police car glides down a hillside drive adjacent to the highway and appears behind me. *Had to cue the cop,* I mutter to the sky.

At her insistence, I get out and pick up the cup, look around for where to put it, ask her if I can cross the street to throw it away at a gas station.

"Worth it," I say when I return, and the officer hands me a ticket.

She puts her hands on her hips. "Want me to search your car? Could be somebody's got the munchies for a reason."

I should mention that I never, ever, litter. So, fuck me that I get pulled over the one time I do.

I buckle my seat belt and start the car. "Unless you're going to arrest me for having classic literature and bubble-wrapped Waterford in my trunk, you're wasting your time."

The officer returns my license. "You kin to Mickey Chambers?"

"Michael, ah, Mickey's, my husband." (That ridiculous stage name. Sounds like the mouse. Goddamned Drake insisted, though. None of us call him that in real life.) At times like these I don't feel ambivalent about strategically taking Michael's last name. I would have pulled the Chambers card earlier, but the officer had seemed provoked by my "fancy" car. It happens.

"I saw his fall on TV," she says. "He okay?"

I drop my head and don't even have to pretend to cry as I say yes. After a moment, the officer leaves my peripheral vision, returning with a packet of tissues. She pulls out one after another and hands them to me until I can compose myself enough to glance up at her.

"Go ahead home, now," the woman says, taking the damp ticket from my limp hand and ripping it up.

I silently thank the country music gods for this act of mercy.

Though there are a few news vans still outside our gates, they are now appropriately distanced, so I make it through without incident. I don't think about what my makeup must look like as they snap photos.

When I enter our house proper, I'm so happy to be back in my own space that I shed my sweaty, tear-dampened shirt and my jeans, too. Since the top of my car was down, the lousy air conditioning didn't do much good. I should get it repaired, but I'm not home enough for it to make that much of a difference.

Bernita follows, picking up my clothing, asking questions about Michael.

When I don't answer, but instead head for the fridge and grab a Bud Light, one of the perks of Michael's product endorsement I actually use, she stops her spew long enough to ask, "Rough day?"

Her sharp edges make me feel less guilty for the times I've asked her to clean the hair out of the bathtub drain, though I'd do it more often myself if she didn't bitch about it. What is it about the role of housekeeper that she doesn't get?

When she's earnest, she's more homely than usual, with her teeth that need orthodontia (I've offered), that endearing bob of hair both the color and texture of hay, and her perpetual wearin' o' the scrubs. I especially hate it when she cooks in them, but she pretends she can't understand my preferences so she can do what she wants. They're adorable on her, but she reminds me of a doctor just after surgery in them. Gross. I still hate them. I flee to my bedroom.

Patrick blows in and closes the blinds. "I know you don't care about how I feel, but there's a yard filled with guys outside those curtains."

I fold my arms and give him a glare aimed to melt his moderately sculpted muscles. It's too bright for them to see in, and who said I'm ashamed to show my body?

As much as Patrick likes to think he's a style maven, he wears his pants too tight and his ever-present scarves creep some of my acquaintances out. That said, he's a skinny sweetie with brown hair and strategic highlights, starched (any color or pattern; he has them all) button downs, and lovely wide belts. Yes, he's judgmental and pretentious but so? He loves country music even if it doesn't love him so much. I, in turn, love him for his loyalty. Or used to.

"I'm *wearing* underwear. By the way, I have several shopping bags in the trunk, if you could bring them in. Careful, I bought more stemware. Michael's family is coming in."

He laughs. "Two dingy triangles of underwired pink up top that have almost come loose from their moorings, and a square of, I think I might swoon, ivory *cotton* on the bottom with (he whirls around me) dental floss in the back is proper underwear now?" He glares at my body as if he wanted to go at it my underwear with a needle and thread. Or at my stomach with a lipo wand.

Being without clothing is not the nakedness that bothers me, although my arms involuntarily cross my stomach, I notice.

"Have you heard from him?" I steady my hand on the dresser.

Patrick's expression answers. I open my mouth to bark at him for not cluing me in, but I know he'd only say again that he had been protecting me, and he would be partially right. I'm sure this will not be the only time we dance upon the head of this pin.

I walk into the bathroom and, maneuvering quickly, toss my underwear behind me, causing Patrick to flee.

Once alone, I stick my finger down my throat. A rush of already digesting ice cream. It's no use. Just as well. Do I really want to go there again?

A better question: will I be able to prevent it?

My muscle memory tends to bring it on of its own accord when I'm stressed, anyway. But ice cream is tricky.

I stand upright and dry my eyes and I remember the goodies in my trunk, the ones that won't inflate my ass.

"Don't forget the bags," I text Patrick. One should never underestimate the comfort of filthy lucre, of vices large and small. They are what make life. Say it one more time.

I run a bath, shake in pomegranate-scented bath salts and double down with pomegranate bubble bath.

Sipping the beer, I push the "call" button on my phone, leaving yet another message on yet another band member's phone, being careful not to say anything press worthy, just in case. Those drunken choruses of the song "We Are Family" on the bus hadn't meant anything? Shocking.

My head throbs. Eventually, I pull myself out of the tub like primordial ooze.

I tug on hip huggers, still cotton. Putting on a bra always pleases me, making my silhouette into a ship's masthead. Simple jeans and a blue, V-necked tee paired with nothing but pearls, the gray ones Michael bought me when he went to Japan, are enough for my planned backyard evening tonight.

Until today, I had been looking forward to the fundraiser. Patrick and I have spent hours coordinating with Ride 'Em's director. We've called in every favor possible in town, collared every musician of note within 100 miles we could, country or no. We've gone begging to every business in Nashville for auction merchandise. Last year we raised thousands, and in this second year, we aim to double it. It's doable. Ironically, especially, now. Scandal is peoplenip, you know.

With Patrick's bossy gene in high gear, I sit back in an Adirondack chair with a Bud Light Lime, an even more preferable member of the Bud family. Bernita hovers, tentatively offering to sit beside me.

"What, are you going to hold my hand? Just keep 'em coming," I say. I don't need any pity from those soft brown eyes, but I do require alcohol from those hands.

With a sigh at the hurt expression quickly hidden on my housekeeper's face, I pat the chair beside me. She sits. Her nose rabbits like she wants to say something but can't remember what.

The yard teems with workers, tents, chairs, and bunting. Banners, signs. PA. Podium. More. The day dissolves and refracts in the heat like the modernist "plot" of a later Woolf novel.

I eat at some point, bland chicken and noodles with mashed potatoes, from a plate foisted upon me by Bernita. My mind registers that the food isn't as good as usual, but I'm still cognizant enough not to say so.

My finger fruitlessly masturbates the phone. I drink more and laugh about nothing.

"I tell you not to let her tour with you," Bernita says, shifting in her chair.

"Michael stare when she sing. Then he close his eyes like she bring God down on a cloud with her voice. I tell you this more than once."

I rest my head on her shoulder and she touches my neck

79

like she's patting a meatloaf smooth in the pan.

Waving my empty, I am soon in possession of another bottle of beer and after slamming back a large part of it, dive into the saltwater swimming pool where a splash informs me that Patrick has joined me, speaking in that annoying "You're drunk and I'm not," placating tone, begging me to get out, to at least hand him my pearls.

"Pearls come from the water, jackass. This won't hurt them."

He makes some argument about the string they're on, but I don't listen. He's wrong and I don't have to explain why.

I demand cake. Cookies are produced instead, which I shy at Bernita and Patrick and then I hand feed the remaining ones to the men who have "taken a break" to gather around the pool. "Here, puppy," I say, going from guy to guy and tucking a cookie between their teeth, shutting their jaws and making the sign of the cross.

Cake eventually does arrive, along with a handful of forks, because I'm Briscoe. Everyone in the house eats directly from the rectangle, plunging in forks, separating the skin of icing from the tender cake flesh. Consuming the flour, egg, sugar as if they are the individual components, not understanding the beauty they have become. I call them philistines aloud, and they are, because they don't even know what I mean by that.

Someone (me, I'm pretty sure) leads a rendition of YMCA, spurred on by the tiny denim shorts of one of the men, who I press into service as the "C."

"Michael," I whisper as my hands form the M, and I collapse poolside, weeping. I'm only vaguely aware of Patrick waving the men back to their jobs as he gathers me into his lap.

"You smell like a piña colada. And by the way, tell them to go home now. I'm not paying overtime." I push off him and flop into a chair to his right.

Eventually, Patrick and Bernita march Drunk Briscoe inside.

"You're not my mother," I say.

I reach for my phone, but I can't call *my* mother for sympathy.

"How could he?" I moan.

"Shhh…"

"You never want to listen to me. Why do you hate me?" I ask the woman who is always freshly brown. The deep woods, fake-and-baked hayhoo.

Bernita pulls my sheet up to my neck. I kick it to the floor and frown at her until she leaves the room.

I call Michael, leaving him messages in every vein. Angry, desperate, threatening, sad. If it weren't for the ramifications I knew Mr. Selfish Himself wasn't even contemplating, I'd cancel the meet up with Rhonda and hop a plane regardless of what Benny suggests.

If Michael and I divorce, this silence will stretch out forever. We've had music, battles. Songs, arguments. Jokes. We've never had silence between us before.

Patrick brings me red Gatorade and a gaggle of ibuprofen tablets he insists will stave off a hangover. After I chug a quarter of the bottle of liquid, I stick out my tongue to glimpse the bloody colored tip, try to touch it to my nose, succeed, make Patrick attempt the same with his own – he can't. I make the fun of him that he deserves for his stubby tongue.

"Don't you have a meeting with Rhonda in the morning?" he asks.

"Listen, you've earned your wings. Now go away."

But he and Bernita (who of course returns) both sit with me, he on the floor, her on the edge of the bed, and tell stories

81

about their lives to keep me company like we are enduring a blackout. Which I am hoping for: for me to black out. How else can you escape yourself? Suspended animation. Self-induced coma. Why isn't there an OTC pill to create those? Because these two are in the room, I can't sneak off for a gag fest and my stomach is doing a countdown to ass expansion. Eventually, I can bear it no longer and flee anyway.

When I'm back, I can't make out a thing they are saying with their Droning Employee Podcast, but something inside me knows they are trying to be kind. They're on their phones trying to call in reinforcements for tomorrow, as we're expecting attendance to be at the maximum.

"You both deserve raises," I say. Their eyebrows sky. So, I'm not exactly generous. Hard to believe you're always going to have enough when you've been faced with the fear of eviction umpteen times in your life. I have money hidey places: in books, under the mattress, of course. Multiple savings accounts in multiple banks. Just in case.

If you haven't had to do homework by candlelight and pretend to enjoy it, you have no idea.

"I'm serious. Get me some paper."

Bernita hands me my ever-present hookbook from off my nightstand (I only use my phone for notes when I'm out and about, then I transfer them to paper – pen and paper were good enough for my dad). I scribble a reasonable facsimile, I think, of: "I, Briscoe, of somewhat sound mind and notably unsound soul, do hereby declare that Bernita and Patrick have earned a raise of $100 each weekly, effective immediately."

"Fair enough?"

The pair nods a little too enthusiastically for my conscience. Bernita folds the paper and puts it in her pocket. Maybe I should have doubled the amount, but I'm not that drunk.

****

A noise around two a.m. causes me to wake reflexively and check my phone and I find a text from Michael. I hold the recently purring animal to my aching chest briefly before clicking on his message.

He is fine, had just been stinkin' drunk, sorry for not calling but no reception, coming home soon in time for the benefit as originally planned, and we will talk more then. He's fine, please forgive him, etc.

I leap out of bed and riffle through the kitchen junk drawer to find rubber gloves to duct tape to my hands. The orange fingers droop like a lank rooster's comb and I can't resist shaking them at one another as if they are puppets, but at least this prevents me from answering right away. I climb back into bed, determined to try to sleep. Funny, it dawns on me as I almost drift out again, how he had enough service to text but not to call.

Before, Michael's stupidity was "only" physical. The times I found out about, anyway, he'd been drinking, been stupid, with no-name groupies who could be paid to go away. Michael and I talked with a discreet celebri-pastor a few times who told me I needed to be with Michael on the road all the time if I expected him to "behave himself" with all of that temptation around. So...I allowed myself to be persuaded to become Michael's road manager/guard dog on a more permanent basis as soon as I graduated from college.

I called Michael's first (known to me) indiscretion, "The One with the Nipple Ring." Let's not go into how, but I now own the woman's nipple ring. I had it sterilized and made into an earring that I wear as a piercing high up on my right ear.

83

The second, I called "The One with the Fellatio Oratorio." This fan with multicolored hair and a short jean skirt had these *expensive* shoes, and you could tell the way she repeatedly wiped at them while she waited in line to meet Michael that they were the only ones she'd ever had. I thought it was cute, until it wasn't.

Don't worry; I didn't take them from her when I found her affixed to Michael like a hood ornament. Didn't take *both* shoes, anyway.

I planted basil in her right devil-red bottomed high heel (you know the brand) to remind me that marriages must be taken care of. The basil died. I let it rot in the shoe.

The infidelity didn't crack us as wide open as you would have expected. But his sound changed, gained some bitterness. You can't trespass against yourself and it not show.

I told him I'd make him regret it in ways he'd never dream of if he ever cheated again. No need to elaborate, not to him, not to you.

I had thought Michael's improved behavior since those early "mistakes" was genuine, perhaps heartfelt, and not due to my eagle-eyed supervision. He seemed sorry, tried to be nothing but polite to even the most ardent fans after his indiscretions. Until V., I've had no further reason to doubt him.

I sit up, bite off the tape, rip off the gloves, and start packing an overnight bag. How dare Michael think he can get by with not talking to me?

My head tilts *and* my body, a reminder of the evening's overindulgence.

The blouse in my hands falls onto the bed as I recall I have Rhonda in the morning; I can't miss that meeting unless I want the true story (which I'm assuming she has more than a strong whiff of) to be on the front page of *On the Nash Front*.

I call everyone in the band in turn like I am loading them on the bus and doing roll call. Repeatedly. No one answers. I had only wanted to get an ETA, something nice and businesslike, a way to reassert my manager self into the mix.

It takes some effort, but with Patrick's reluctantly texted help, I get online, open the phone account for the band and crew, and disconnect all lines but mine and Patrick's. Let the bitches buy burners.

I dial V., but quickly hang up.

I turn my useless phone off and flop backwards onto the bed, arms outstretched.

My eyes close, but I can't sleep. At some point I feel the weight of a sheet once again and murmur my thanks without even opening my eyes. I know exactly whose overly bronzed hand brushes mine, but I don't feel like talking.

After she leaves, I fetch a cup of coffee, turn on my computer. I'm more sober than I ought to be, but that's due to the heartache. I write, knowing full well this will have to be heavily edited. Writing is the only thing that calms my mind.

The lighthouse is more than a literal destination. For those who know Woolf's work (or what a metaphor is), this is evident from the book's title. What exactly this lighthouse symbolizes, however, or who, is open to interpretation. Several candidates emerge.

Is Mrs. Ramsay the lighthouse? She's the beacon of warmth and hospitality that everyone gathers around. She's certainly a possible candidate.

Much like Mrs. Ramsay, Michael makes you forget there is anything sad in the world, any kind of illness, poverty, war, tragedy. He's a heat source all his own. He's constantly on.

One could see the lighthouse as phallic, and therefore perhaps

Mr. Ramsay more closely resembles the lighthouse. Yes, with his intellectual, tepid, illusory celebrity, with his gaggle of sycophants, he could be the one everyone wants to surround and yet, because of his lack of emotional depth, because of his emotional immaturity, that's as far as it goes.

The man himself knows he can go no further with his theories, but he thinks he has hidden it from others.

One could say that the idea of the lighthouse offers illusive (and elusive) peace, a semi-mythical shelter for both the children and Lily in the novel after the center of the book disintegrates as the bomb of war scatters and separates the Ramsays from their children, and from one another.

The story meanders, then, further afield as the reader tries to regain equilibrium. Just as the family loses its center with Mrs. Ramsay, the reader loses the expected thread. While the story free floats among characters from the beginning, it all comes back to Mrs. Ramsay until she abruptly exits the story. Lily doesn't return to access the lighthouse for ten years. When she tries to get closer to the lighthouse now that the one who was the lighthouse for her is gone, she does so, although clearly, she has chosen her own path by not marrying and by pursuing her art professionally.

Or, should I say, that's what the passages looked like after I edited them. I found a long line of gibberish where I left off and assume I passed out over it. Literally.

Chapter 6

Take a headache, twin it, add the twin to the first headache, multiply it by two, and that is how incapacitated I feel when I wake, despite my brief caffeinated jag of writing the night before. So, no gym. I attempt to ignore the panic ignited because: YESTERDAY'S FOOD+LACK OF EXERCISE. The way I know my head will pound with each lunge, the prospect of each goblet squat bringing on a groan, decide me. I'll eat less today instead.

Funny how less weight, less eating, makes you more in others' eyes when you're a woman. That is stupid, but true. Even feminists have to acknowledge reality to battle it. To be more you have to weigh less, at least in the current cultural climate.

Patrick has left the thing that I have asked him for on the table. I reach for it and blast out the door.

By swallowing two cups of coffee in succession handed to me by Bernita, coupled with a trio of ibuprofen, I make my meeting.

At the Pancake Pantry, I reluctantly remove my sunglasses (definitely not needed as early as it is; It's 7 in the morning; what was I thinking?) as I come in through the kitchen (as always; oh, right. That's why I was wearing them.) to avoid the line of tourists out front. I shout howdy at the cook, who flips a pancake and raises the spatula to his forehead in a salute. The aroma of frying food that usually causes my stomach to growl produces a different sensation today.

Rhonda rises when I approach her table, and we pretend to kiss one another's cheeks as we sit on opposite sides of the booth; I also pretend I don't see her eyeing my purse.

Her hair almost matches her brown eyes. Her features are sharp. Attractive, more or less my age, that tipping point where you discover whether or not you're going to get what you thought you would in life: career, love, money, or give up and buy a dog. Body by MMA, Hot Yoga, or trending-of-the-week class. She wears a Saturday date outfit befitting her age and profession: dark jeans and a turquoise tunic, chunky statement necklace, red platform sandals. Your Pinterest-worthy-basic-in-Nashville look.

When Rhonda turns her head, I note the upper half of her hair is pulled back and anchored with a black plastic claw.

I ask Heidi, the server, how her kids are before asking for sweet tea, try to squeal over the photos she pulls up on her phone. All I can grasp is that the youngest (curls, brilliant green eyes) will be in first grade after this summer. I really try to focus, but this is not that morning, and I pat her on the back in case she notices. I don't think she does.

Rhonda and I both order the sweet potato pancakes without glancing at the menu. Because why would you order anything else here?

My breakfast companion grimaces at my beverage order like she's afraid my chunkiness might be contagious and asks for water.

After the water is delivered, she drags on the straw like the beverage might have anti-fat properties. Far be it from me to point out that the pancakes aren't exactly a carb hater's haven, not even with the health halo of the sweet potatoes. Then again, Rhonda has ordered them to pretend she can eat whatever she wants and keep her shape while also showing she can control herself and not eat more than a few bites. I know this game, and while I'm not above it, not today.

I drink my sweet tea, grateful for the hydration.

"Did you get the statement?"

"I did," Rhonda says, sucking on her straw. My hung-over ears protest.

We speculate about a music exec and his breakfast partner hiding in a corner booth and what that might mean, about trends in music.

I thank her for meeting with me so early, but she's a journalist. They take what they can get. She says she understands how busy we must be with the benefit coming up tonight.

She pulls her lips from the crimson-covered plastic straw.

"Some more water over here?" I call to keep the woman across from me from making that ghastly noise again but talking so loudly is as painful as hearing the sound would be, so it isn't a win.

As if we don't both know that Rhonda is employing the drink-as-much-water-as-you-can-hold-to-avoid-eating trick. You don't eat because you don't want to be judged but the people who are judging you are eating. They're judging you, so you won't judge them.

I return the nod of a lanky studio musician Michael and I know, Chad. It's a mistake because the man and his pronounced Adam's apple bob over to ask with "concern" what happened to Michael, after I have introduced him to Rhonda who presents – no other word will do – her hand to him.

"Oh, he was being a good ol' boy when I wasn't around. Had a few too many and fell," I say.

When Rhonda finally releases the man's hand, he squats tableside, revealing gym-hammered quads wrapped in jeans. He cracks his knuckles, and the noise fireworks throughout my foggy brain.

"How is he?"

"His pride was hurt way more than his arm," I say, a jag of terror imagining Michael permanently damaging his arm throbbing through me. I'd have to have Michael put down if he couldn't play. He'd *want* to be put down.

Chad offers to fill in for Michael if needed at the benefit (of course he has a motive for coming over), leaning in for a hug. I return it, briefly, and discover his arms are as tight as his legs. Holla.

If Michael thinks I am naïve, he's wrong. I get it – the world is full of fit bodies and fine minds, of lust of the body, the mind, the soul. Bodies everywhere. The hardened ones, the comfortably softer ones. Bodies all capable of giving and receiving pleasure. Of covalent bonding, unpairing, reconfiguring. But see, that's where I thought marriage vows came in: if they weren't needed to keep us monogamous, we wouldn't have them. We ask society to keep us accountable in moments just like this by marrying.

Or maybe that's just how I see it. Apparently Michael, not so much.

I pat Chad on his chest, mistake number two. The physical contact with a human threatens to bring tears to my eyes; I pop my sunglasses on as I thank him for stopping by.

Chad mentions he might have a news story for Rhonda about an up-and-coming band. She texts him her number because she'd like to hear more. Right.

"So," Rhonda says as he leaves, though she watches him until he's out of sight.

Just then our food arrives, pancakes the color of gentle morning sunlight on mellow orange bricks.

I fan my napkin conspicuously over my blouse before bisecting the pile of powdered sugar and cinnamon dusted cakes and overfilling my mouth, noting Rhonda's discomfort with pleasure.

I remove my sunglasses.

"What do you want to know?" I ask through my stuffed mouth, closing my eyes to savor the taste, though the calorie meter starts running.

"Is it true about him and Velvet?"

I chortle and shove another bite in, watch the pitiful animal of hunger scramble across Rhonda's face as I chew. She saws at the soft cakes before her as if they are an enemy, then does little more than move them around.

"I thought you were a reporter, not a gossip columnist."

I peg Rhonda as a chew and spitter when she's alone. I almost offer her the unused coffee cup on my side of the table.

No one our age(ish) in this town is without an eating disorder, even if it is "only" perpetual dieting and/or being exercise obsessed. It's so prevalent it's not even really acknowledged.

"I have a source. A credible one."

I eat one more bite, double dipping into the restaurant's signature cinnamon cream syrup, another moment of joy in the presence of my enemy before having to speak.

"You've barely touched yours," I say to acknowledge Rhonda's achievement as I decide on one more one more bite. Then I wipe my mouth and throw my napkin onto my plate. Excessive Southern incivility is always followed by a show of power. Bank on it.

I pick up and swing "my" purse from side to side. Her eyes follow it.

"This is for you."

"Excuse me?"

"I saw you eyeing my Kate Spade bag at the Forks Chili Cook-off last month. I happen to know she's one of your favorite designers, so here's one for you. And I also put a little something inside it for you to spend on a worthy cause, whatever that might be."

I shove the handbag towards her, smiling. It's a clone of the one I own. I had Patrick track one down. I'm sure it wasn't easy, given the time crunch, but he managed. I gave him no choice.

She hesitates for a moment before tugging the bag towards herself.

I grin, but it falters as I notice a familiar mark on the bottom of the purse.

"I've got to be going. So much to do for the benefit. We've got to get those children some more horseflesh. They say riding gives them self-confidence and someone to talk to."

Rhonda glances into the purse, reaches inside. Her lips move. I could have saved her the trouble of counting: 2K.

I throw some bills for my food down, rise, don my sunglasses. She won't be able to let me pay for her meal, not openly, since she's a journalist, but she can sure as hell covertly take my bribe.

Only once in my car do I begin shaking. I wait, watch as Rhonda gets into her Buick.

"Chump change," I whisper. The handbag is a classy touch if I do say so myself. I am aware a Kate Spade bag isn't upper rung, but it's the most a local news reporter can carry without suspicion. I do bribes right.

I exhale and mime a hellacious explosion to my right, where Rhonda is parked. "Kapowie!" I exclaim as Rhonda takes off like she's pulling a bank job.

I remove my sunglasses for a minute, groan, put them back on. The town's population would decrease substantially if I could do away with everyone who pisses me off.

Where is that tight-thighed Chad?

I dig for more ibuprofen in the car's console, find a couple that aren't too fuzzy, dry swallow them, and press the gas pedal.

It's only when I'm almost home that I realize Rhonda has won after all: I forgot to ask her who her source was. No matter. I'll ask her tonight. There's no way she'd miss the benefit, not her or anyone else from the media in town.

When I return to the house, Patrick holds a cardboard dessert container aloft in the living room: "Chocolate strawberry cheesecake."

"Isn't it a little early for cheesecake?" I say, hoisting it by its white ribbon, a box of instant forgetfulness. His high-pitched squeal and my own desire to bury my face in the dessert make me hesitate as I go towards the trash.

I note his untended sideburns, his wrinkled shirt.

"No! Dustin and the blond?" So the cheesecake isn't really for me? For a moment, that probably matters more than it

93

should.

His boyfriend is a guest on a reality show where men who are straight are "friends" with men who aren't. The show pushes to see if they can kindle a flame or even just a moment of someone questioning their sexual orientation.

"Yup. And the whole world's going to know, which might be the worst part. I begged him to quit the show – I could tell he was getting close to that jacked *Jim*."

He wails into the sofa. Into the silk pillows. I locate the tissue box, thrust it at him with a "Here." How can I tell him to stop ruining my fine French pillows without sounding like a total vag?

"Dios mio la chulupa pita…" Bernita enters the room with a feather duster.

"For the last time, you are not Latina, and I know enough Spanish to know that's not it," Patrick yells. "It sounds like you're ordering fast food from God. And this is the 21st century – buy a Swiffer, for God's sake." He tosses a pillow at her, and I rescue it and put it on the chair farthest from the sofa.

With another gust of unintelligible syllables, Bernita leaves the room. I put my arms around Patrick and open the pink box, show him the multi-swirled treat with the chocolate on top. Who doesn't love food packaged like a gift? I hold up my finger while I leave him long enough to get a fork.

When I return, I dip into the cheesecake and give him the laden utensil. He takes a big bite, hands me back the fork. While he tells me the story, I eat the rest. His eyes narrow when I scrape my fork against the cardboard bottom.

"Yeah, I know it was my purse I gave Rhonda," I say as I drag the fork heavily along the bottom one more time.

"You have a new one coming tomorrow. It was the best I could do on such short notice."

I shake the empty container at him. Then I hug him, as if I can squeeze his pain from him. I try not to panic that it's already so late.

When he begins answering the dings on his phone, I figure he's reasonably okay, and I dictate a list of what we need to accomplish yet. When he tells me he has his own list, I defer to him. Just as long as someone has it all under control.

Chapter 7

My feet intermittently sweep the wooden planks of the porch as my body swings in and out of the sunlight and my fingers continue typing. "Find My Friends" on my phone claims that Michael is only ten minutes away. My *phone*, not Michael, not his minions, tells me, regardless of the fact that we have a media appearance scheduled for later this morning. I've been watching my phone like it's Doppler radar. Knowing roughly where Michael is happens to be part of my job as his road manager, so I track his phone in case he is ever lost, left behind, or kidnapped. *Of course* I haven't used it for any other purpose, ever. Wink, wink.

To find him, I had to reactivate his phone. Didn't mean I had to turn back on the phones of the rest of the band or his useless roadies, so I didn't.

I've approved the final benefit to-do list, and Patrick's outside commanding workers and volunteers in the backyard. I'm keeping a low profile until the event starts.

I have to do something, anything, besides stare at the app to see how close Michael is to getting here, so I write.

As noted before, Woolf's sister, Vanessa Bell, was a painter. Woolf was so close to her sister one could see them at times as one. Which means Lily also stands in as Woolf herself in the story. (Rumor has it that Virginia and Vanessa decided that Vanessa would paint, and Virginia would write. It could easily have gone the other way.)

Woolf examines what happens when a pillar is removed from a family.

Despite the doubting, secondhand observations about the nature of the Ramsays' marriage, it can't be denied that there is a deep and abiding affection between them, a connection that any momentary taciturnity or fleeting irritation can't eradicate.

In the distance, a cloud of gray becomes a bus the size of a fist. Upon seeing it, I jump up to head indoors with my laptop, turn at the doorway, pause, then rush inside.

The Prevost's brakes steam to a stop outside the front door.

Somehow, I am at the sink. I pick up and wet a sponge, run it across the counters, stare out into the backyard. Behind me I hear the front door open, and the sound of Michael's bus slippers shuffling in the foyer like twin timid dogs. They slide their way into the kitchen with its acres of marble counters. I glance sideways at Bernita.

After a moment, the bus sighs away.

I find myself sunflowering towards Michael as Bernita intercepts him with a hug when he saunters in with his duffle bag.

While he and the housekeeper embrace, I eye the sling on his left arm, his pale face with its squinched up features, disheveled red hair. Then those green eyes turn towards me, and I whip my hair in front of my face, so I won't notice if his face glows when he sees me. I sneak a glance and ignore the way he winces when he shifts his burden. Who cares that when he drops his bag his shoulders sag? So what that every line of his face says, "forgive me?" His eyes, always wide, initially

97

shine (I can't help staring at him now) with joy but drop at encountering my scowl.

He bends over his bag and brings out a Tiffany blue box and offers it to me. I admire it before giving Bernita the stink eye. That greeting seemed way too sympathetic.

"You're fired," I say to Bernita as I open the back door. She knew, too, didn't she? At least now I won't have to pay her that raise. My chest feels like I've just fired a shotgun. There is, apparently, no loyalty in heaven or on earth.

"You're not fired," Michael yells behind him as he follows me out the patio doors, sliding the glass closed at Bernita's automatic behest: "Muchacho, paluga door now."

His hand nearly touches my shoulders as he reaches out. I unwillingly wilt towards him as he smiles and places the box on the grill in front of me, and I try not to see it, gazing at the white tent farther away instead.

If you've ever had the prospect of Tiffany's in front of you, you know what my pulse is doing about now.

I feint as if I'll pick up the box but switch on the grill instead. He reaches for the knob but his hand lands in the flame; he doesn't flinch. I switch it back off.

"Let me see," I say, inspecting his hand.

It's as calloused and warm as ever.

He closes his right hand over mine, and I shut my eyes before jerking loose.

"Whatever's in that box better be expensive." The outside of the box is barely charred, so any jewelry inside will be fine. Considering, what else would he dare offer?

I flee to the yard where workers pop table legs into place and then upright the tables as gently as if they're flipping ballet dancers, drag chairs across the lawn as if they're doing the tango with them, poking holes in the perfectly maintained grass. A couple of volunteers fuss with Patrick over the best place for the cash bar.

When Lily can't understand Mr. Ramsay's work, his son Andrew tells her to think of a table. After that she always pictured one perched in a tree when she thinks of his philosophy. I toss my love up into the tree for now, hoping it will be safe until I decide what to do with it. Is love a separate being or a refillable commodity? Do you only have so much? Or is it pumped fresh for each relationship? Does it disappear or dissolve when you're done wrong?

Normally, I'd complain about the condition of the grass, but I don't have the energy to do more than throw my hands up at Patrick in the distance, who shrugs and raises both eyebrows, nods toward Michael as if to ask how it's going.

I shake my head sharply. He pulls an exaggeratedly sad face.

Walking in the grass stirs the smell that usually stays so close to its base, that secret aroma of growth in progress. Only now do I think to stop and motion to Patrick to ask how he's doing over Dustin, but his back is to me.

In an adjacent pasture, the neighbor's goats lend a pastoral air with their stubby horns and faux innocent bleats. Don't let them fool you – they are armed sheep. Once when I was at my mother's, a rogue billy goat chased me. I hid in the outhouse until she came to rescue me.

I wander over towards the goats to escape the workers' stares.

"Look at those baby goats," Michael says as we face the fence.

He reaches for my hand. I put both of mine behind my back.

The bells and bleats send up a song that soon has Michael humming along.

A guttural noise catches my attention, and I realized that Michael is bleating me an apology:

"I'm sorrrryyy…I'm sorrryyy." My face trembles, but it's not something to laugh about, my countenance says when I eventually master my muscles.

The goats line up at the fence, waiting for him to bless them and he does, bending to scratch heads, patting some. Even they seem aware of his celebrity.

"They stink. And they sound like a woman who needs to clear her throat," I say.

He crooks his finger and motions me closer as he hums. My pesky feet don't listen to me when I refuse.

The smallest goat, piebald, ducks between the rail, and I bend to pet her. She butts me right in the eye with a nub.

I fold in half and Michael bends down to check on me while I cry harder than necessary.

"Briscoe, baby," Michael says as he inspects my eye. Once we determine I've not been blinded, he raises his good arm like a preacher doing an altar call and sings my name again.

Worker ants still buzz, setting up poles, twining lights around the fence.

"Stop it."

He's waving his arms using his stage motions.

"Let's go inside and talk," he says, extending his arm, but I bat it away. He doesn't want to talk. He's just afraid I'll make a scene.

We slowly cross the yard, pausing at the fenced tennis court with its sagging net and surface fissures. Michael was enamored with tennis briefly, so I tried to learn how to play. My serve sucks, but I have a mean backhand. Then we went on tour and abandoned everything that wasn't on wheels. This apparently includes our morals. Or his, anyway.

I text Patrick to for god's sake have someone at least weed that disgraceful patch of concrete. And I ask how he's doing and if he's heard from Dustin. Though he's only dated Dustin for like two months, so I'm not sure how serious it is anyway. Still, not my call. Patrick feels things deeply. It's one of the things I like about him, when I'm not pissed at him.

I pluck a piece of long grass and poke myself in the arm with it.

"Janice says you have to tell your side of it, Michael. We have an interview arranged."

"She told me."

"I'm going to pretend I didn't just hear that you were in contact with her and not me."

He sticks his hand in his pocket.

I share my notes on my meeting with Drake with Michael and he shakes the fence with his good hand, although I don't tell him yet that he's supposed to write the album with Velvet. Am I punishing him by not telling him he's about to get something he's never dreamed he could, or am I giving myself just a little more time before everything changes forever?

"We had a dozen gigs left," he mutters. He hates missing a show.

"And you were coming home today for the benefit– why didn't she just do the show? What happened?"

"Ben said to let him know what he can do to help you with rescheduling or whatever." "Reschedule? You should just be thankful that Drake didn't drop you."

That doesn't mollify him any more than it does me. And he didn't answer my question about V.

Even though Michael caught Drake's interest early on, he

had to go through development. As in, see a vocal coach to learn to preserve his voice long enough to do an entire concert because he held nothing back. Learn what to say, and not say, in public. Learn how to dress, something I gladly helped him with. I'm not trying to be all stereotypical, but I just happen to be fashion savvy and he favors tee shirts and jeans. And flannel. Which is fine for country, but they have to be of the right quality and not recently picked and sniffed off the bedroom floor.

No one took me seriously when I argued that Michael shouldn't be singing what he was early on. It wasn't called bro country yet, and it wasn't entirely that yet either, but it was well on its way. Michael has always relied on performing more than content. On melody more than message. His music is emotional junk food, not that anyone has noticed. But he could do so much more.

I turn away from the fence, giving it a swift kick myself, then grabbing my sandaled foot.

Don't say I'm too chicken to press him on why V. left early. Say that even a jaded heart hurts twice a day.

Hopping on one foot, I say, "You've got to get a shower; we're due at the TV studio in an hour."

He tries to take my hand. As we walk (I limp) back to the house, he pauses at the grill and pokes at the charred blue gift box with a spatula, flips it onto the implement and holds it out to me.

"What's in it? A necklace?" It's too long for those matching earrings.

"A pinecone."

Where are my legs and if I find them, how do I get them to move?

102

Later, I find the package on my nightstand. To this day, I haven't opened it.

****

Our collective line to the press, ironed out before the interview on a hasty conference call between me, Robert, Michael, and Janice, will be that Michael drank a few with the "boys" and that no one realized how inebriated he (including himself) was until he got onstage. Someone offered him a 252 and he hadn't known how potent it was on top of the couple of beers (yeah, right) he usually has. It spiked just as he headed onstage.

That Velvet wasn't there that night was indeed due to a family emergency and no other reason. Her dear uncle is terribly ill, the last of her family, you know. In her worry, she just packed up and left. The uncle is doing fine, considering, thanks for asking. (No specifics are offered.)

I hold Michael's right hand on camera during our interview (secretly pinching the skin between his thumb and finger) and smile. I say that Velvet and I are close from being on the road together and that the internet rumors resulting from her abrupt departure are "preposterous."

My spine aches from sitting so straight. My face hates all the smiling.

"Actually, Velvet's been a mother figure to me." I feel her stiffen and I pat her crepey hand. Target achieved.

The China doll beside me with its blonde curls, blue eyes with flecks of brown, like two Earths framed by invading spiders blinks in protest at the maternal characterization of herself. She has hot flashes lashes; she's never still. Some insecure women hoist their enhanced breasts in tight shapewear and hail every ship that passes. She just does this blinky/winky

103

thing. It always gets her what she wants, apparently.

"More like a sister, agewise, wouldn't you say?" she crows as if she's got something stuck in her throat. "We share makeup tips and fashion, all that fun stuff."

Anyone with sight knows that's not true: my face is lightly made up, even for the camera. I emphasize my eyes and my mouth and let the rest go, except for special occasions. And I don't own a thing studded with rhinestones.

"You're the only women on the tour bus, aren't you? So do you stick together?" the dutiful host says. I'm not about to ask Robert how much he paid this guy to lob softballs.

V.'s smile shows nearly every one of her teeth, the long bones of a crown roast.

"I hate it when Briscoe isn't on the bus. You can't imagine how many fart jokes I have to endure."

Only Velvet could use the words "fart" and "endure" in the same sentence. That really tells you all you need to know about her. "Fart" was for the press; "endure" is who she really is. Mot juste, y'all.

Actually, V. has her own bus and driver, though her bus is ancient and cranky and it's ridiculous that she even starts it, as much as it must cost to maintain. (It used to be her and her parents', so sentimental attachment? More likely stubborn, hangover vanity. If you don't have a bus you feel like you're one step away from traveling in a van and sleeping in Super 8's, getting booked at nothing but gas stations.)

Sometimes she has to ride with us, say, if her bus breaks down. When she does, Michael and I lend her our bedroom and huddle together in a single bunk. I actually look forward to those times.

V. leads our laughter now with a great, fake bray. I'm

104

reminded again of what an old pro she is.

My shoulders touch the back of the chair for what feels like the first time all day.

When she and Michael rise to sing on the show (with Josh, Michael's lead guitarist, playing acoustic, since Michael can't play right now), my smile nearly matches hers. Any part of mine that happens to be real has to do with how that rhinestone cowgirl outfit ages her.

At the end of their chorus of "Forever," I have to swallow several times and hum my favorite Saturday morning cartoon theme song from my childhood in my head, but I manage not to cry.

Robert nods "stay steady" from the wings when my mouth starts auditioning to speak all on its own, and I soften my face, not knowing where the camera's eye is. You have to assume it's omnipresent.

I bet Robert made her wear that ridiculous pink cowgirl hat with the sequined headband just for me. I gingerly pat my head and raise an eyebrow. He grins. (Don't get me wrong – V. loves excess, but she wouldn't want to wear a hat on camera because of the unflattering shadows it might cast onto her face.)

The song is over, and it's back to the interview with the guy in the cheap sports jacket.

"Was your label embarrassed by your fall, Michael? Or is there more to the story of your tour's cancellation?"

"*I* was embarrassed by my fall," he says.

I give an oral version of our press release. Again. Every time I say it, it seems more real.

"How long will you be off the road with your arm?" Michael is asked.

105

"While I heal, I'm going to focus on writing and recording my next album."

The guy in polyester smiles, and I make a note to refuse to let Michael be interviewed by anyone wearing anything subpar again. People might think that's the best interview Michael could get. Not even. This was Drake's choosing, because Drake, too, though still powerful, is a tad old school.

The interviewer says (I'm not giving his name; he doesn't deserve the shout out, but you know who I mean), "Some are saying online that your injury isn't as bad as it appears, that you are being asked by your label to cancel the tour for other reasons, reasons to do with…"

Robert, across the set, sits upright.

"Then those people should see me try to button my shirt without help," Michael says.

Mr. No Expiration Date Suit tries again, and again Michael dodges, though this time I think I can smell the guy's hair singe. I smile and touch Michael's shoulder lovingly. All potentially on camera. Wisely, the reporter gives up.

"What's next for this duo?"

I'm not naïve enough to think he means me and Michael.

V. looks down with false modesty and moves her shoulders.

The question hovers as we stare back and forth without speaking.

Then V. flings her arms wide, bangles jingling: "Cue the music."

We laugh.

The interview ends without the announcement about the album of duets being made. It's only a temporary reprieve, but a welcome one, at least until I speak with Michael. Something about the lift of V's lips when she refuses to look at me makes me think she already knows.

But before we leave the air completely, the benefit is touted. Something, anything, to change the narrative.

After we remove our mics, I force myself to stay still long enough to speak with those from the studio audience who come forward to shake our hands. A couple says to me that they will pray for me and my marriage, which reveals they've been listening to gossip, something their simple, dated clothing tells me their church would disapprove of, and I'm tempted to say so.

According to them, I'm not submitting to my husband as I ought to, or he wouldn't be turning to "demon drink." They say it with an air of righteous concern. Regardless, they ask for both my and Michael's autograph. Not that I get asked so much for my autograph, but it happens often enough that it's not strange.

"I'd submit to *you* anytime, Sugar," I say to the man with the excess fried chicken gut and the Pentecostal Pompadour as I scribble some numbers alongside my name (it's actually the number of the dry cleaner just down the road) and hand it to him just to piss off the weekly wash-and-set haired woman with the better-than-you face.

I can feel the man checking out my ass as I walk away. I give it an extra twitch and hear behind me what I'm quite sure is the sound of a man being whacked with his wife's purse.

Studiously ignoring Michael in the car, I press Patrick, Bernita, and a bevy of volunteers into service to be sure things are ready for tonight. "This has to go perfectly," I tell them via phone and text. What was once a charitable act is now a potentially career saving one.

"Don't worry, reinforcements are coming," Patrick writes.

"I so owe you something pretty," I tell him.

"Not anymore. I just ordered something," he says.

I don't ask what. Right now, I would pay him almost anything, and he knows it.

****

When we get home from on our Damage Control interview, Michael opens his lips, but my hand flies up. He disappears, and that's all I want. There's too much to do.

My phone buzzes with a text from an unknown number that turns out to be Ben pleading for me to let him have access to his contacts, so he can alert them that Michael's not going to be showing up for gigs. I turn all the phones back on and call him to say that I know how to do my job and that I'm doing it.

It feels good to yell so loudly that my throat hurts afterwards. Although screaming at Ben is what it must feel like kicking a kitten: No matter how angry you might be at the time, afterwards you're sorry. Especially when you remember you were off for the week, and you put Ben in charge. And that he gave you a heads up (through Joy, but still) about your husband. And he was the only one.

No one else in the band thanks me for turning the phones back on. Ingrates.

I change into work clothes and head out into the yard to inspect the progress of Patrick and crew. We toil until late afternoon, when Patrick tells me he's got it and runs me indoors.

"You need some rest," he says.

I have no idea where Michael is. Again. I text him with no immediate reply and I decide that's for the best. I don't bother checking to see where he is. Nearly as soon as I curl up in bed,

CHAPTER 7

sleep comes.

Chapter 8

I wake to someone pounding on the door.

"Two hours until show time!" Patrick says, jiggling the doorknob.

As much as I want to bury my face in my pillow, I get out of bed.

"Can you do my makeup?" I ask as I twist the lock and let him in.

He claps. "Is it bonus time already?" His face is sweaty, and his eyes exhausted.

I put my hand between his to stop the noise. Then to make up for it, I pick up an empty beer bottle that Bernita hasn't had time to remove, and fellate it.

He gently pulls the bottle from my mouth.

"If that's all you've got, we seriously need to talk about your technique sometime," he says as he walks away, taking the bottle with him

The sensation of cool glass lingers on my tongue.

"Where's Michael?"

"At the cabin." He says it quickly, while looking back over his shoulder. "I sent him there to hide out, just until tonight."

"Did he drive himself?"

"Yeah. He insisted." He's halfway out the door.

"Hey? My makeup?"

"BRB." Be right back. Will the English language soon be reduced to acronyms? Abbreviations? Nothing but letters? IMO, perhaps. Maybe there's a song in that somewhere? I have mixed feelings about it, though I use them, too, when I find them convenient.

I don't trust Michael anywhere by himself right now, but I comfort myself with the fact that Velvet left *him*. She's not likely to come for him, especially after the PR today. If she does, I'll come for *her*, no matter about her tragic past.

My instinct is to not explain what makes her so tragic, what it is that tempts me to give her a pass. And I do feel hella sorry for her.

Back in the day her family was a musical trio. This is awful, but a nutso fan got a gun past security and shot both her parents dead. They were onstage in Atlanta, doing an outdoors show, and the guy just leapt up on the stage and shot them both point blank, then himself, before anyone could react. Neither of her parents survived. He didn't either. No one knows why he did it. He said nothing, left no note.

Velvet was at home recovering from having her appendix out or she might have been killed, too. She had apparently encouraged her parents to go back to their concert schedule without her after her surgery. At 25, she figured she could recover just as well without them. Afterwards, it's said she blamed herself for not being there, for telling them to tour again.

It took a year before she went back on the road, and rumor has it she only went back out then because she needed the money. Fans rushed to support her and have ever since.

Although her parents' fans have begun to age, so they don't exactly go to shows anymore. The good news is, they're not of the generation that pirates music or signs up for Spotify and its ilk, so they still buy plenty, even if it is off TV shopping channels.

While her parents' tragic deaths don't excuse her, and I still hate her for all the things, yeah, there's that.

Ever since then she's been hyper religious, as far as I know, except in the matter of committing adultery with my husband. She believes she has this divine purpose, is the Joan of Arc of music, was spared for a reason, and though she only ever lightly talks of this in public, it's evident in all she does, if you know where to look.

My mother's atheism might have something to do with my mixed feelings about Christianity. She and my father disagreed about it. While he never went to church, he believed in God, especially in relation to nature. He taught me to bless my food and pray before bed. He made sure I went to church every Sunday until I refused. When my mother moved out, I was scandalized one night when I was staying with her that I'd forgotten to say my nightly prayers.

"I think the big guy will forgive you just once," she said. Then we had a talk about him, about how she thought I was old enough to know that, in her opinion, God was no more real than Santa.

"You'll do the world more good if you know that. You can better know how to encourage and comfort them if you know the fallacies of what they believe without telling them you don't share their belief. Err on the side of mercy and kindness, Briscoe. We're all the god there is in this world, and who doesn't need both of those things?"

****

Bernita gets the task of picking up Michael's parents and sibs from the airport for the benefit, though she protests. None of us says we know their last-minute arrival is on purpose and relieves us all. There is a tenuous relationship between Michael and his North Carolina family. They don't seem to know how to handle his fame, landing somewhere between being proud of him and offended because he's "stuck up," though they don't say that. It makes me sad, but not, at least not visibly, Michael.

Michael claims there's nothing wrong with his relationship with them.

He *is* close to his only brother, Brent, who has autism. If I ever forget who Michael can be, I only need to see him with his brother to remember.

His family seems comfortable with me. Maybe because I treat them the way I treat the talent, making sure Bernita cooks their favorite foods, having Patrick fill the guest bedrooms with locally produced lotions and soaps, fresh chocolates, a fruit basket, which Michael's mother will say she prefers to the chocolate, though she will secretly eat all of the chocolate we make sure to leave for her "on accident." There is always a bouquet of flowers.

I've been texting with his mother today, assuring her that he's fine, having assumed, correctly, it turns out, that she had received the same Michael silence I had after the fall.

His mother texts to say they have landed safely and are on their way here just as Michael and I begin greeting our guests at the gate, making sure they know where the bar is before saying hello to the next group. Because of his sling (he's been taking it off as he pleases throughout the day, though no

113

one needs to know that tonight), Michael isn't shaking hands, which also means no performing for him.

When Michael arrived back at the house from the cabin smelling of smoke a scant hour ago, I had Patrick herd him into a tux. It's overkill, sure, but I have only seen him in one three times, none of those times at our wedding. I fully expect him to sneak off and change as soon as he realizes it's a black-tie optional event, but for now, I get to gaze.

My strappy red dress has a wide, flowing skirt with a moderately plunging neckline. I can't abide sheaths or tight-fitting clothes without movement. I've dressed it down with cute, expensive-as-hell Roman sandals, but I regret them the moment I stand in the receiving line feeling short and text Patrick immediately for heels, but he doesn't respond. While I had thought the shoes both sensible and whimsical, they come off as tacky, not to mention they give me cankles. How did I not notice earlier?

The guests stare at us as they arrive as if expecting to read the truth on our faces. Just watching for a tear or a sob. My professional face is as thick as V's pancake makeup. I take it as a personal challenge, not cracking.

I have forbidden V. to perform; she's to make a brief appearance and then go home early to care for that sick uncle. It's bad enough I have to let her inside our gates. Don't blame the other woman, I remind myself. Even if I didn't, no one wants to see their husband's walking glory hole, do they?

Too, too soon she's going to be a daily part of our lives. I signal for a glass of champagne and manage to juggle it along with my greeting duties. Not that it takes me long to swallow the glass's contents, to motion for a second, to glare when Michael tells me to pace myself. He's right, so I slow down.

The band and the roadies mingle with their wives and girlfriends and avoid me. As they should. Joy goes in for a hug when she and Ben arrive. I spend several minutes pointing her in every direction except mine, finally succeeding in interesting her in bidding on a trip to Paris before giving her the slip. She has another scarf around her neck, and I'm tempted but decide to leave it alone, especially since Bernita has been dusting with Joy's Hermes scarf, which has given me unending mirth, but is awfully wasteful.

Bernita arrives with Michael's parents, brother, and sister. They have opted to stay in a hotel this time, saying Brent has a hard time settling down after a long night so I booked them at the Renaissance before they came without a complaint from them. Or us.

Beverly and James hug their son, afterwards embracing me a little more enthusiastically than they did Michael, not that he seems to notice. His mother checks out his arm, but he plays down the injury.

"You know better than to drink before a show," she laughs.

Macy hugs her brother. "Glad you're okay," she says. She's always polite enough to me, but apparently, she and Michael were close when they were young, and I'm not sure she's ever truly forgiven me for daring to marry her brother. I pretend I don't even know she doesn't like me. Hence the texts I send her occasionally, and the swag I pass along: full-sized samples of cosmetics, boxes of designer clothes I'm done with, items I've been asked to share pics of on social media, whatever. I'm not trying to buy her off. I'm just trying to not let on that I am aware of her petty-assed jealousy.

Her nose is a twin of Michael's, but other than that, I see no resemblance.

115

Brent crushes his brother to him, says he saw him fall on TV.

"Yeah. I'm okay though. See why you shouldn't drink?" Michael laughs while holding up his arm in its sling before turning to me. Brent guffaws and whispers loudly that he does drink sometimes when their mother's not watching.

"Why don't you go check out the silent auction items? We'll be sure to squeeze in some family time afterwards," I say to the group as another gaggle approaches our receiving line of two. "I'm sorry; it may take some time before we can join you. Wait, Brent? You ready to help Michael out later?"

He nods solemnly, and their sister takes him towards the tent.

Before long, a string of country stars entertains us with former or present chart-topping songs, our guests willingly doing double duty. Nearly everyone who has a song on the charts is here. Carrie, Brad, Jason, Keith (sans wife – will I never meet her?), and more grace the portable stage, by turns, one song each. Though I am acquainted with them all, I can't claim to be friends with any of them. It's hard to be friends with anyone when you're on the road so much. And tonight, my mind is anywhere but here.

Beverly's face shines beside me, and I see the evening's glamour as she must, until I spy Michael hovering near V's table. He pretends to talk to Robert.

I turn my head and catch Drake staring my way. I smile to let him know that I'm playing my part.

Harmonicas wah; steel guitars with tears in their eyes wrench emotions from us that couldn't be got at any other way. My blood pulses along with the standup bass. Country people aren't afraid to feel. We're not afraid to tell you about

116

our problems in song. Even here, even now, in this group of super sophisticates, no one laughs at a tear here or there being wiped. It gives me a welcome release that I couldn't otherwise get by with here. I'm careful not to go beyond what everyone else is displaying, though, even if I'd like to sob. I don't forget for a second that I'm being observed by pretty much everyone.

A vigorous fiddle sounds its enthusiasm. Violins became fiddles in the proud way that country refuses to be highbrow. There's something beautiful about that kind of pride, knowing you could claim something that you don't. Taking something that belongs to another world and making it so completely your own that you – the world — call the same thing another word entirely. *That's* transformation. That's us.

There's plenty wrong and raw in me tonight, but country people are optimistic. We sing our woes, but only because we believe something better is coming. We purge the pain, and trust that God will make it better in the end.

Michael hops onto the platform at the invitation of one of his favorite musicians who is wearing his trademark polka-dotted shirt, and Michael sings on a couple of songs and plays air guitar, much to the crowd's delight.

Melodia bullhorns us all out to the pasture where volunteers lead several yawning kids out on horses. The children wear matching shorts and tank shirt sets of florescent green, and one of the older children holds a sign with the organization's name as they circle. The littlest ones hold tightly to the reins with both hands, though they are each guided by an adult volunteer.

As paddles are politely raised and lowered during the horse auction, I tug at the skin on the back of my right hand. I've worked for months on this with the director of the nonprofit,

Melodia Myers. Patrick has been more involved than I have, he would say. Whatever. Same difference. I just need this night to end.

Michael brings his brother onstage to help thank everyone and quizzes him about horses. The sandy-haired, slightly overfed man of 30 goes on about horses until Michael changes the subject by asking if Brent likes country music. Everyone laughs when Brent responds by shaking his head vigorously back and forth not unlike a horse. Michael pretends to pout. They're adorable together.

I drape the shawl that has appeared on my chair over my shoulders. I never question where these courtesies come from. I just avail myself of them.

Shifting our attention to the auction tent, Michael urges the crowd to bid, bid, bid, and toasts the group. There will be dancing later, too, he informs us: "A chance to hold these lovelies tight...even if you're not married to them." Everyone laughs except me. He leaves the platform, but as he heads towards me, I find myself possessed with the idea of bidding on something, and I beg his mother's pardon and flee from my seat.

Tables of items to bid on outline the interior of the white tent: gift cards for chain stores and boutiques, services, from vent cleaning to vocal lessons, and every country star's wife's jewelry or clothing line has donated something.

Sidebar: Why does every third woman in Nashville start a jewelry or clothing business? Why must we all have jewelry boxes full of inferior "one of a kind" pieces bought for outrageous sums so we won't offend someone? We all know what we're getting for Christmas from one another.

"What do you think?" Macy says, reverently putting a

necklace made of lopsided clay discs up to her chest from the collection of the spouse of one of the better-known singers.

"It's so you," I say. "Here, let me bid on it for you."

After the riding exhibition, Michael saunters over and we do our hourly touch and smile for appearances, although if my entire body could vomit, it would.

We even manage a fauxversation with Robert and Velvet. During it, I mention V's earrings, admire her nails that are so long I can't imagine how she performs basic sanitation on herself. Then again, I actually play guitar while she uses hers as next door to a prop, so I guess she can afford to wear those things. (Michael wouldn't agree with that assessment of her playing, but I think we know why he'd be so quick to defend her. If forced, I might even say she can play adequately, but I wouldn't give her an inch more.)

Robert asks me to dance; our quick twinned glances tell Michael and V. not to even think about doing the same together.

Robert flexes his forearms in his rolled cuffs, which I reflexively admire. We smile as I tell him how pissed I am about how the interview went, and he explains he had to give the guy some leeway, and that Michael knew ahead of time what the tough question would be, so he could dodge it. I gotta admit, skulduggery is just as sexually charged as you'd expect.

It would serve our spouses right, it crosses my mind and, it would seem, his, as his arm at my waist says so with a squeeze, but no. I don't have a real appetite for anything but revenge.

I remind him that I want V. to leave right after dinner. He agrees to get her out as soon as she says that she couldn't eat another thing.

119

"Great. So that will be just after she splits an amuse-bouche with you, right?"

He laughs and steers me; I steer back, sending us out of step for a moment.

As much as I despise V., I like Robert. Whether you come down on the side of it being weak or brave of us to love our spouses, it certainly makes you as vulnerable as a mama pig's teat at feeding time to allow yourself the emotion, and I whisper as much to Robert, who tightens his grip on my waist once again. If we were alone, I'd bury my face in that broad shoulder and cry myself dry.

We sidestep to avoid a rut in the yard.

I tell him that we have major logistics to discuss for the upcoming album, but not tonight. He tells me about a call he got from someone who had heard from Rhonda. I say I will deal with her ass as soon as I see her tonight.

"Hey, did Drake tell you he's going to announce the album tonight? We'll have to stay for that."

I stop moving and Robert sways me until I begin moving again on my own.

It's hollowing me out, having to be in the presence of a woman I despise and pretend nothing is wrong.

When the song ends, Robert leads me back to my table, to Michael, who puts his arm around me as I sit. Human bodies are supposedly approximately the same temperature, but this blaze across my shoulders is treble that of Robert's. The purifying properties of fire obviously aren't what they're said to be.

The food is blessed on mic by the senior pastor of Paradise who takes the opportunity to tell us how (cliché) we are to (cliché) in this (cliché).

120

Jessie arrives, late, as planned in my rushed text to her earlier today, and I introduce her to Julie, ask Julie to take her on at the record company rather than Al doing it. Julie says she is happy to and is tactful enough not to ask questions. I tell Julie I can be there for the signing if she wants, but she says no need, she will oversee it personally.

Michael and I hit the buffet as much for something to do that doesn't require talking as to eat, filling our plates from the smoked pork, tangy slaw, sweet barbecue beans, great hunks of honeyed cornbread, and a glorious selection of cakes, from sheet cake to hummingbird. Servers provide long pours of tea and water. Why should Nashville pretend we're a caviar city when we make our money singing about beer and hot dogs? (Though there is plenty of caviar in this town too, we don't advertise it.)

The cash bar is unsurprisingly popular, despite the free wine being circulated.

After we eat, we wordlessly go in opposite directions.

The strawberry shortcake has scarcely been identified by my tongue, which is trying to judge it as friend (for its taste) or foe (for its calories), when Rhonda turns up with a man who seems vaguely familiar. I greet her with a handshake that makes her squeak and I urge her and her "feller," who turns out to be the owner of a radio station conglomerate, to make a plate. His media ownership means I have to be nice to her, at least in front of him. Some business obligation of his made them late to the benefit, he apologizes.

"That's fine. Rhonda and I have a bit of unfinished business ourselves," I say with a forced smile, but Rhonda looks perplexed. I say we'll speak later.

I keep my eye on her, and eventually I see her talk to a server who points at the two Portapotties on the lawn (these are nicer than some home baths) and then towards indoors, I follow her inside and watch her enter the room indicated by Bernita, who is wiping down the kitchen counters. While putting my fingers to my lips as Bernita lets loose a string of protests in her Englishese, I jiggle the bathroom door just off the kitchen with no success.

A hair pin plucked from my head opens the lock. I ignore the curl that tumbles into my face. You learn a lot of useful skills on the road.

I let myself into the room. Rhonda looks up, startled, tells me to get out of there.

"Robert told me you made some calls even after we talked, after my generosity. Leave us all alone or I swear..."

"You swear what?"

I pull up photos on my phone of her taking the purse from me, of her peeking at the money, a stack of green visible. Patrick to the rescue, again. One of his friends was planted at the restaurant and took the pictures for us.

"Besides insisting that you quit poking around for real this time, I have to ask: who's your source?"

She stands, holding up the hem of her dress. Her posture says she doesn't want to do this. Her smarts know she has to answer me because these photos could end her career.

"Someone on the road with you, of course."

"Who?"

She sighs, pulls up her underwear, and steps away from the toilet. Going to the sink, she washes her hands.

"He called you Heebie Geebie incessantly, if that tells you anything."

A familiar, most charming corruption of my nickname,

Head Bitch. I know exactly which roadie that would be. Randy.

She opens her purse and pulls out her lipstick, twirls it upwards and slowly covers her lips with crimson. "You'd pee yourself if you knew why V. really left that show. You didn't ask me that, and I don't believe for one minute you know, or you wouldn't be here tonight."

Even though I am desperate to know, I walk out the door, leaving it wide open.

I barely even hear Bernita as I rush back out into the yard and command the nearest guy in white and black to remove the dirty glasses from a nearby table. Turns out he's a songwriter and we have a laugh as I apologize, and I know I will forever be that bitch in his eyes now but he is oh so nice to my face so who cares tonight?

Even if I weren't married to Michael, this is a high stress job. It warps you; you forget that the life you're living isn't the same as everyone else's. You do things like, I don't know, walk in on a woman urinating. Marrying power changes the world in ways you've never anticipated.

A tray of mini cream puffs wafts by on an anonymous hand, and I stop the server long enough to pluck one off his tray. Don't mind if I...did Michael just shake his head at me? I pick up another, and stuff one in each cheek before dismissing the server. Michael rolls his eyes. I give him my kill stare that I know half infuriates him/half turns him on. Then I chew on the soggy, custard-filled bits that are only partially defrosted.

Where is that caterer? I whirl around, looking for any place to reject this nasty mouthful and see Michael laughing his ass off at me. I chew valiantly, but get the punishment pastries down.

When I realize how truly awful the dessert is, I hunt down the server with his tray of nasties. "Give me that," I say, taking the platter. "Tell the caterer I said not to send any more of those out." I prance over to Michael and offer him one as if the two men standing with him (boring music execs, low level) aren't there.

"No thank you. I'm watching my figure," he says, eyes still laughing. At me.

"I insist."

"Really, I'm..."

But I've placed one in his mouth and now he has to chew. Except it doesn't seem to bother him at all.

"Frozen pastries! Who does that to delicate pâte à choux? I will never use this caterer again."

Michael swallows.

"It wasn't so bad."

"It wasn't so...is that how you want our party to be remembered?" My eyebrows must be at treetop height by now. My voice is.

"No. I want it to be remembered for raising the most money ever for Ride 'Em, the *benefit*," he says sotto voce. Has that ever gotten me to lower my voice? Ever?

"With all of the wonderful things in the world to eat, I see no need whatsoever to eat soggy desserts," I say.

"I don't know, the custard was pretty smooth," he says.

One of the men beside him reaches to take a puff, but I stop him.

"You don't want these. They taste like old twat. Unless you've got a yen for that?"

The man withdraws his hand as if I've licked it.

"*Custard filled*, Michael?" I ask before handing him the tray

124

and tromping off to locate that highly recommended woman who probably bought these treats in the freezer section at Costco. No referrals for her.

Not ten minutes later, Drake makes the announcement. He calls Michael and V. to the microphone with him, and they say how thrilled they are at the prospect of an album of duets.

Patrick sits beside me and lets me squeeze his hand so tightly that I worry for him enough to let up. He also whispers for me to hold on, hold on, hold on. Then, precisely seven minutes after the announcement, when the music has started back up and the dancing recommenced, he walks me slowly inside where I barricade myself, alone, in the bathroom in my and Michael's bedroom. After a time, he knocks on the door and when I emerge, he wipes my eyes and reapplies my lipstick.

"Let's go back out now," he says.

"I don't think I want to."

"You don't want to tonight, doll. But if you don't, tomorrow you'll wish you had. So they know now what you already knew. So you have to pretend it's a good thing. It sucks. But you have reasons for wanting to do this, and I know you can."

I lean on him and don't scold him for calling me doll.

"What souvenir are you taking from her?" he asks.

I try on a smile. "Maybe her husband."

When we sweep back outdoors, I snatch a glass of wine from a circulating tray and take a turn around the yard, making sure I've greeted everyone I haven't yet. Under any circumstances, it would be exhausting. Now? Nearly impossible. Spreading my fakery out millimeter by millimeter, however, makes it easier.

I eventually lose my momentum and find myself in a chair by the firepit with a glass of wine and a shoulder rub from Patrick, who has somehow temporarily separated himself from that celeb hound, Dustin, who has done every tacky thing possible tonight except ask the stars here for autographs.

This has been the longest day in history. All I'm looking forward to is sleep, at some point. And yet I haven't had to deal as long as people are here, so I am also grateful for the day that won't end.

After the guests leave, Michael's family gathers round with (more) wine while we visit.

"Just stay here tonight," Michael urges them politely.

"And let that fancy hotel suite go to waste?" his father says. "Besides, I promised Brent a dip in the hot tub."

Although everyone knows it, no one mentions that *we* have a hot tub.

Bernita and some of the servers hired for the night bring leftovers in and put them on the dining room table. We all make ourselves plates. Who had time or energy to eat properly earlier in the heat, we say to justify our hearty snack.

We take loaded plates back outside and gather by the lighted pool.

Pleasant, topical conversation with those left behind opens onto relaxed spans of silence and I sink down knowing nothing more will be demanded of me until morning. I don't have to speak except to say goodbye if that's what I want. (It's what I want.)

Inevitably, Michael brings an acoustic out and attempts to plunk on it, but winces and puts it back in its case.

"Ma Chambers, where did Michael get his musical talent from?" I ask the question out of politeness, though I'm too tired for the ritual.

She smiles, and I know I will be spared speaking for the

126

next while. Again, I hear the story about how she was almost a child country star, how her parents owned a saloon, and she sang in it on Saturday afternoons. How Buck Owens came through town and begged her parents to take her to Nashville to be on the Grand Ol' Opry. How her mother refused.

Michael's mother would have been a household name had she gone (naturally). She would have been as big time as Michael. And she regrets that Michael hurt himself because they could have performed together at this benefit if he hadn't.

She's got a pleasant enough voice but unlike V's, it's going noticeably brittle with age. And in a town like this, you don't want to be pitied.

Michael's family leaves around midnight.

Patrick smiles at me and touches my back after they're gone. "You doin' okay?" he asks. Dustin's sympathetic smile asks the same, and while I appreciate the effort, I barely know him, so I also resent it. What has Patrick shared with him about me?

"Peachy. Y'all should go on home."

I hold Patrick's hands, and we push against one another's.

"Tell him I'll kick his ass if he doesn't treat you right from now on," I whisper.

He kisses me on the cheek before they leave, and I permit it.

****

After everyone is gone, Michael and I dodge one another.

He swathes the sofa with a cover and adds a pillow; he stretches out on the concealed leather.

"Good call," I say as I pass him to go to our bedroom. "Let me know if you need anything." I turn out the light.

Like a gin and cyanide.

I don't ask him why he doesn't take the guest room. I don't care.

127

Text alert. Though I can scarcely keep my eyes open, I read my mother's message. She has belatedly (no shock) heard about Michael's onstage "faux pas." She writes: "Is this one of those times when a woman needs her mother? Let me know to expect you, and I'll put a clean sheet on the cot."

Note that she doesn't *know* whether I'd need her or not. Her people skills aren't exactly stellar. She's living alone in a lightning rod. I once made the mistake of asking what she does for, er, companionship, as isolated as she is.

"I go into town once a month for supplies on my bike," she said.

"Are you saying you bring someone home?" I prepared to lecture about the dangers of stranger sex.

"I buy a package of batteries, if you get my drift."

Ugh, I did. I couldn't help but be relieved, though, that she wasn't bringing home randos.

"Michael's fine, but…" I write, delete, wondering if giving my mother the gift of technology was wise.

Because she doesn't need much, it's hard to give gifts to my mother. When I send her something nowadays, it's usually a book. I'm the only reason she's ever read a book published post 1990—we trade off choosing books to read and discuss online. That way I still get my fill of olden moldies, which I adore, and she reads something more recent.

A couple of Christmases ago, I bought her a Kindle that she scoffed at until I showed her how much easier it is to search a book with it. It's so much more efficient, but then you miss dipping randomly into, say, a Woolf novel and that's a shame because when you do, you always find a delicious sentence.

Right after I bought her the Kindle, Mother sent me emails every day for a week: "Number of occasions Woolf used the word 'art' in her work. Occurrences of the word 'knife' in *Lighthouse*." You'd think that would bore me. Nope.

I ask Mother outright to come to me instead and "help me with my thesis."

In grad school, I've been loosely supervised. The school and I came to a nontraditional understanding, the agreement facilitated by my mother, to accommodate my traveling role as Michael's manager.

They created an online/low residency option for me. They said they'd make it work, but they'd appreciate it if I didn't mention the details to others. Now, ahem, my advisor is still crawling up my ass, insisting I get her a rough draft by the end of summer. At the time that Molly (the advisor) issued her edict, I hadn't thought that would be a problem and had welcomed the deadline as something to keep me busy between our arrival at gigs and sound check, the empty hours.

While I wait for Mother's reply, my eyelids close incrementally even as I text Patrick. "What are they saying online now?" I'm not about to check for myself to see if our spin has worked, how the clips of the benefit landed.

"Brent went over well."

That's something.

"And your dress was amazeballs!"

We shoot another couple of complimentary texts at one another. More media gossip. Overall, the response is apparently more positive than not.

"Where are you?" I text.

No reply. He knows I want him to make an after midnight run to some godforsaken part of town for food.

"I'm buying. Hot chicken? Ice cream?"

Again, nothing.

Oh, right: My Colossal Ass. I guess I don't deserve to eat.

I type on, immersing myself in Woolf. Sonic's chili cheese fries will just have to wait.

What? My taste buds don't know I have money, and even if they did, I'd remind them that the moment I can't appreciate chili cheese fries is the moment Jesus just needs to come on back and pull me up in the air with him for that midnight ride church folk get so excited for.

"You did a great job with the benefit," I text Patrick, in case he's pouting that I didn't crown him Lord of all Parties. No reply.

This food is still heavy in me, like a faux baby, for all that I do worry it's too late. It feels like an intruder, and I want it to leave my body. Somehow, though, I also have the urge to add to it. I hadn't had any episodes, not full-blown ones, not in the longest time, not until the V. thing blew up.

The food is supposed to comfort me, to keep me company, to make my worries disappear. That's not what happens. It fills me for a few minutes, but then the self-loathing, the regret, the knowing I am wasting food whether it stays in or not that others so desperately need sneaks in.

I tally how much food I have just now, uhm, disposed of and tap out a donation to Second Harvest of Middle Tennessee, a place my father and I were not unfamiliar with during the lean times, and that now, ironically, distributes *Thrive* soup regularly.

Mother texts, finally, about my request for her in-person help with my thesis. "Give me a day." She refuses a plane ticket, saying she'll drive her Jeep because, have I forgotten, she needs to bring Virgil with her.

She texts again to say it's going to take her an extra day–I don't ask why but assume she is having trouble finding someone to check her bear traps or some such while she is gone.

I tiptoe out to the living room to check on Michael, who is frowning in his sleep. I stifle the urge to pick up his Martin made of Brazilian rosewood leaning against a nearby chair and whack him with it. That would be a terrible waste of wood, especially endangered wood. Instead, my hand, mine, reaches for the throw along the edge of the sofa and covers his bare feet. His frown disappears.

My love didn't up and cheat; *he* did.

Michael kicks the throw off his feet in his sleep, and I bend over to retrieve it. He touches my cheek.

"Briscoe," he says.

"How could you?"

His breath hisses out, his move toward reconciliation degrading already into anger. If I don't accept his "apology" with my whole heart the moment he makes an overture, then he's angry and it's on my head.

"It just happened."

"Oh, is that right?"

Confirmation.

He turns over, away from me.

No damn body ever died of a broken heart, so I guess I'll live, no matter what it feels like right now.

He rolls back over, grabs my hand, and I let him. He's crying, and I refuse to ask if it's because Velvet has deserted him, or because he knows he's hurt me.

You don't pretend a tiger is a cat. If you do, you will eventually be sorry. Or eaten.

We have sex on the sofa. It's not an apology, and it's not

forgiveness given. It's just another section of the conversation. Though I have this disgusting feeling that I've just comforted him for his loss.

After, I am awkwardly curled beside him on the leather. "Why did she leave the concert?" Why do I do this to myself? Why must I know everything?

He shakes his head. I want to know, want the waiting to be over, but if he thinks I can't handle it, this guy and I who tell each other everything, even hard things, because the music depends on it; if he won't tell me now, it's bad.

Obviously, it's bad, whether he tells me or not. But I can't believe he won't talk about it.

Instead, he kisses me, and I let him.

When I wake, the throw that was on Michael now rests at the foot of the bed. I smile as I think of the sweet words he whispered, and I ignore the words he did not say.

I also read a text from Patrick who reminds me that I asked him to ignore him if I asked him to go get me fast food, and he also sends me a link to some zero-carb nonsense plan, which sounds even worse than his usual low-carb regimen. Looking down at my stomach, I decide to give it a try it.

I make my way to the kitchen in my black camisole and my black pajama bottoms sprinkled with pink hearts. I am aware that I dress like an Instagram influencer, but so what? I get swag sent in the mail, stuff I actually like, sometimes. Sometimes I keep it. So what if Patrick sometimes takes pics of me wearing stuff and posts photos? So what if he tags the company? So what if that means I get another free box? And another.

There's something about free swag. I can shop all day and

it barely registers, but let me get a freebie with my makeup purchase, and I go out of my mind with joy.

Bernita is busying herself at the toaster, slipping in wide slices of homemade bread. I cover my ears, so I won't hear myself say:

"Just eggs fried in coconut oil for me today."

If you weren't looking closely you wouldn't see her eyes roll towards Michael, see her pop up the toaster lever and return the untoasted bread to the platter where slices of wheat congregate.

Now that's just a waste. Anyone knows that bread that's been heated at all is no longer fit for eating without toasting. Toasting, sheening with butter, coating with insulting amounts of strawberry jam or Bernita-made grape jelly spread over the transformed surface...

"Patrick's eating plan?" Michael asks as he watches her crack a brown orb and release its contents into the large ceramic-lined skillet, takes in with a glance the half pout on my face. He wears the worn jeans and tee from yesterday. His face prickles with what wants to become a beard. Trust me–it won't.

I slide onto a stool beside him. "Yup. No more carbs this month as usual but with a twist: I can have one cheat meal a week. He didn't say how long my cheat meal could last, though. Or how much I could eat." I pretend to be gleeful, but the idea of moving my lips, my jaw, tires me.

My hands reach for Michael's mug of coffee, and I am grateful that it's fully loaded with cream and sugar. Out of sight of Bernita, his hand skims my thigh. I move my leg off the rung of the stool and prop my leg up so that his hand rides higher.

He's never made a secret of the fact that he believes I would

133

be even "hawter" (his word) if I lost twenty pounds.

A plate of crispy eggs lands in front of me. Bernita tells me a string of things the yard crew didn't do to her satisfaction as if taking all the air for herself will keep me from speaking.

"I'm not going to bite the mister, so calm yourself," I say.

I don't thank her for the eggs or for the mug of coffee she gives me as she takes Michael's from me and hands it back to him.

"I had an idea last night," I say. A hook came to me in a dream, and I vaguely remember fumbling with my phone and singing into it. Hadn't I almost woken Michael to get his take on it?

With the right person, writing songs together is as good as making love. One of you starts unclothing by sharing an idea, or maybe a few notes. The other builds on it, strokes a note, kisses it with a phrase. Then the rhythm rises. Your climax is the song. Once you've written with someone, you can't claim not to know everything important there is to know about them. Clearly, this does not have to be sexual. Clearly, sometimes it is.

I lift my fork and shove in the food.

Michael eyes me over the top of his coffee mug. Then I remember that he's been writing with V., that he's now obligated to continue his word orgy with her, not me. My face reddens and I change the subject.

"Where's your sling?"

He shrugs.

Which is shocking, because he milks every ailment — the crew calls him Honey Boo Boo behind his back. I think it's easier for him to express physical discomfort than other forms. He saves his emotions for his songs.

He bases many of his songs on the country holy trinity: G-C-D. In the Nashville Number System, that's 1-4-5, you know. Which allows anyone to easily transcribe keys. It's shorthand for those who aren't music theory heads. If you ever see someone putting up fingers on a hand when performing live, they're showing the band where to go next, not waving. It probably means they're playing a song not all of them knows. Or changing keys.

"I have a honey-do for you today," I say.

He motions to his arm and begins rubbing it exaggeratedly.

"Don't worry–it only involves a firing."

His face contorts.

I tell him Randy, a guy I've never liked anyway, has to go. "Rhonda confirmed it."

"After breakfast," he says. I know Randy is one of his buds, but then they all are.

Michael gives Bernita a list of items to pick up at the market for him, which should clue me in; he never does that. I didn't know the man could write a list.

She says she has to supervise the chair pickup, but he tells her the crew outside has it covered, which definitely tells me that trying to get rid of her.

After she leaves, I say, "Shouldn't we call your parents and ask what time we're doing lunch before they head home?" Then I make to hop up.

He drags my hand through the yolk on my plate as he grasps it.

"You've literally got a captive audience. What is it you want to say?" I bat my eyes at him.

"This rumor about me and Velvet…"

My eyes aim to stun. "Rumor?"

135

Michael drops my hand and crosses his arms.

"It's not like before."

Does Michael know that what he's saying is that the others were nothing, but this one wasn't? (Isn't?)

Is he saying that?

"Wait until you hear what we've written. I could never have done it if, if…" his eyes won't meet mine.

The counter shakes in response to my palm while the stool trembles with the movement of my body.

"I didn't know artistic Viagra could be administered via vag."

He grips my hand with his weakened left one. *Feeble, feeble humans.*

I push against him; I wrap a leg around his stool, and he holds onto me while I tangle the other leg around him.

I unzip his pants and then mine, peeling away the obstructive clothing. Beyond him, in the yard, workers tug at the ropes of the huge white tent as I mount him. The tent collapses.

There is triumph in his touch, mad zeal. Something about the crinkling of his eyes, the same crinkle he gets when he stares at…

"Wait," I say, jumping off. "I know that look."

I put my forehead against the top of his head. Goddammit.

His lowered eyes admit all. I'm not the one he's thinking of. I leap off him.

"Your parents will be expecting a call soon. Lunch at Puckett's before they fly out?" I ask as I zip my pants, adjust my breasts back into my bra.

"Sure," he says, voice as flat as a can of soda left opened overnight.

"Your mother adores their sweet potato fries and green

beans with bacon," I say from the sink. "Why don't you give her a call and tell them we'll pick them up?"

Why do I keep imagining I am married to a complete human being, no assembly required?

****

The benefit, once everything has been counted, has raised nearly twice as much this year. RScene publishes photos of all of us beautiful people. A few shots of myself actually please me. Regrettably, those are only on their website and don't end up in the print copy.

Michael is silently forgiven by Nashville for his stupidity, though no one knows exactly what it was he did wrong in the first place.

Benefit over, Patrick diligently looks for a suitable "green-house" for this album in waiting.

While I'd like the home court advantage, just having had V. in the yard for the benefit causes me to ask Bernita to smudge the lawn for me. She walks around outdoors waving a long, lit match and mumbles, but I have no idea how to do it either, so it works for me.

"What about this five-bedroom just outside Leiper's Fork?" Patrick asks, waving a photo on his phone of a fancy log cabin that, he informs me, also has an ice cream parlor and a home theater. There's a full, unfinished basement that should work for music making.

I take his phone and scroll through the pictures, note the house's high Airbnb rating.

"As long as it has enough room," I say before turning back to my laptop. "You and Bernita get it ready, okay? I don't want to be there one minute before I have to."

It vaguely occurs to me that the bedroom count might be off, but I figure I'll leave it to my scouts to sort. Every home should come equipped with a Patrick and a Bernita, complete with wireless remote control, dust cover optional.

After having fallen asleep while writing, I startle awake and rub my face, feeling the imprint of the embossed letters from the cover of *The Waves* on my right cheek. From somewhere below, the salted scent of music finds me. Just as Mr. Ramsay depends upon his wife, I know Michael depends on me, how could I forget. His music says as much.

My arms flutter, my feet tap, commanded by his notes. He lures me with the promise of bottomless mysteries of the soul, of emotions I've never experienced. His fingers fly and I am up and out the door, seeking him from room to room; he is using nothing between his fingers and the strings. I'd hear it if he were.

Here am I.

The notes roll.

Where is he?

Bernita, oh what is she doing in front of me with her open mouth and sounds that are not his, "fish," did she say and that is what is wrong with this world is everyone is worried about the fish, but I will not listen, and he is where, not in this room, not in this one either and yet he must be close by, and Bernita is – *shut up, shut up, shut up.*

Now, *here,* I sink down at his feet, my hair spreading across them.

I know now how sorry he is. And I can afford to forgive him because he wants to be forgiven.

Michael puts his pick in his mouth to finger the notes. He

plays the fretboard with enthusiasm, liquid lightning.

I part my lips, open them…nothing comes out.

"Just something Velvet and I came up with on the road," Michael says when he finishes.

"Of course it is." I ignore the pity on Bernita's face and find someplace, anyplace, else I have to be.

Like at my laptop. Drinking a Coke Zero Sugar, I go to it and type like I'm aiming to press the keys through the other side of the computer.

Mr. Ramsay, dandy, philosopher, believes himself to be failing at what he sees as his life's work: advancing philosophy. He has contributed to the field, he admits, but not enough. What he doesn't see is his inability to be the father or husband he should be to his family while he's pining for recognition and a legacy. He torments them with his moodiness and his insistence on being right. Often, he doesn't seem aware anyone else exists. We don't get even a glimpse of a warm and fuzzy encounter with any of his children. Even on vacation he can't get out of work mode. Freudian notions aside, it's little wonder that child James wants to stab his father.

I backspace and take out that last sentence. Mother would have a conniption.

Instead, after they lose their mother, he makes a journey of contrition to the blasted lighthouse with two resentful, motherless teens, the two younger children, who still don't want to spend time with their moody father who tries, too late, to make up for his contrariness.

The egotistical motherfucker seems, after his wife is dead, to finally realize his error.

But did Mr. Ramsay really repent of his ways? I'm not inclined to like misters just now, you might say.

Chapter 9

Our physical shift to the rental house goes smoothly enough, mostly because our own house is close enough that we can return to get anything we forgot in minutes, and because the Airbnb is furnished, of course.

The construction has the expected high ceilings. Its kitchen has slick modern stainless everything, offset with a porcelain farm sink, a subway tile backsplash. It's fully equipped, which I appreciate. A wicker basket of fruit welcomes us.

In the living room, brown leather furniture dotted with colorful pillows faces a huge TV. End tables and a coffee table are unremarkable metal and glass. The house has a knockout view from nearly every window: tree-topped mountains, a sky begging me to come out and play. Dense woods on one side. A fenced pasture on another.

The bedrooms are lightly themed: one has a canopied bed, almost as if you're outdoors, one suggests nautical, complete with an invitingly striped loveseat. One has two sets of bunk beds, nothing foreign to our band, for sure, but the treehouse painted on the wall might not be their speed.

I choose a highly textured room with a king-size bed, and Michael nods from the doorway. From a quilted bedcover of plum to feathered pillows of coral, it's a glorious nest of a bedroom, but more importantly, it's the one furthest away from the others and it has a large bathroom at one end. Every bedroom has its own bath, quite a luxury after living on a bus. Not that it makes up for having to do this heinous thing that I will pretend is just an extension of our touring scenario, with a few changes, of course.

"Where V. will sleep?" Bernita asks. Michael and I glance at one another, away.

While I want to give her the room with the bunkbeds, especially since Robert says he "can't" stay here with us after all, I know even I can't get away with treating her that way.

Patrick consults his phone.

"Can't she commute?" I ask again, but no. The muse will strike when it strikes. We'd best be ready to grab her by the heel when she shows up. Drake was right about living together during this.

And having experienced V's lack of punctuality firsthand, I'm not willing to chance it. We don't have time to waste. First you'd have to contact her, then get her awake, showered and shellacked, fed, get her here, round up the others…it would be like herding cats.

I point a finger towards a pleasant enough room nearer the bunkbed room featuring traditional cabin decor, with a brass bed, a cabin pattern quilt, and a large rag rug.

"I'll get our suitcases," Michael says and leaves the room. Of course he and I are going to have to share a room. Patrick puts his hands up and follows Michael.

Bernita mutters that this is all a bad idea.

"They have to write this album. Otherwise, it's over. Your job, mine, the money, the fame. It's done, do you get that?" I take off my shoes and toss them into the closet.

She shrugs. Yeah, if only all of that were of no consequence.

"At least he carry your stuffs," she says, bumping my shoulder with hers.

She's right. Michael doesn't ever carry anything but his favorite guitars. When he returns with my suitcase in one hand and his in the other and places them on the bed, rubbing his shoulder, I thank him and massage his arm, not asking myself what his sop means, or mine.

While I'm forced to wait for my mother's arrival, I don't have any such luxury regarding Velvet. Robert delivers her in all her glistening glory the day after we move in. From V's sequined butterfly sleeves to her white jeans (a mainstay of the Nashville over 40's set), down to her rhinestone studded stilettos, she shines, radiating artificiality. Her undersized head sports an oversized hair bump – who still wears those? Her jewelry, likewise, would be visible from any venue's backrow.

Trust me, her style does not represent our town as a whole.

Her silicone-plumped breasts press into my chest as she air kisses my cheeks before I can stop her. She clasps my hands in hers and smiles as if we are at a party.

"Stay for dinner?" I ask, beg, Robert after extricating myself from the cedars of Lebanon smell of V.

"Sorry—Natalie needs me at the studio." Their daughter. A singer as well, though she won't have anything to do with V's or the family's music, though no one says why not.

He deposits V's suitcases in the foyer and promises to be available if needed, before leaving.

I immediately text him hell for not going through this with me. Convenient studio scheduling.

No reply. So Robert.

Strummed steel filters inside from where Michael plays guitar, his feet in the pool, his voice in the soft yet resonant zone matching the graceful flight of his playing.

V. walks to the window facing the pool and as she stares out, her head falls to her shoulder. Her lips tremble with what I'm pretty sure will be a confession, maybe an apology, as she turns to me.

"Bernita!" I bellow. "Please show Ms. Wickens where she'll be sleeping."

"Please, I need to say this."

"Someone will bring your luggage to your room," I say as I release the handful of my necklace I've been clutching.

"You've got to hear me. I told him no, that I would never…"

"Bernita!"

Drying her hands on a dishtowel, my angel of the house somehow manages to get the woman out of my face in time.

I pace and steal a beer from the fridge and decide to take my ire out on my laptop. I don't know what else to do. This is no vacation home situation.

Charles Tansley, the incredibly insecure young man who gets inside Lily's head by saying "Women can't paint; women can't write," is poor. Mr. Ramsay's shadow, he initially gains Mr. Ramsay's attention through his intelligence. Alas, his snide remarks about women don't seem to seep into Mr. Ramsay's consciousness. Who knows what view about women Mr. Ramsay holds anyway; he doesn't seem to do anything to encourage his wife to do more than serve and adore him. He interrupts her quiet reading time without a thought. He seeks unremitting reassurance from her. Tansley's open hostility towards women and the arts may be just a given in

Mr. Ramsay's eyes.

Perhaps Tansley's ire towards women could be compare with today's incels who hate women because they feel that women don't give them a chance because they, the men, aren't handsome or wealthy enough to date. Any woman, then, especially the beautiful ones, are denigrated by these men who feel unworthy. Tansley would likely have been a keyboard warrior for the group, had the internet existed then.

There is no "object" of beauty in competition with Mrs. Ramsay in the novel. She is the lovely (albeit around fifty years old) grande dame of the house. Though the younger girls are pretty and shiny, no one's looks eclipse Mrs. R.'s, which are doubtless enhanced by her warmth. She manages to be all things and still charm the entire company, men included.

Lily alone seems to have mixed feelings about her hostess, but that's mainly because she can't sort her own emotions regarding the woman, and because the undercurrents of nasty, testosterone-laden thought swirling in the house are troubling her vision.

If only Lily knew that Mrs. Ramsay, while fond of Lily, privately speaks belittlingly of her and her painting. She acts as if she thinks her too unattractive to marry anyone but someone as old as Mr. Bankes. Mrs. Ramsay thinks of Lily's work as her "little paintings."

My fingers slow. V. said no to what? *To what?*

I drill at my laptop.

Mrs. Ramsay, as far as we know, kept going in the direction she had begun until one morning when she did not, could not. We aren't told what she died of, but we do know it happened abruptly. Her poor children.

For the first time since I was twelve, my throat aches as I think of mothers. I want mine to get here, and soon.

144

✳✳✳✳

My eyes open to the sound of a rooster crowing. A groggy glance out the window reveals the noise to be the horn of my mother's Jeep.

I pat the other side of the bed, but Michael isn't there.

Scrambling into a robe and flipflops, I run outside to greet her just as she descends from the vehicle in a worn military jacket (though she claims to be an ardent pacifist!), and a dusty driver's cap.

I rush forward into the first bruise of light; *she's impossibly thinner*. I try to hug her, but the matador adroitly dodges by reaching back into the Jeep; Virgil II, her aging Jack Russell, tumbles out. I crouch to pet her crotchety doppelganger but rise as Mother tosses a battered leather suitcase to me. I bend my knees to support its weight, a wise move.

"This must weigh 50 pounds!"

My mother grins: "Books," we say together.

She pulls a small camouflage duffle from behind the seat. What, does she frequent a military surplus store nowadays?

"Clothes?"

My remark is anticlimactic, and her curt nod tells me so. The air is morning damp, chilly almost, but it won't be for long.

Virgil II sniffs at my feet, whimpering for affection. Though I know he alternates between snappish and sweet, I oblige him with a cuddle that's more for me than him.

By the time we reach the kitchen, Michael has hauled a carton of eggs, a large skillet, and butter onto the counter.

I haven't tasted his cooking in months, if not longer. It's not like cooking on the bus is really a thing for either of us, but here he is today at the stove.

My mother greets Michael with a kiss on the cheek, stealing a piece of toast when it pops up. She has always shown more feeling for Michael than he warrants, even though she doesn't give a damn about his music or fame. He's a man, therefore she's a fan. (From what mother has let drop since I made the mistake of inquiring about her sex life, she has had more than her fair share of visitors to her cabin.)

So much for hoping she'd give him hell.

I show Mother her room and heavily deposit the book-laden suitcase on the floor.

"Take your time settling in while Michael finishes breakfast."

Toast between her teeth, she unzips her bag and rummages in it. I leave her to it.

The sun eases into the kitchen; coffee and bacon scents radiate from the room.

"She doesn't know everything," I whisper to Michael. "No need to be so nice."

"Are you trying to keep my stuffed French toast all for yourself," he asks, cracking an egg into a bowl and whisking it.

"Try to keep me from eating some," I say, though instantly I remember all that has brought us here, and my smile dissipates.

You'd think toasting the bread first would unalterably change the texture of the dish, and you'd be right. It adds a crackle to the finished product. It enhances it.

I sit listening to the sound of butter awakening in the cast iron skillet, hearing my mother walk about above us, imagining the faint hum she customarily emits when engaged in activities that please her. She's probably placing her books in the bookshelf and alphabetizing them, separating the fiction

146

from the non. No doubt her clothes are still in their bag.

A willowware plate is deposited on the counter in front of me. Michael jiggles powdered sugar over his creation as if releasing dice, causing me to choke on the mini cloud.

I take a fork and knife from the basket with the floral liner further down the counter.

Michael watches me cut that first bite.

"Mmm ... you used cinnamon bread." Cinnamon toast: 150 per slice. Egg: 70. Butter: 110. Syrup: 100+. Bacon: I quit counting.

Virgil's extended paw asks for my toast. I surreptitiously allow a bite or two to fall. I happen to know he eats mostly people food anyway, along with the odd squirrel or two, supplemented with roadkill.

Mother joins us, and Michael ceremoniously hands her an orange Fiestaware plate. She, too, prefers the counter with its bar stools. Her appreciative moans as she eats punctuate her polite replies to Michael's inquiries about her trip. She accepts a cup of coffee, tapping rhythmically on it between sips.

We eat, pretending we don't see the others tossing bits to the dog who has taken to yipping when we don't feed him quickly enough.

Virgil growls again, but in a different key, when Velvet appears, completely dressed, eyelashes already on duty. She blinks: coffee, stat. Michael rushes to get her a mug, and I scarcely squelch the urge to trip him as he passes me.

Velvet fingers the lashes of her left eye. She stands at the end of the counter in mules and a multicolored kimono with a fur ruff with her mouth wide and successfully separates the lashes.

"You didn't tell me you had a new maid, Briscoe." Mother rapidly empties her mug of coffee and hands it to V. "More, please."

My mother would never call a woman the demeaning word "maid" unless she suspected something. Maybe she paid more attention to my emails than I thought.

Michael hastily hands Velvet the mug he's fetched for her.

V. blinks. Her lips press against and then recoil from her mug, press and recoil.

"Do you sleep in those things?" Mother asks, pointing at V.'s eyelashes.

"More French toast?" Michael slides an underdone piece onto my mother's plate and furiously sprinkles it with powdered sugar.

Velvet scans her coffee as if there are tea leaves at its bottom.

My mother winks at me.

We're all going to be together for weeks. Civility will be required, and I reckon I'm the one who has to indicate that. Or pretend I'm for it. My mother has never been controllable, something I'm banking on.

"This is our esteemed guest, singer Velvet Wickens. Remember, she was touring with Michael? You must forgive my mother, V., she's all alone on that mountain of hers most days. She wouldn't know Al Pacino from an alpaca."

Before Velvet can reply, Mother extends her hand.

"I'm Julia Buttersford Jenkins of the Massachusetts Jenkins. How do you do," my mother, (who everyone knows as Jules), says in her most silver-plated manner.

V. takes my mother's hand, then releases it, wipes her own on the counter. She grimaces. "Syrup."

My mother smiles.

This sequestering might end up being just the teeniest bit bearable after all.

Chapter 10

At the first opportunity, I corner my mother and more thoroughly explain my concept for my thesis. If she weren't who she is, she'd be sick of it, having lived at its periphery for so long. Instead, her eyes brighten.

I pretend not to see the pity she feels at my study of Woolf's views on marriage. In a way that I intend to be imperceptible but that the moving of her head to the side shows she catches, I shift our conversation to how Woolf might have written differently today. She pretends to take me seriously.

"I suppose if *Lighthouse* were written today, Woolf might have added modern conveniences such as cell phones, might have included social media references."

"Would she have finished her novel-essay that she ended up dissecting and tossing all over the place if she were writing now?"

My mother's reply is insightful and pointed: "You sometimes have to decommission, and slightly humiliate, older literary fiction to make it applicable today."

She continues: "Woolf saw the contradictions inherent in combining the two formats. She realized she would bore people with straight essays, with preaching, afraid they'd flip to the novel section, ignore the social commentary. I maintain that she began to care about the characters and wanted to give them more fully realized lives, hence the novel, *The Years*. Today, she would likely have combined the two and perhaps even made them into a multimedia presentation."

My mind adores this talk so lovely, dark, and deep.

Just last year my mother and I attended a Woolf conference.

Mother's emails leading up to the ask were uncharacteristically adorned. She writes about the approach of fall, the squirrel activity in and around her cabin, (which she knows interests me), and, oh yes, she will be attending a Woolf conference that weekend.

"Your research would benefit," she says.

I write back. "Is that your way of asking me to go with you?"

Almost immediately: "If you want to."

"You don't have cancer or something, do you?"

"You wish!"

Do I want to share a room with her for a weekend in some predictably armpit hotel? Michael and I just happen to not be on the road then, a fact that is obvious if you track his tour online, which makes me suspect my mother's been sleuthing. Unless I invent a business meeting or a mystery trip, I have no excuse not to go, and she knows it.

I discover through some online sleuthing of my own that my mother is the plenary speaker for the conference. Somehow, she neglected to mention that.

I agree to go to the conference.

Turns out my mama is a fish in Woolf circles. As in a big fish. As in THE academic rock star – scratch that, the equivalent to me is country star – at this conference. Here in the marbled and chandeliered lobby of the Marriott (town undisclosed due to lack of relevance to anyone with a pulse) with its 60'svibed conversation pits and multiple check in/out kiosks that will eventually put desk clerks out of work but to which my mother and the line of introverted academic conference goers gravitate, we are stopped every three feet by people who "just want to say hello" to my mother.

"This is like being in public with Michael," I say to my mother. She basks in the adoration, unable to hear me. Which, truth be told, shocks me, misanthrope I thought her to be. When we register at the table with the ubiquitous ruffled skirt, we are handed packets of material and a bag of swag. I dig in to see what Woolfies consider fun freebies.

I immediately toss the lanyard with my name on it back into the limp canvas bag when it comes into my hands. There's no way I'm going to wear that. Maybe I'm a lit geek, but there's no reason to be branded as one outside of the conference. I try not to think about the irony that the bag advertises books but is in no wise sturdy enough to hold more than a couple of paperbacks.

The bag also contains sticky notes advertising a small press (keeping those, thank you very much), stacks of brochures (I promptly toss mine into a nearby recycle bin), a handful of hard candy that is not worthy of bearing the title. These I put on the nearest table. I've seen better candy at parades. (I do keep the chocolate ones because inferior chocolate is, arguably, better than none.)

At the bottom of this cave of limited wonders is a finger puppet of Woolf. Now this I can get behind. I put just the tip of it on my finger and gesture it at random people, who smile or look away. This puppet alone is worth having come here for.

My mother talks to a reverent crowd and shoves a stuffed

manila envelope at me that the woman in front of her has handed her. I buttonhole the woman with glasses as thick as her manuscript: "Have some respect for trees. Send an attachment to her email address like all humans do nowadays," I say, thrusting it back at her.

She sputters, adjusts her slipping bun, and walks off, but my mother grins.

To the right of the registration table is a screen scrolling conference events. An image of my mother fills it for a moment, one I've never seen. It's probably a decade old. In it, her cheeks are fuller, and her eyelids haven't thinned. Her eyes seduce the viewer. She knows all about the male gaze, so that pisses me off, until I wonder if she's subverting it.

Feminists, don't we sometimes either say we're subverting or doing something ironically, to make the thing acceptable for us to do? #TelltheTruth;ShametheDevil

While Mother is being fawned over, I head to the bathroom where a trio of conference attendees with mom bobs whisper about which of the scant male attendees will become my mother's dessert. Apparently, she has a "reputation."

Even enlightened women can't handle a woman with a healthy sexual appetite. My mother's single. So what if she loads up at a conference?

"Maybe she brought someone with her," I say, flinging my hair over my shoulder. They gasp like a Greek chorus. Obviously, they don't know I'm her daughter. I nearly let them off the hook, but why should I?

One of the women grimaces, revealing a jag of lipstick on her teeth.

I reapply my own lipstick, kiss the three women on their lips one after another before leaving the room wiping my mouth.

I pop my head back in the room and make a squeegee motion to the woman with the red hair and redder teeth.

"Your teeth," I say. "It's not a good look."

For the record, I'm straight. But no one was complaining about those kisses, guaranteed.

I live tweet the conference. No one has mentioned a conference hashtag, so I make one up (#NotAfraidWoolf) and add the year, thus creating yet another connection between the play and Woolf which will have me and other researchers cursing. But it's irresistible.

Your imaginary honor, an indulgent aside: I adore Albee's writing, but the fact that he called the play "Who's Afraid of Virginia Woolf" is difficult for those of us trying to search the internet for real Woolf information. For the love. As for my conference hashtag, I plead delusions of momentary wittiness.

The conference session titles, despite (ok, maybe because of) their overblown names, actually tantalize me:

1. The "Oh!" in Orlando.
2. Painting: The Sister('s) Art in Woolf (This construction must stop, btw, that whole word with a parenthesis on it. It's ugly and unwieldy. Just stop. Yes, YOU, conference people. No one else does that. It was clever for, oh, a minute in the 90's, if my mother's past conference programs are any indication. What, you don't read voraciously all things Woolf that your mother brings home? Then you are no true fan, and you may leave now.)
3. Leonard's Later Loves
4. Forum and Function: Roman and Grecian Influences on Woolf's Work

154

5. Veni, Vidi, Vita??

This is only a smattering of the creative titles. I may have to revise my opinion of this group. Then again, surveying the majority of the drably dressed, maybe not. Vibrant colors don't cost extra, do they? Dear God, I look like a lone poppy in a field in my red dress. (I might be exaggerating, but not by much.)

At the podium right now, every ounce of personality drains from my mother's voice as a bland midwestern newscaster possesses her. I'm proud to say that she is not wearing tweed, though she is wearing brown. It doesn't look bad against her perma tan. Her embellishments begin and end with a turquoise necklace (She knows how I hate the stone. It reminds me of rock bubble gum.).

She clutches the stand before her, raving about Woolf's ambition to write a novel-essay.

Was she concerned that the essay made the novel part too dull? You'd have to jazz up the story around it, wouldn't you? Or make it so closely related it was inextricable from the plot. Though of course, she hadn't intended to write the novel at all. It had been meant to illustrate the essay.

I've been talking with my mother about this off and on for years, but something leaps out at me this time, a possible connection between it and a different Woolf novel, *Lighthouse*. And the topic for my thesis, which I've been struggling to find, lands on my shoulder, just like that.

My mother's voice struggles with that lower, calmer pitch she's attempting, and I almost giggle aloud. Holy fuck am I going to give Mother hell over her "accent" later.

Why would Woolf want to write an essay-novel, novel-essay,

whichever you prefer, in the first place? What is the point of something that is half true, half not? Why can't a novel instruct on its own? I learned to live and love from reading.

Did Woolf like that it was a unique form, or did she feel she couldn't say what she wanted to say with "just" a novel? But Woolf re-created the novel, in my opinion, so she is allowed to do anything she wants with it.

Mother has moved away from the Plexiglas podium and is waving her right hand. She stamps her foot, raises her voice, heightening her cadence, preacher style. This is why they love her. This is why she's scheduled for a TED Talk this fall. (TED-X, but so?)

It almost doesn't matter what you say when you've got that kind of passion, and yet what she says does matter. To me, to them. The flavor is back in her voice, and I forgive her for her bland beginning.

Dad and I used to watch a local Christian channel on TV sometimes, just for kicks, and when a preacher made a particularly good point, the audience would rise, sway, raise their hands, point. If they really liked what was said, they would throw their shoes onstage.

I find myself rising and flicking my jacket over my head at my mother. I wave that Woolf finger puppet like mad. More than one woman mimics me, and my mother glances my way, hands on her hips. Instinctively, I buckle into my chair.

"She knew more than anyone how to explain the human condition."

More people rise, and I join them.

Her charisma climbs. We're enthralled, all disciples of Woolf and, by extension, my mother. I've never seen this happen at a conference, not that I've been to very many.

"Tell it," someone calls. Nowhere but in the South would a Woolf conference get this reaction. I wouldn't be surprised to see someone take a Glory Lap.

Did Woolf think she'd be so sliced, diced, and plucked? Did she want this kind of attention?

Why yes, I believe she did. The way she pushed form yet in a more sensible, compact way than Henry James. The way she exhausted a sentence first by dissection, then, not satisfied, by vivisection. She resurrected those sentences just to pull them apart and put them together again, according to her drafts.

She tortured ideas with cigarette smoke, by drowning them in her bath, by not letting them rest until they softened under her hand and allowed themselves to be shaped.

What must it have been like, writing a novel, then not a novel, then an essay-novel, ultimately stripping it back to a novel?

I type notes feverishly on my cursedly small phone screen; I glance up when I hear the applause.

There is a Q and A. My mother opens her eyes and smiles invitingly, but only I know it's a fake response. There are sure to be some stupid questions mixed in with the inevitable pseudointellectual ones. Does my mother sound like someone who suffers fools gladly?

A hand goes up.

"Yes?"

"Did Virginia Woolf, like, really not want children?"

My mother's faux smile disappears.

"It was more that it was inadvisable, due to her mental health, as I understand it."

Another hand.

"Does that mean she used some kind of birth control? Do

157

we know what kind? Or did she just not have sex, except with Vita?"

"You'd have to ask her." A nervous twitter flushes through the crowd.

Mother's chest heaves. There's not a thing I can do.

From the back, without a lifted hand: "I read a rumor that she had an abortion. Do you think that's what really killed her, and they threw her body in the river to cover it up and claimed she killed herself?"

"We're done," my mother says, unclipping the mic, not addressing the ignorance of facts, the half-formed suppositions, the incorrect knowledge of Woolf's age at death, well beyond childbearing years unless she was the biblical Sarah; Mother's brow says all of these things. Her words boom as she hunches, her adopted Southern accent now fully deployed: "We're here to talk about a writer who changed everything. She broke and restyled the novelic form irrevocably, pointed out injustices perpetrated on women by society, and bested many, no, most, men's writing *forever*. And all you want to do is speculate about her sex life and her lack of children? When was the last time you were at a lecture about a man without children and someone asked why he didn't have kids? Did anyone ask if he pulled out? Did anyone want to know if his lovers had abortions? Women, don't blame men for not respecting your research, if your questions today are any indication of the sort of work you're doing."

Admittedly, a mic drop isn't the same when it's done with a lavalier mic, but still, she lets it fall and storms offstage.

I give her a few minutes before following her to our hotel room where I find her sprawled on her bed.

I do a slow clap from the doorway, but it's lost on her.

"I'm serious."

"Mmm," she says, her fingers moving as if she holds a cigarette. She quit a decade ago because she said it was too difficult to climb the tower when she'd been smoking.

Her lips tighten, and her face grows melancholy.

"I'm ashamed of having carved my life from someone else's, as you once suggested I have done. I've spent my career immersing myself in another's work, creating something of my own from it, only to have a room of social media reared, pop cultured tarts negate everything I've attempted in their thirst for literary gossip. As if they couldn't google their questions."

I sit on the edge of the bed but turn away. I feel for her enough not to challenge the use of the word "tart" as she would if I used it.

"You've built a house of original criticism on her foundation. You've helped a generation see and appreciate Woolf anew, present conference excepted. I think that first question just opened the floodgates of speculation."

"Social media encourages casual scholarship. Owning a mug with an Austen quote on it and brandishing a plume in your profile picture doesn't make you a scholar."

She's heard me say that, but I don't mention it. "I see you've checked out Instagram."

I can see how many of these attendees could appear to be poseurs. Some surely are. However, I will take casual engagement to none at all.

She rolls towards me, her brown eyes pink all around where her hands have been pressing against them, her skeletal, tanned face earnest as she gently takes my hand.

"Briscoe, don't be like me. Have a family. I'm not supposed

to say that to you, but *I* felt my scholarship wouldn't be taken seriously if I were a mother. I followed Woolf's example. What they reminded me of today was that maybe Woolf didn't have a choice. Maybe she would have chosen to have a family if she could have safely, and her killing the angel of the house had more to do with killing her hopes and dreams of a typical life. Justifying why she 'wouldn't' have children. I followed mindlessly in her footsteps like that was what I was supposed to do. Maybe she didn't have a choice. *You* have a choice."

I pull away. "What is this, an after-school special for feminist families who suddenly see the light? Don't undo your whole career's work with one misguided pity party."

It doesn't slow her.

"I ran away from you, from your father. I thought I had to be alone, focus on my work. Now it's all I have. They reminded me of that out there. They reminded me that I sacrificed something I might not have had to. I have no one left."

"You have a *daughter,* you ridiculous, calcified cow." We both laugh. I kneel on the floor beside her and stroke her hair until she pulls away.

Though I have to force the words out of my tight throat, I say as I sit up on my haunches: "I've never felt bitter. Being without you made me fearless. I may have missed you, felt disconnected, wondered occasionally if I had done something to run you off, but you have been yourself. *That's* the mother I needed. And I don't for one minute think you have lived the way you have because of Woolf. You love your life, your freedom. If Woolf was your excuse to do what you needed to, then good for you."

The omniscient me can believe this. *She's* mature and has never woken up at night crying for her mother.

160

"What if I never have grandchildren because I was never a real mother to you?" Her face wrinkles and sags.

"Babies are big balls of need. I'm not sure motherhood's for me. Trust me, I have all of the responsibility I can handle right now."

She sits up and curls her tan legs beneath her.

I shake my head as the surprise seeps in. "I would have bet good money that I was the only woman in America who felt confident that her mother wouldn't pressure her to have children. Until now."

We laugh.

"You really don't want children?" she asks.

"Any nightlife around here?"

That evening, we go dancing. My mother has no rhythm, but enough joy to make up for it. I say nothing about her dry-heave dancing. I just orbit her, as always, her hula hoop.

That curly-haired grad student named Marshall whose company I left her in at 2 a.m. is probably still wondering just what happened to him. I, for one, don't want to know.

Predictably, my mother and I never speak of it.

Chapter 11

W e don't exactly ease into things on the musical collab front at the rental. Give Michael a guitar and an idea, and he's off. When he wakes now, he picks up his instrument and starts beating it, wanders the house troubadour style until he finds me. Or V. There's something of a rock star's country side to his music at the moment, all bright strings and heavy playing, intense vocals, about whatever it is his brain has concocted during his sleep.

Today, the living room gradually fogs with sound; you allow yourself to believe the grandeur of the notes can become a part of you and they temporarily possess you, wrapping you in the warmth of fresh strings being fretted by firm fingers. It's the mundane, ordinary wood and metal turned miracle.

My eyes seek Michael's, but he is too busy (im)pressing the coiled wire and V., who is all eyes and appreciative rigidness in a corner, to notice. (See how disruptive that above parenthetical is?)

Eventually, his playing turns to dreamy musings. I've glanced to be sure he's turned his phone on to record the session, something he sometimes forgets. Nothing worse than watching a song disappear, never to be recaptured.

Now he shifts to what I call "Michael's Song," because he has no name for it himself. It's an original series of arpeggios, faintly classical. Nothing you'd expect him to play. It's technical and complex, but also alluring, and it has no lyrics. Unpretentious but gorgeous.

I'm transfixed, as always, when I hear him play it.

A voice blankets words over the melody, unbidden, and the song turns country instantly. My body tenses as if I'm about to be in a car wreck.

This song I've always thought of as more mine than the one he wrote to propose to me, is being violated in front of me, but I make myself hear the unexpected colors emerging from it with V's voice. There a *yes*, there a near miss, but she rides the tune perfectly, dammit.

As she sings, I hear myself gently redirecting the lyrics, taking the first word she says and softening it, her nodding. I write out a line and hand it to her, and she sings it, glances at me as she changes a noun. It fits.

This song was sacrosanct. I wouldn't have dreamed of touching it, but it turns out that was my opinion, not Michael's. Possessiveness gains me, gains the world, nothing. And yet I feel sick in parts of me I didn't know could feel.

Michael's eyes remain closed, his head directed away from her. His fingers grip the guitar, his foot punctuates his playing with a tap-tap-tap.

My hands clench. Her voice is nothing but a genetic fluke, DNA gone right. Doesn't make it any less seductive if you ignore the words straight from the fairy's Thesaurus she apparently uses to string her songs together.

Frilly words lack substance, lack grit and truth. They don't mean anything more than the tepid images they evoke. There is no truth behind them; truth always has heft and a hint of darkness or intense joy. And yet no, these aren't the words she would typically use.

For nothing was simply one thing. James's words in *Lighthouse* spring to mind.

My mind leans forward, my body back. I don't attempt to change her word choices again, not now. I allow the phone's voice recording app to capture the moment.

Michael's face shines, and trying to tell myself his thing with V. is merely a creative crush taken too far is impossible.

Her voice soars, taking us heaven high. Michael stretches towards her voicing, his notes urging her back down until she dips impressively deep, revealing that unsuspected range she seldom needs to use. The notes crescendo upward again into a trill before tapering off.

My hands extend blindly for Michael's phone, looking at it only long enough to stop the record button. "Well hell, I feel like I've just been in the presence of two simultaneous orgasms, and neither of them was mine. How disappointing."

I leave the room before either can say a word.

If only I could have draped Patrick around my neck and dangled him down my back, the effect would have been perfect. He'd have loved being a part of that snap.

I put my sunglasses on and head outdoors, dip my toe in the pool. I go back indoors, retrieve my bag from the living room, sit in a chair, and wait for my laptop to start. When it does:

Much has been made by others about sight and eyes in this novel, and I'd like to specifically point to Mrs. Ramsay's physical short-sightedness and its metaphorical role in the novel. She needs glasses and won't wear them. As a result, she isn't sure what she is seeing sometimes, which is a signal to the reader that she might be an

164

unreliable narrator, even if she doesn't realize it. (Though she is not, strictly speaking, a narrator, she's as close as we get to one.)

At the beach, attempting to write letters while the wind whips her writing paper about, Mrs. Ramsay encounters figures who aren't who she thinks they are. This is the primary problem with her: her inability (or refusal, perhaps) to see the truth except in those moments when it engulfs her in private. Later, Lily is able to complete the postmortem, to "see" things not the way Mrs. Ramsay would have with her public mask of chipper positivity, but to view them as only an outsider with a privileged peek can. The veil is pulled aside and here stands Woolf as Lily once again, condemning while also commemorating her (Woolf's) mother for the domestic life she chose and lived, Woolf's child self needing and having appreciated that, her womanly self asking if it had been a worthwhile way of spending her short life. With her writerly objectivity inevitably marred by filial subjectivity, Woolf tries to make sense of her mother's life as a woman and mother while also examining society at large's view of women with the same text, another method of questioning her own choices.

Mrs. Ramsay's choices and attempted influence may have appeared ordinary for her time. Were they? Her thwarted ambition caused her to recruit other women to become wives and mothers as if to convince herself she'd made the right decision for her own life. She wielded secret power over her accomplished husband: she often refrained from exerting the influence she knew she could, while sometimes using smaller, pettier means to exploit his insecurities: for example, he wanted her to say she loved him, but she didn't like to say it aloud and so wouldn't. She didn't sprinkle the word around the way she did her attention to everyone else, but she looked at him in a way that told him how she felt instead, and he made it enough. It would have taken so little.

Instead, she "saw" life for him, painting him a pleasant picture every day from her appearance to her public positivity. Perhaps it's not her sight, but his, we are to doubt.

I pick up my phone. Robert doesn't sound surprised when I call him, when I tell him I can't do this, and that he needs to tell Drake so. He lets me go on until I finish, then he tells me he will personally shave V.'s head in her sleep after the album is done and bring me her hair. The image makes me laugh so hard I cheer up and tell him to bring Natalie over to dinner soon.

He updates me on Natalie's album. She's so talented that I can't help but wish for her all of the luck I don't want her mother to have. After our goodbyes, I am able to return to the living room. I even bring out my guitar, though no one says anything as I join Michael's strumming.

"Aren't we cozy?" my mother asks as she passes through. She insists I join her for a walk, and I do, grumpily running the bottom of my shirt over my strings and returning my guitar to its case. Except for discussing which way to head and when to return to the house, we are silent the whole time. Just before we arrive at the front door, I ask her what the point of the walk was.

"I heard you on the phone with Robert. It's not safe, going from fury to pretending everything is fine in so short a space. I can't watch you do this to yourself. You can't sit there while they ignore you."

"In case you hadn't noticed, there's more on the line here than my ego." I remind her of what I – what we all – have to lose.

She pushes her light brown hair off her sweaty forehead.

"I have failed you utterly if you believe any of what you just said."

I walk into the yard. She follows.

"It's going to hurt either way."

We pick up the bean bags for the ridiculous game with the dirty name, "Corn hole," that the guys play, and we lob them at the board with circles cut out of them.

"With all of the literature you have read, how can you still believe love conquers all?" she asks.

"With all that you have read, how can you continue to discount it? It's the one universal desire, the one universal experience. We can do without many things, but we will never thrive without love of some kind."

She tosses the bag, misses the hole.

"There has to be the capacity to process love in the one you love for it to be reciprocated."

I long to launch a bag at her face, but refrain.

"Which of us are you saying doesn't know how to love?"

"When you were a child, you always admired those singers and actors who were over the top. Overly emotional ones. I blame myself. I know I tend to be too rational. My sense of humor might be lacking. I might have been more academically minded than not, back then. Your father, such a good man, was quiet, non-demonstrative. It seemed like you were always searching for a heater, you know?"

"I still don't understand." I toss the beanbag from hand to hand, note its weight.

"You've been around music and books for so long that you might be imagining something that's just not there. He's a performer. I think he's been performing all along."

"Dad told you that Drake wanted Michael and me to marry, didn't he? He wasn't supposed to say anything to you."

Whirling around like a shot putter, she releases the sack, and it bounces off the board.

"I believe Michael cares about you as much as he can care about anyone. It's just not in him, darlin'. It's no shortcoming of yours. Better if you remember why you're together in the first place."

I see now that what I took for her liking him is really my mother willingly being taken in by Michael's charisma.

I toss the fist-sized bag I clutch into the pool and head into the house.

Once inside, I choose a bottle of beer and go to the in-home theater. Patrick and Bernita join me, and my mother follows, at a distance. I hear her whisper something about Michael and V. to them, and she excuses herself.

"Virgil isn't the only guard dog," Patrick whispers.

"I never asked her to do that."

"Madres wants to does she does," Bernita says.

I shrug and put on *Casablanca*. I don't like the film, but I need a reason to cry in the dark.

As the screen dims momentarily, I pull the theater-sized package of *Twizzlers* that I lifted from the candy counter on my way in from beneath my shirt, and pretend I don't hear Patrick's disapproving sniff. I cough to cover the crinkle of the package and turn my head away from him to chew.

When I toss the empty package under the seat, I tell him not to pause the movie as I rise to rush to the bathroom. He pulls on my arm, but I break free.

I make it back just as Bogie says that one famous line which makes me cry and I cover for it by telling Patrick that Michael and I don't even have Paris, which sets us to giggling for some reason. He squeezes my hand, and I reciprocate.

"Hey Patrick…"

Bernita, not one who can endure inactivity, is long gone, even before the movie was over.

He cocks his head towards me.

"You know I love Michael, right?"

"Girl, please."

"That doesn't make me pathetic, does it?"

We rise and head for the door.

"I know one thing it makes you, and that's well off."

He's not wrong.

✳✳✳✳

To and fro, to and fro, my mother swims. Funny how limited places offer unlimited opportunities: you can swim forever to nowhere in a pool.

My hands slowly shuffle the pages of *Orlando* from left to right, but my eyes aren't committing, so even though I adore the novel, I set it down. The yard swing's weathered bottom beneath mine, its rough chain beneath my hand, ground me as I watch the day wake.

I take up my mug with its clever literary quotes, pick up my book and read for the (insert what's to you an annoyingly ridiculous number of times; the number here is, I think, seven) the passage before me, pretending I can indulge in this without hearing what wafts outdoors eerily, unbelievably early, this morning.

Hey, I've earned this mug. I've actually read the books quoted on it.

I have no idea how Michael got V. downstairs so early. More likely, they never went to sleep. I can't tell you if he came to bed or not, because I passed out from heat exhaustion as soon as I got into bed. That's what happens when you don't face

169

the music. (Please. I get to use this cliché if anyone does. And it actually applies here.)

Our lives right now: they play a section of a song. Stop, pause, go over it again. I only catch the harmonizing of their voices. They do songs, I listen, critique, suggest. They'd do a fine job all by themselves if they weren't both so emotionally invested. As it is, they don't know how to critique what they're creating.

I, on the other hand, do, and I'm trying not to at the moment. Coffee launches over the rim of my cup as I slam it down.

"AirPods to the porch, stat," I text. *Winky face.* My boy Patrick does not answer. He's not an hourly employee, especially not at this hour, so I can't technically complain, though I'd like to.

Can I bring *Orlando* into my thesis discussion? The novel's so deep, so fanciful, unlike anything else Woolf. Perhaps it made sense to who Woolf was then and who she was attempting to be. She felt stuck in expected roles. She felt constrained by society's rules. Literature's rules. And she wanted freedom for her friend and lover, the inspiration for the book, Vita, so she gave it to her by recreating her as Orlando. It's a highly feminist book, but I want to convince myself that *Lighthouse* has all I need, so I do convince myself.

A blur of blue enters from the right. By now, I am not at all surprised to see Mother's limbs emerging from her cotton cocoon, but I am nervous knowing there is nothing under there to protect the world from her throw-back bush. She has taken to wearing a towel when anyone is around, at least most of the time.

She motions for me to make room for her, and I refuse. "Not while you're half naked."

She shrugs and sits on the ground, which is worse. Her body leaves wet marks on the helpless cement that supplants the grass around so much of the house. Shifting limbs expose more of her than I'd like to see, though, to her credit, she attempts to tug her towel about her.

I cross my legs in the swing beneath me and pick up my coffee.

It can't be past 7:30 yet. The day will be long and sodden with sound.

As I open my mouth to ask her about *Orlando*, she motions for my coffee, takes a sip, speaks.

"You know why you're in charge of the album?"

"I'm not." Not exactly.

"It's because Drake knows you can't bear any more than he can to allow Michael to put out bad work." She hands me back my mug and sucks on her knee, revealing way too much thigh.

"Stop that!"

She pauses. "You do realize you're both infantilizing me by trying to control me and also telling me that as an older woman, I'm not desirable? I only point that out because as women, we owe each other more."

Before I can reply that almost sixty isn't *that* old, she motions to the book in my right hand.

The noise from the basement floods further onto the deck as they test a song at a higher volume. It recedes as they pause and try again. Unfortunately for me, the acoustics in and around this house are good.

My mother raises her voice. "How many times do you think we need to read a book before it intertwines with our genes? And what do you think of *écriture féminine* in general?"

Voices crescendo. My heart rate rises in tandem.

"Who are you, the Sphinx? I've got my own questions, thank you very much." These are topics we have covered before; she's trying to distract me.

I toss the book as far and as hard as I can, and it impressively reaches the driveway. I manage to miss hitting my mother with it, but then I wasn't aiming for her, was I?

Rolling onto her knees, she reaches forward and places her hands on my shoulders.

"I already told you, you don't have to do this. You don't owe anyone anything. No one has the right to ask this of you. Come with me and Virgil back to my cabin. We'll work on your thesis for the whole summer, and it'll be ready to submit right on time. Screw it–I still have plenty of friends at U.N.–we can get you an extension if you need it. But this is not a decent environment for you to live in, let alone write in. It's making you sick again."

Again? You mean she noticed before? Why didn't she ever mention it?

My imagination takes me into her Jeep, holding Virgil, winding our way onto those country roads that would take me anywhere, please, but here. Straight up Blair Mountain to Mother's cabin, raising the chain behind us.

Me, my mother, Virgil, probably Patrick because he couldn't bear being left behind, and Woolf.

My insides clench as tightly as my hands.

What Michael and Velvet put out will be garbage unless it's tempered. Sure, it's beginning to have raw beauty, but they can't see clearly right now. Drake knows it. It won't matter to fans at first; at first it won't matter to Michael or Velvet either, because they won't be able to identify it as that, not until later. Heat of the moment writing always seems good.

Because Drake's rushing it out to add to the controversy, the rumors, while also squashing them (ambiguity everywhere) he would allow them to put out absolute garbage if necessary because in this case it's the promise of the product more than quality.

Unless, as my mother says, he knows I'd never let that happen. Not only for my reputation, for Michael's, but because musical history is bigger than any of us. No one will care in, say, 50 years that my husband fell out of love with me, probably not even me, but people will, I hope, still play the music, still get something from it. What happened to me will be no more than a footnote, especially if I don't pick at it, if I cover it up, because why wouldn't I? Do I really need to contribute to the ugliness of the world? Do I really need to condemn something I understand, just because it doesn't match with the world's expectations, with my own? Is my love such a thin reed it can't endure?

From the first time *I* kissed *him,* I knew my feelings for him were my responsibility, not his. I'd always feel more, because his "feeling" was a source, like electricity.

"You ran away to write *your* book, *Jules,* but you never finished it," I say. She knows nothing about the music business, nothing about a traditional marriage.

She sits back, arranging her towel when I make a face. Sighs in that annoying, wise owl way she has.

"You're going to either help them complete this album and make something beautiful of it and lose your marriage, or you're going to save your marriage and tell Drake to go fuck himself."

"If he needs help with that, all he has to do is call," says a voice.

Patrick yawns as he pads over, pulls up his droopy-bottomed pajamas, and reaches out his hand, revealing my AirPods.

"Perfect timing." I take the case from him and insert the buds gingerly in either ear.

When the two eventually make their way inside, I retrieve *Orlando* and smooth the slightly dented cover, stroking it as if I can undo the damage.

Michael and Velvet's music and conversation intermingle below, and I strain to hear it better.

I place the book and the AirPods on the ground beside the swing, then I squat, rise, and squat again next to the open basement window, pretending I'm doing my RDA of the exercises. I even bust out a set of burpees while eavesdropping.

V. interrupts Michael to discuss a line she's written, something "spiritual" even he is having trouble swallowing.

I pull down my Lululemon tights and I back my ass up against the screen. "What my husband is trying to say is that God doesn't want to sound hokey." The sensation of the unexpected movement of the mesh behind me and the realization that I am falling are one as I end up on the floor right in front of the two of them. And it's not my bare ass that's on display.

"It's still a bad line," I say as soon as I can breathe. I refuse help, tugging my bottoms up as I rise, relieved to be unharmed. While V.'s face blanches, Michael can't stop laughing.

"You could have gotten her hurt, pulling the screen out like that," V. says.

"You *pulled* the screen out?" I ask.

"I was going to catch you, but I missed."

My expression halts his laughter.

Thank God I went for a wax earlier in the week, leaving me

the shape of a heart down below, if you must know. Though why I would bother hiding that from you when I've revealed so much more, I have no clue.

Michael makes to follow me up the stairs, but my raised hand tells him not to bother. He touches my shoulder, apologizes again, but I am having none of it.

Instead, I shoot back up the stairs and outdoors. I plunge straight into the pool. It's not until the next day that I'm mildly tender from the fall.

Chapter 12

Michael and me, the early mix:

After I introduced Michael to Drake, things accelerated.

First, there was applying the polish Drake said Michael needed before he could officially take him on. We made demos of his songs and had him attend every open mic in town and beyond. He joined every songwriting group, attended the opening of every convenience store, played "I'll Fly Away" at an outdoors tent revival without so much as flinching. Hey, in Nashville, connections can be made in every genre.

He learned that people were connecting with him through his songs and not just the abstraction of the emotions he was singing about. That he was a healing influence, almost. He even learned to connect in return, at least onstage.

Sometimes I'd perform at the smaller open mics, too, sometimes not. His desire and talent were stronger than mine, so I started working extra jobs to give him more time to write and play, to get his career going, since we were all convinced that Michael had "it." And though Drake never said it, he didn't have to: my strength is my songwriting. My voice is pleasant enough in certain ranges, but otherwise I sound nasal, and not in the fun, blue grass way.

Once I graduated from high school, Drake said he could no longer keep me on as an intern, but that he had a better idea: as manager for Michael. The problem was, though he thought I could handle life on the road, he said it would be best if Michael and I married. Otherwise, people might talk.

"Would those people be my father?" I asked Drake.

His grin said plenty. Although I don't think my father thought marriage to be a magic elixir against hurt and gossip, seeing what he had gone through, I think he wanted to be sure Michael took care and not advantage of me. Insert affectionate eye roll here.

Getting married at eighteen is ridiculous, but I was young, in love, and convinced I held the future of an element in my hand.

I'm still not convinced that I don't.

While helping Michael, I also attended Belmont, that finest of music-focused schools. Mostly online through their video conferencing option, with obligatory tests and meetings being fitted around Michael's touring schedule, to my relief. I know they were so accommodating because of Drake's recommendation of me. Just as with U of N, I was asked not to broadcast our arrangement.

I made it work. I was able to count managing as part of my schooling, another internship with college credit. Actually, I taught plenty of my classmates the practical side of music in our online class forums. I think I could've given a master class in that. There's no substitute for trial and error.

Michael and I had already moved in together to save on rent before we married. (My excuse, when really, I wanted to see his face every morning.) Initially, he played the "dues circuit:" weddings, parties, barbeques, whatever. He worked at Gruhn's Guitars briefly until he kept saying a guitar brand that the store stocked was worthless. He was promptly fired when the manager overheard him.

He went from playing free gigs and weddings and the like to being on the bill with other acts, as Drake and I started quietly promoting him. Then Michael began opening for names, people whose bus he might or might not be invited onto after the headliner's show, but that he could put on his résumé, get his picture taken with, anyway. Get close enough to gold and you reflect the shine.

I reached out to neighboring states for shows for him: Georgia, the Carolinas. Saying you were from Nashville was key. He began doing fairs and festivals, and soon he was co-headlining. Then, after several songs from his first album received frequent radio play (later, of course), he became *the* headliner.

When Drake officially signed him, Michael was already established as a reputable opening act. I'm taking more than a little credit for the days I had to roll him out of bed and tell him to get his pants on. It didn't matter if a gig were large or small, who he might offend if he didn't play, in the beginning he would only play when he wanted to play. I had to explain to him once that he could not blow off a gig at the Ryman.

It took me inviting Jim McCully over, one of Michael's music idols who had once been huge in country music in the early 90's who had no career left, a guy who played at a café in a hollow near Hendersonville for tips at the time on Saturday nights. Jim was a friend of my father's, though even his connections couldn't land Jim any work because of his reputation for being undependable. Jim sat with Michael, and they drank and played poker an entire Saturday night. I only heard bits and pieces, but after Jim left our cabin, Michael promised he'd do whatever I suggested on the music front. I sent Jim word to go to Gruhn's and buy a guitar and have them send me the bill.

Jim's wife called a few months later to say he had passed of liver failure. She said she didn't even put a notice in the paper, afraid they'd dredge up his bad behavior without crediting his good. She asked if we wanted the guitar back. I told her to sell it and keep the money. Not that we couldn't have used the money, but musicians don't usually have great burial insurance.

Not too long after the news, Michael and I began traveling in a dented Eagle six sleeper with a rent-a-band who'd done mostly studio work up until then. I asked my father to join us, but he politely refused. Michael didn't try to persuade him.

Michael and I disagreed over his songwriting style, the way he gravitated to a clever hook nowadays (important, but), to a crowd-pleasing lyric. For the man who didn't want anyone to tell him where to be when, he began tilting towards public opinion when it came to harnessing his gift. *That* I did not encourage. Pandering is the worst form of artistic compromise.

The pay-your-dues tour continued. Grub pubs, rural bars in states where public smoking was (is) banned but not enforced, with a cigarette machine in the place while there's a door saying not to smoke within eight feet of the door that you can barely read for the smoke. Tiny tables surrounded by flimsy wooden chairs, beer glasses and cigarette ashes, crumbs of unidentifiable batter that should be called generically "fried food" but is usually an unspeakable part of the chicken or a batter dunked vegetable. Graffiti in the reeking bathrooms, poster tack or Scotch tape holding random poster corners, the only remains of the cover bands as stale as the cigarette smoke that churn through weekly.

Playing, singing, traveling. Loving. Writing. Hotel rooms: good, bad, indifferent. Our growing collection of mini hotel shampoos and body washes enchanted us less and less as the bag filled, until we began leaving them behind. Cities were mostly alike except for a signature restaurant or a "must see" attraction. We "saw" most of the states, even had photos taken in front of many famous landmarks, but what I remember is the blur. How each day rammed into the next like it couldn't wait its turn. How we anticipated the concerts: him because it was life. Me, because for a few hours afterwards, after a meal, after a couple of beers and a shower, we would end up in bed in our pj's watching dumb TV, reviewing the night as I snuggled into him. He was mine for such a small amount of time on the road. When I was managing him, I was his boss. When he was in public or on stage, *he* was in charge.

In bed though, we were us. I could tell him how exhausted I was. How I couldn't wait for our two-week break. He could admit that his throat was killing him, and that if he were asked to smile for one more photo, he'd refuse. (We both knew he wouldn't. It took a while, but he values his celebrity now almost as much as he values his music.)

Sometimes between shows he'd listen to music, both country and not. His sound is technically country, but if you examine it closely, it owes a lot to everything he's ever heard. Lead Belly, Django, Willie Nelson, Those Pickin' Wickens–V's family, Brad Paisley, Blake Shelton, Jason Isbell. Father John Misty. The Beatles. Les Paul. Even the Bee Gees. Naturally, he reveres all classic country. Ironically, the only music Michael can't tolerate is pop. I say ironically because don't tell him, but there's even some of that in his music. He just doesn't know to call it that.

If you can work out to a song, it's part pop.

I said what I said.

When we weren't on the road, Michael played his LPs for hours and talked about growing up, the albums apparently spinning his childhood memories back into the air, but I didn't learn more than surface things about him. Like that his mother baked the best gingerbread men, using a cookie cutter handed down from her grandmother to her. Or that his father smoked one cigar a week, after church.

The Wickens family fascinated him, both when he was young and now. He'd play V's family's albums for me, inevitably causing my stomach to clench because someone who knows that much about anyone besides a dear family member is, let's admit it, obsessed. I listened over and over again with him anyway not because I loved the music (which is, to be fair, excellent, but not my style), but because I wanted to understand him better. The tears that filled his eyes when he heard the twin but divided by a fifth swoop of the mother/daughter vocals of the Wickens, the automatic movement of his feet to the rhythm: you can't know who Michael is unless you understand the music he loves.

I thought I could figure out where his gift had come from. Could figure out how to help him maximize it by enduring his worshiping of his heroes. Instead, I found myself vaguely jealous of this family. The few times I'd seen V. at the label she'd been breezy and not exactly friendly unless you counted the Southern boa of accent and affectionate pet names she uses to blow people off. That's okay; it made it easier for me

181

to know how to handle her when we were on the road with her. Or so I imagined.

He, I am happy to say because I don't think he would have survived had he not, made it to a couple of her family's concerts, though not the fateful one. I can never tell if he is sorry or relieved he wasn't there when he talks about it. His parents took him to see them. (Did I not mention that Michael's mother was speechless when she encountered V. at the Ride 'Em benefit up close for the first time? That his father blushed as he shook V's hand? My apologies. It was a busy night.)

On the day Drake officially signed Michael, Drake arranged for Velvet to be doing a silken, scented walk-through of the office to meet Drake for lunch. He introduced the two of them and then whisked V., off after she had congratulated Michael. He still managed to ask her three in-depth questions about her music before Drake led her away.

Michael's calculated questioning of her achieved its purpose: it made clear that he was no amateur fan. It resulted in V. patting him on the chest as she left and calling him Sugar. I half expected him to get her invisible handprint somehow tattooed on his chest. Still, I was happy for him. I hated that he tried to dim his enthusiasm as he watched my face. I wasn't worried, not then.

Inevitably, someone had the idea for the two of them to tour together. (Someone named Robert, I would discover, agreed to by Drake). Ticket sales weren't solid for V. at that time, hadn't been for a while. Sure, her and her family's royalties were anchor income for the label, but if Velvet was to continue her career, which meant winning new fans, concerts were the way to do it, she was told.

Like buying your husband an LP for Christmas without considering it means that you will have to listen to it every day for weeks, I agreed for us to meet with Velvet, Robert, and of course Drake to discuss a tour.

Velvet, turned out, was reluctant to be paired up.

"I've never had to *open* for anyone," she said, wrinkling everything possible on her face, which isn't much.

Ego ruffled, settled. In the end, she allowed the men to convince her with wine and talk of stronger ticket sales. At the mention of money and increased popularity, she sat straighter in her chair.

Truth be told, I found myself a little starstruck the first time I met her back when I began interning, before I saw how she treated others; regardless of all the celebrities I'd met by then, meeting her was different; her family *is* early country music, a second Carter family, and while I used to roll my eyes when Michael played Wickens records, privately I thought the clarity of Velvet's on-the-brink-of-adulthood voice (which she has maintained, regardless of her age) on her solo album wasn't terrible.

Actually, I found myself attempting to imitate her when alone, thinking that maybe I could hit those clear, crystal notes. I could, some of them, but mine sounded like they'd been dipped in flour and tossed in grease.

I know what I am and what I am not.

One night right before Michael and Velvet began touring together, Michael stacked his copies of the Wickens' albums in a bin from the oldest to the newest, forming a flip book of their history. Black and white photos of five people (including a couple of the father's siblings early on) became a group of four. Three albums later it became three, then an offshoot: parents

183

only, child turned teen (three albums) doing a solo album, all three again, four as a spouse joined, then back to two on the parents' covers; two on the daughter's, one featuring the granddaughter, one of the granddaughter's only solo album to date, and so on.

Michael explained the changes in personnel and the changes in style thoroughly. Down to dates. Down to conjecturing about things no one could know unless you had been there.

So and so had work done on their teeth *this* year – notice how the buck teeth disappeared? *This* was the album that came out the year so and so was caught in a parked cab with a sex worker on Broadway (Nashville's Broadway, that is.).

Fans of the Wickens (including Michael) pretend to know every nuance, every shape-shifting story and variation, arguing in online forums about "the truth." I've caught Michael doing it, too, blushing as he saw me glancing over his shoulder.

"What? She wore pink satin on her first album cover, *Country Time*. Anyone knows that. It just looks peach."

Apparently, there is no musician, studio, clothing color, hair style, or method of album cover lighting in the family's history too small to be discussed. Michael remembers more about V.'s musical history, more of her personal history (shared onstage and in interviews by her, that is), than *she* does, if their later discussions are any indication.

This is the year the logo of the record label was changed. And here, see, *this* is a second pressing – you can tell by these numbers in the corner. The font of the recording label changed with *this* album.

The font? The font? Who cares about the font? Too many people, that's who.

The whole reason Michael began playing guitar was seeing

184

footage of Jimmy Pickin' Wickens bashing his big ol' Gibson J-45 on TV when he, Michael, was a boy, so I get why the family is important to him.

But when a woman has your husband by his imagination, there is no loosening her grip. You're now the meatloaf and she's the filet mignon. Nothing wrong with meatloaf, but meatloaf can't be steak, no matter how hard it tries.

A week after Velvet agrees to the tour, the four of us have dinner, Michael, me, Velvet, and Robert.

Michael interrogates V., seeming unaware of her reluctance to discuss her early work. His eyes widen as he fires questions, his hand with the serving spoon pausing multiple times until the scalloped potatoes fall back into their bowl.

"I thought the strings for that album were recorded here in town at Studio B. Wasn't (insert a studio in London; though Michael remembers, I don't) used for the album before, though?"

"That's right," Velvet says, her shoulders softening.

He corrects her about a musician whose name she's forgotten or disputes her timeline a few times, and he seems both shy and proud, wiping his hands on the tablecloth repeatedly, even though I've pointedly handed him his napkin twice. He's never had a problem using a napkin before.

They tiptoe around her parents' demise with an "after," and "since." His tact in that surprises me.

"Is it wrong that I'm jealous?" I whisper to Robert behind the wine glass in my hand, though I could have bellowed, considering how absorbed the two of them are in their conversation.

"Comes with the territory," he says, taking a long drink from his own wine glass.

To pass the time, we flirt lightly, discover our mutual enjoyment of beach thrillers. Even then (V. laughs, head back, and Michael mirrors her head's tilt) something tells me I might someday need an ally more than I need to extramarital with someone whose daughter is literally my age.

"And do you ever have the urge to build a bonfire with the family's albums?" I ask, motioning for him to refill my glass.

"I actually have a target out back of the house nailed to a tree and a box of scratched copies I've found at thrift shops and on eBay. When she listens just a little too long to an album, I just go pull out an album, hang it on the nail, and shoot it up. How do you cope?"

Michael tells V. what the drummer from her family's third album is up to nowadays, and she says that the drummer was the first guy she'd ever kissed.

"I'll let you know," I say.

Chapter 13

Michael listens to the woman beside him as if V. is giving him instructions on how to defuse a bomb. His face is a letter read, folded for decades, and unfolded. Each jut of his hair could have its own name.

As they try to work out a line, Velvet's head swivels between me and Michael.

"Flowers fold their petals?"

The effort to keep my eyes still dries them out.

Michael shrugs, noodles in that annoying way musicians have whenever they hold an instrument.

She mentions calla lilies with a raised eyebrow.

"Think innocence interrupted by experience," I say.

"*Little Lamb?*"

"Blake also wrote *The Tyger.*" I so badly want to say cougar, but my tone says it for me.

Her hand troubles her pen. Beneath her thick makeup, her face ripples.

I return my attention to my laptop.

Day melts into day.

Another writing session.

Velvet drags the feather on her pen across her cheek.

Michael twists a tuning peg, plucking the string until it sounds a D. She laughs, Michael smiles. He sits forward, cradling his guitar, his sleeping child. She reads to him. I don't listen, this time.

Something about a passage I wrote earlier niggles at me.

I head to the kitchen with my laptop under my arm and pour a glass of iced tea. Sun tea, to be exact.

I add some rum.

The thing about hunting down symbolism in a book is, you can do it all day. One thing becomes another; personal associations become entangled hopelessly beyond what the author could possibly have intended. We find, create, mysteries and biographical references where there both are and are not any. Because the subconscious writes, too. A writer may say she doesn't intend something, but can we really believe her? Do we want to believe her?

Or you depersonalize the human experience by writing symbolically about everything. See, it's *a* marriage. That works for literary analysis, not for real life, not unless you're more cynical by far than I am.

My mother joins Bernita and me in the kitchen. Mother asks about my essay and sits beside me, but I can only nod as ideas chase one another. Slowly, I become aware of the subtle scent of celery.

I hand my laptop to my mother and move towards the platter of deviled eggs and celery sticks.

"I hope you bought enough food for the coming horde," I say to Bernita while watching my mother. The band is coming this afternoon, and they'll be bringing their appetites as well as their instruments.

Mother has surely read the section by now. She scrolls up.

Frowns.

"Che, ya" says Bernita.

Mother throws herself back in her chair and places her hands just below her ears on either side of her throat.

"Yes," she says quietly. "Very good. Some might find it a bit too speculative, but as a rough draft, an intriguing start."

She glances at something I can't see.

"You've got a creative bent, atypical for academia. You might want to calm it with some qualified uncertainty. Anything you claim you have to be prepared to defend. It has to be tight, darling. Tight, tight, tight. Even then, the committee will grill you."

I bite into a devilled egg, dimly notice the tasty tang of mustard, deposit it back on the plate, lower the plate onto the counter. Pick up a stalk of celery, sniff it, bite into it.

Her voice constricts. "I suppose it's your songwriting that allows you to make those creative connections."

Placing an egg on a clean saucer from the pile on the counter, I hand it to her. She picks it up and slurps its insides. Puts the white back on the plate and hands it to me.

"What if you tied this to that …" she says, motioning to words on the screen, scrolling feverishly.

Beyond us, out the window, Michael and V. amble. She doesn't have a parasol just now, but she might as well, with that simpering walk of hers.

My eyes barely need to meet Patrick's as he comes into the room and follows my gaze.

"On it," he says, stopping long enough to make up a plate of deviled eggs.

"Mother, I have a riddle for you," I say. When her eyebrows raise in anticipation, I give up. "Never mind," I say, watching

189

out the window as Patrick proffers the plate to the walkers. They both decline, so he eats the eggs beside them. Their irked expressions do not move Patrick, who strikes up what looks like quite a conversation.

Bernita hands me my plate and I lift it, take a look at V., and put it down.

"What was it you were saying I should consider?" I ask my mother.

****

Later in the day, Michael's band tumbles out of a circus of vehicles, and I relax as the house swells with people. Michael claims he needs them here to begin rehearsing. A thin pretext for having his Nashville "mafia" with him, but I suppose it makes Michael-like sense, cart before the horse though it is.

V. has been complaining about not having a personal assistant, but she relies on college interns who leave over the summer. She usually has a passel of hangers-on who do things for her, though, and their absence surprises me until I find out that Robert has forbidden her to clutter the house with her yeasayers. I send him a handle of Jack and a pair of my underwear for his thoughtfulness. He responds with a text saying "Wow, thanks," accompanied by a photo of the pink panties half in and half out of a glass of Jack. I reply with a wink emoji.

How do people survive without a sense of humor?

After the band and I acknowledge each other's existence, grudgingly on my part, sheepishly on theirs, we have drinks around the pool, which turns into an impromptu party.

Three drinks in "Let's rank," I slur, not as quietly as I should. Patrick claps. Usually, I wouldn't permit such objectifying behavior, much less participate in it, but I'm feeling mean.

And, let's face it, these traitors deserve it. We sit apart because I'm not ready to play nice, literally, or figuratively.

"Ben: five."

"Five? Be nice. Six."

"Really?" he says. "With that hair? Couldn't he at least hit it with a bottle of Just for Men?"

I shrug. "I think he's brave, being in music and still going natural." If anyone deserves mercy, it's him.

While he's the solidest, most dependable bassist I've ever heard who can play anything with or without a chart in front of him, he's not your melodic bassist. He's a great anchor, though, in more ways than one.

Hoot cavorts, smacking the water with his forearms, spreading droplets like a gleeful child. He's personable, 20, with a cap of curls and he brays instead of laughing. His killer arms pulse with the energy of a drummer like Londin. Though no one drums like Hoot, Michael's constantly having to motion for him to bring it down a little.

We call him Hoot because his eyes are huge. He doesn't seem to mind, and the look suits him. His freckles suit him, too.

His drums are always lined with lights, tacky fun, not that gimmicks are necessary for someone who knows what he's doing, and he does. But he's all about having a good time. I admire that.

He started out in gospel but moved over to country when the family he was playing for divorced, which usually means you're kaput in gospel. I gather he's pretty happy to have made the conversion.

The rhythm guitar player, Josh, is one of the Lost Boys of Sudan. He fled during the violence post-independence.

191

Michael went into the local Wal-Mart to buy a heavy-duty extension cord one day a few years back and came out with Josh. According to Michael, Josh handed him a cd once he heard he was in music. Josh said he was looking for a better opportunity and that Michael wouldn't regret taking him on because he was a hard worker, open to learning, and a spectacular guitarist. He told Michael you had to be the first two things or no matter how talented, you were no good.

Michael asked him to pop the cd into a store stereo and one minute in, Michael hired him. Josh went from the store to the stage within a week.

Josh plays country with a jazz flourish. One of the first things he did when he moved to the U.S. was to learn to play guitar right alongside learning English. His horror stories of his escape (told matter-of-factly) have caused us all to cry.

Nothing causes Josh to worry or lose his composure. He has a solid sense of right and wrong and won't do anything that comes even close to offending his ethics. Except ignoring this Michael and V. thing. Maybe he didn't know.

Yeah, right.

He once literally saved my life when I was choking on an olive from a Bloody Mary. Add the Heimlich to his list of skills.

"I have begged Joshie baby repeatedly to join my team," Patrick says.

I elbow him. "I know that, silly boy. So he's what?"

"Eight-and-a-half with a bullet."

The man's physique *is* impressive, for such a slim guy. He and Hoot are always having pushup contests.

Josh stays in tip-top shape, and I'm sure it has something to do with the march he and his compatriots had to make across their country to get help. He's determined to never be caught weak or poor again, he says–he saves every penny he can, living in a house with at least 5 other guys when he's off the road. On the road, he buys jars of peanut butter and loaves of bread and saves his meal stipend. Sometimes, I make him buy a real meal. Because while I acknowledge that peanut butter is nearly the perfect food, Hunky Man cannot live by Chunky Jif alone.

"I'm so happy that you're drunk enough to rate," Patrick says.

"I believe in equal rights, and men have the right to be ranked."

He laughs.

Tomorrow, I will be horrified at myself for this sexist pastime.

I roll onto my side. "What about V.?" She has taken herself and her My Fair Lady hat out of earshot, apparently offended by our game.

"Not going there," Patrick says.

"Not drunk enough?"

"Nope."

"That tells me all I need to know."

"For her age, right?"

"She's ancient though. If she hasn't had surgery, damn. Explains the parasol."

Unaccountably, Velvet returns and sits by me, stretches her legs out and tries to make small talk about her bathing suit, a one-piece that has a Lycra midsection panel so strong it causes even her flat stomach to muffin. In a black sequined one piece! For bonus points, it squishes her meh breasts. They're fine for fake, I suppose, but not nearly as spectacular as my 100%

organic ones.

"The Moulin Pooch," I mutter.

"What?" she asks.

Patrick snorts into his drink.

Her monstrously bedecked garment belongs in Vegas; I harrumph and turn over onto my stomach to keep it out of my sight. I twist my head to the side, cradle it, and hum as the voices of various members of the band float in and out of my ears.

About the band: Michael isn't *in* a band. He *has* a band, hired to play his music, which is a creative decision and not because he's a tyrant. It means he has total control. Well, he mostly does.

The house teems with musicians: in the bathrooms, in the kitchen, on the sofa. The pool area, the yard. The men flow into every available space, admirably while unintentionally preventing any occasion except in the bedroom for me to have to be alone with Michael. Or for him to be alone with anyone else.

Red Solo cups, wet towels, stray articles of clothing populate the place like lazy frat boys. Ever-present wet footprints, puddles of water, guitar polish, picks, drumsticks, and the like, are everywhere.

Strange women pull away from the driveway in unfamiliar cars at all hours, women that I'm not supposed to see, as if we have forbidden Hoot and Josh to have visitors. (We have not.) Dating apps, I assume, bring them plenty of company. Neither of them is ever in town long enough to have a steady relationship, except Ben. Knowing Joy, I'm not at all surprised that Ben seems fine being on tour so much.

194

Truth be told, I'm grateful the women sneak away so I don't have to eat breakfast across from them. They're just enough younger than I am that they have tauter skin, and I resent it.

I have threatened to make them sign NDA's, but Michael says not to worry about it. That's just what he would say.

My mother says I'm not old, that 28 isn't old, and she's right. Country is realistic about age in a way that rock is not. Especially when it comes to men, the craggier the better. That doesn't mean that those performers with their barely-of-age faces who keep coming up season after season aren't just as popular, as I've said before. Good thing country music is loyal.

When they're not having assignations, the two younger band members spend just as much time playing *Doom* and *Fallout*. I play *Sims* with them sometimes, but otherwise, games aren't for me.

Sometimes, we have actual conversations, and goof by the firepit. I run around stealing hats and being chased for it, participate reluctantly in counting how many marshmallows they can fit in their cheeks, and all such nonsense. Michael and V. never join in.

One afternoon, I toss Hoot's keys into the neighbor's pasture where there *might* be a bull. After he hops over the fence and back he holds something in his hand and smears it on my face, swearing it's more than mud. I hop up and chase him, but once we get away from the crowd, he lets me catch him. He holds my shoulders and lowers his head towards my face, but I jerk free and walk back by myself.

✳✳✳✳

I tell Michael more than once that the songs need to be ready faster, ready for rehearsing, at least. He doesn't reply because he knows I know how it works. There is no recipe for art. But

195

there is a deadline, and I'm tired of the constant onsite B.O. and wrestling already.

Patrick and my mother are not.

My mother seduces the masses. I had no idea that she of the hairy armpits and legs felt so deprived. I'm tempted to tell her that you can't save orgasms in a hump like a camel stores water, but she'd only cackle. Or worse, she'd turn all Jenkins on me, East Coast cold and blow. You never know which you'll get–best to avoid frostbite by provoking neither.

****

"It would have been so much easier at our house, in my own studio," Michael complains as he and one of *Lightning's* sound engineers discuss the smallest amount of equipment that will do an adequate job to lessen the load of what they have to bring in.

I bristle when he glares at me.

They agree on what they need, down to soundproofing the basement for our sanity, the engineer tapping the order into his phone. Without it, every stray background sound would seep onto the recording and up the stairs as well.

I try not to associate soundproofing the basement with all of the horror stories I hear on the true crime podcasts I listen to, but when I see Patrick's eyebrows go up, I know he's thinking the same. We giggle in horror and clutch one another's hands.

In the studios I used to go to with my father, baffling was the gray egg-crate foam, not the beautiful sculptures of any color you can get today. Nowadays if you look up, you might think that what you're seeing is just an architectural feature, when it's really about function.

I almost ask Michael to order the egg crate, but I know I don't have to. He would never touch the other fancy-pants materials. He's only strategically superficial.

Instead, I ask, "Can't we at least paint the walls first? Bare drywall is depressing."

Ignored. Request denied.

Michael and the engineer call the record label to sign off on the supply list, and no less than Drake promises to have everything needed sent over the next day. The soundproofing, we are told, will be brought over later today and installed ASAP.

Within no time of her arrival, V. began apologetic rituals towards me: bringing me iced tea (unsweetened, because who would want it any other way, she must think), offering me pieces of her jewelry (oh god no!), and wanting to show me how to wear eyelashes (thanks, but I don't think so). If she hadn't slept with my husband, I might have tried to like her and her bent-headed, silent, prayers over every meal, her insistence on saying "a few words" directed upwards whenever things aren't going well. There's something about the inherent innocence of someone who believes in God, especially when you realize that it's because of her belief she's tormenting herself.

As angry as I am, I almost pity her.

I test my admittedly naïve theory about the situation on Patrick as we sit together on the cabin's ice cream counter. The room is tricked out like a 50's sweet shop with its checkerboard patterns and '57 Chevy wall decals. I want to show disdain, but it's cute.

Plucking a sugar cone from the stack, I spin it between my thumb and finger as I gesture towards the music, having to raise my voice to be heard. "They're just in a creative fog, something outside of reality. I don't think it will last, do you?"

Patrick picks up a thick piece of my hair and begins braiding. Silently.

A tug on another section of hair says he is adding to the braid.

"Am I wrong?"

He puts the hair down and touches my shoulder. "It's not that you're wrong. I'm just not sure that you're right."

"Imagine you were dating Michelangelo, and he was working on *The David* with, say, a partner."

No matter how many times I am corrected, it will always be *The David* to me.

Patrick eyes soften and he smiles dreamily.

I poke him in the side with the end of the cone. "Stop it. I know which part of the statue you're thinking of. Now, what if everything in you told you that if you just waited until he finished carving it, he would be done with the other guy forever?"

He picks my hair up without speaking. I pull away.

"I mean, it's *The David*. What would the world be without it?"

"What, he gets to do whatever he wants because he's a genius?"

My eyes water, my heart beats faster, as I turn to look at him.

He shakes his head like he's trying to mix a drink in his mouth. "This album isn't *The David*."

"I kinda think it might be, in its own way. Or I think it *could* be."

I toss the empty cone over my shoulder and hear it land, lift another cone from the stack, twirl it. I can't seem to stop the motion until Patrick stills my hand.

If only thoughts could be halted as easily.

****

It's difficult, writing my thesis with the omnipresent juveniles everywhere. (Great potential band name, right?) My mother attempts to keep them occupied in a way I have not asked for. One by one, over a matter of days, she picks off her sexual conquests.

She's sometimes even available to discuss my thesis with me. When she's not, I continue on my own.

Woolf gives us opposing paths available to women then: While Mrs. Ramsay represents the domestic arts, high art is represented by Lily Briscoe. Holding a paintbrush, she is only able to see Mrs. Ramsay in the scenes, the tableaux, into which Mrs. Ramsay consciously arranges herself and others. The brush, rather than clarifying sight for Lily, distorts her perceptions and makes her see things incorrectly.

When Lily sees life through art, she can't see straight. Sight is definitely a theme in the novel.

Lily is not the only one to see Mrs. Ramsay as sacred in tableaux or framed to look as if her beauty and domestic efforts are art. Mrs. Ramsay is idealized and idolized by those who surround her, and it takes even the perceptive Lily the whole novel to truly see her. Charles Tansley, a guest at the Ramsays' summer home, sees Mrs. Ramsay after a moment of clarity backed by a portrait of Queen Victoria; another guest, William Bankes, sees her as a Greek work of art. On one occasion she is displayed against a copy of a Michelangelo painting.

Here the second half of the paradox begins unveiling itself. Lily is not privy to what is really going on inside. Slowly, Lily comprehends a previously unsuspected interiority to Mrs. Ramsay. Frames can honor and display a work of art, but they can also entrap, can limit, can hide from view a portion of a canvas, a portion that might be the most important, but who would know, if it's hidden?

Mrs. Ramsay hides her feelings even from herself at times, and she criticizes her own intelligence. But while walking with Charles Tansley, she talks passionately about art. Though she says she can't understand her husband's latest book or books in general, she reads poetry by choice and sits quietly enraptured by it. She wishes her children were grown so she would have the time to be sure the local dairies are sanitary and see a hospital built on the island, ambitions which are outside of the normal "domestic" sphere she claims to find so fulfilling.

Mornings generally work for my writing. No one's up but me, sometimes my mother, and the squirrels. She doesn't intrude unless I ask her to, but we often sit together after her (God help us) laps and nude yoga. She won't hear of wearing anything until after her session, saying the neighbors aren't up that early and that no one cares about her saggy skin suit anyway, and, she says, it's not like all of us here haven't seen it.

Way too often I have to hustle her back into her robe or a towel after she's finished. "Regardless, this is not a nudist colony."

During the early hours, I pretend that the day will progress in an orderly, productive fashion. Everything that needs doing will get finished. Of course, it never does.

The chaos of creativity that too briefly cocoons our afternoons is followed (too frequently) by drunken, weed-fueled evenings, the casting aside of the heavy mantle of inhibitions, before we eventually collapse into our beds.

This morning, I opened a window and shut it, opened

it again, shut it, before stepping outside, wanting a fresh impression of the kinetic activity in *Lighthouse*. As I closed the door (unavoidable), I realized I was not giving doors their due in my essay.

Woolf uses a series of domestic objects to represent the Ramsays. Mrs. Ramsay is associated closely with windows, in part in the framing of her domestic activities, Mr. Ramsay with doors. She tries to get everyone to open the windows and shut the doors and can sense when even unseen doors are open. Windows bring in light and air. She is the one who wants to bring in opportunity and sun.

Psychology and literary criticism are kinfolk, I decide.

While she opens windows, Mr. Ramsay slams doors. Mrs. Ramsay invites guests for the summer, encourages them in their work. Mr. Ramsay only seems to want them around to make him feel better about himself, thus becoming, instead of an open door of opportunity, a closed door of egotism. Yet Mrs. Ramsay is the one who repeatedly asks for doors to be closed, windows opened. In a sense, Mr. Ramsay is only giving her what she wants. Her ambivalence about opportunity (hence the desire for closed doors) is highlighted by her near claustrophobic command to open the windows. Some things are to be let in, others to be kept out.

There is also the issue of privacy. While they open their vacation home to all and she publicly frames herself in the window (in part to model for Lily's painting), her true self and marriage are kept behind closed doors where only a trusted few are permitted: Mr. Ramsay, of course, as well as Lily. Mr. Ramsay, the closer of the door. Does he seek to protect her?

The outdoors stretches and rises. Scents and sounds waft out the window as the house's inhabitants wake, too.

I check the power left on my laptop battery: we're good.

201

When the temperature is bearable, I prefer to write en plein air where there's more light, and, for the time being, more privacy. I've bought a shade for my computer screen that mostly works.

Throat clearing and humming alert me to Michael's presence. He sits across from me and adjusts his robe over his boxers, puts his cup of coffee on the table between us, and asks me how it's going.

Sleeping in the same bed with the man you love/hate doesn't allow an emotion a full cycle, short circuiting one for the other until you suspect there are no pure emotions in the universe.

Michael runs his hand through his hair, moves it over his face, his scruff rasping beneath his fingers. That he doesn't know the effect it has on me heightens my desire.

"Did you make the bed?" I ask.

He sips his coffee.

"No."

I check the time on my phone.

He lights a cigarette (he allows himself two a day at the most; his doctor and I would prefer zero) and I take it from him, stub it out.

"Could you give me a hand with it now?"

Unless the man is as thick as his French toast, he has to know what I'm aiming for.

Mr. and Mrs. Ramsay are represented by two other domestic images, complementary items of furniture: Mrs. Ramsay is the throne-like chair in which she knits, and Mr. Ramsay is the knotted table by which Lily's imagination visualizes his work. That Mr. Ramsay is a knotted table is another sign of his irascibility. Though he appears to control Mrs. Ramsay, the truth is that she is the "chair" of their family. He is the titular head only.

The afterglow of my time with Michael remains even after I hear the music start up again, flowing outside, causing my shame to build, too.

It sticks in my mind, in the back of my throat, and demands release.

Afterwards, I brush my teeth and wipe my eyes. I pretend all is well and type on, confining myself to the living room for the moment.

Before too long, the recording equipment arrives in the back of a U-Haul, and the men grunt and nearly have to pry the door off the basement to get the boxy JBL speakers downstairs. The NEVE something or other sound console is the size of a piano. I shut down my laptop and go take a look when I hear how rare this model is. Turns out it's just a big rectangle with sliders. Michael is excited to use the classic equipment, saying the recordings will sound more like V's parents' music. But these are supposed to be demos, not the finished product, and I tell him so.

"We cannot afford to major in the minors," I tell him.

He reverently moves the slider up, then back down as if he is conducting an orchestra. It's not even hooked up yet.

I come back out and hoist a stack of cables onto my shoulder and follow the men downstairs, upstairs, down again.

I've never bothered to go so far as to learn models and exact uses: mics, preamps, channel strips, EQ equipment, compressors, limiters, but I do know they are the *stuff for recording*. Effects. Playback thingamajigs. Headphones. I wonder if Drake is sweating at the thought of sending all of this out of his studio, until I hear the engineer say it's all rented.

203

Michael's eyes meet mine as he ratchets something on the drum set. His right hand tightens the nut joining the high hat to its stand.

A snare drum disappears down the stairs along with a duo of amps and a herd of guitar cases full of guitars worth more than half of the cars outside. Spools of cables. Musical toys of all stripes. Michael is known for his inventive country sound. Consequently, he has never been conservative with his cartage. Lucky crew who gets to carry his stuff, which "the boys" have fetched this morning from our house to add to the borrowed equipment.

I pick up the drummer's throne, one of the few things I am allowed to carry since I once drop an amp and shattered one of its tubes.

The west end of the basement looks like they are setting up to play at a private party, causing the same ripples in my stomach I always get before Michael goes onstage. In public, he strips himself and stands in a shower of light and throws his soul out to everyone like Mardi Gras beads.

You dig deeper, imagining there's more, but by now you are pretty sure that's all there is, and you hate yourself for loving a projection and for how unfair it is to you both to expect more because it is what it is and how could it be more when it isn't?

You hate, too, that you can't fathom the endless night that life would be without him. You wonder what this says about your own capacity to love and be loved.

The engineer and Michael arrange the recording equipment.

Michael tunes his guitar by ear, always, something he has fired people for not being able to do. Cocks his ear, plucks a string, turns the tuning peg. Plucks, turns. He frowns, strums a reference string and the one he's attempting to tune to compare. Continues until it sounds the note he wants. He plays a chord, a series of them, and when he fires off a musical phrase or two, I know he's content.

"You've got a bad case of The Female Gaze," my mother says as she puts her face too close to mine.

Then she gawks beyond me at the man flesh.

"Looks like I'm not the only one."

My mother extends her turkey neck and guffaws.

I attempt a discussion about the Ramsays, just to change the subject: "She makes the marriage seem fine when it's not. Mr. Ramsay is a narcissist with grandiose delusions."

"What's so wrong with that?"

I laugh in disbelief. "He tosses bowls out of windows. He gets angry when someone else wants more soup. He ignores his whole family and walks up and down reciting poetry."

"And?"

It takes one to know one, Mother, I don't say.

I plug my ears while Hoot warms up on his bass drum and opens and closes his hi-hat disco style, grinning all the while.

"Tell me how it's a good marriage. She's pretending all day long." I have to raise my voice.

Hoot brings it back down.

"I'd say she's acting, not pretending, which is not the same."

Before I can ask her to explain, she asks something that intrigues me even more, "But with all of those children they had, why is there no mention of Mr. and Mrs. Ramsays having sex?"

"Mother!" Except I have wondered the same thing.

Virgil growls at Velvet when she makes her way downstairs.

"He's been chewing on my shoes." She puts forward a pink-muled foot, though the slipper wears now more of the memory

205

of fluff than actual. While I apologize for the dog, Mother goes upstairs, returns with a treat, and pats Virgil on the head as she feeds it to him. The humor isn't lost on me, and neither is the loving gaze my mother trains on the dog.

The PA crackles, Virgil howls, and I bristle on my stool. Every movable chair in the house has migrated downstairs to the cement blocked, unfinished basement.

"Again, can't we please paint the walls?" I ask.

Michael sprays on Fingerease and opens the Universe with a flamenco-like strum.

His head rises. "Ready, V.?" He poises his fingers above the frets.

Bernita beckons for me to follow her up the stairs. I refuse. She flaps her hand upwards. V. now stands beside Michael, and I hold on to the sides of my stool as if I'm on the back of a motorcycle.

The lyrics and music fight one another like two cats in a bag. I make to intervene, but Michael has lowered his voice into that sweet register I seldom hear to explain to her what harmony part he wants her to take.

When Bernita motions again, I follow, blowing past her when I reach the top of the stairs.

I return to the living room to write, pivot to outdoors.

Before long, I'm engrossed in Woolf and have two new pages of my graduate thesis along with the beginnings of a heat stroke.

In Mrs. Ramsay, Woolf begins to explore this idea, sketching a woman who apparently not only thinks less of herself than she should, but encourages men to do the same.

Her glove and his boots are related to their primary activities: the glove with the fingers that knit, and the boots with the laces he knots. Mrs. Ramsay is the crumpled glove with the twisted finger. A glove is a covering to protect the hand. We are told Mrs. Ramsay covers her true feelings as she is always covering something or someone in the house.

Lily observes Mrs. Ramsay's roles: she is a mother, thus "feminine," yet Lily suggests she is also domineering and controlling (an iron fist in a velvet glove comes to mind). The twisted finger of the glove looks as if it is pointing, almost accusing.

A covering also performs the function of hiding something. When Mrs. Ramsay comes to Lily's room and insists she must marry, Lily senses there is more to Mrs. Ramsay, some hidden fount of knowledge.

The twisted finger of Mrs. Ramsay's glove is also more than one thing: it is her complex self, though it may also represent her husband: "But in her opinion one liked Mr. Ramsay all the better for thinking that if his little finger ached the whole world must come to an end," Lily thinks. Mr. Ramsay is what causes Mrs. Ramsay's world, her finger, to be twisted. "She was not good enough to tie his shoestrings, she felt" (17).

I analyze, think, brew. Revise.

Only her immediate family and Lily, to whom Mrs. Ramsay has chosen to reveal herself, can see her sadness, her moodiness, and her madness. This woman of composure and breeding, one who rules well her household of servants and children, thinks violent thoughts: "All this phrase-making was a game, she thought, for if she had said half what he (her husband) said, she would have blown her brains out by now" (106). Notice she does not say if she had thought, but if she had said.

Maybe she does think similarly melancholy thoughts, and if she were to express them rather than cover them with her calm knitting and caretaking, she might be tempted to such a violent act.

Hushed sessions between Michael and Velvet are interspersed with jamming with the band to break Michael's "writer's block."

I save myself the argument because there's no way I'll win it. Precious thinks his writing process is the only way it's done. God forbid he should be held to a schedule.

Now various watersports seem to be the way to bring on the songs. Volleyball, Marco Polo, whatever. Somehow, Patrick and I have become the band's audience.

Velvet glides toward Patrick and me with her floral parasol above her head.

I snap my fingers and indicate the glass I empty in the time it takes her to reach us.

Patrick pours me another margarita. Sipping, I slow the scene: Michael in the water, coming up out of the pool, Adonis on a Half Shell. Velvet watching from her chair as he pushes himself up and flings his arms, dispersing droplets, and comes to rest on the cement.

I offer to fetch her a spoon. She pretends not to understand. She said no, I remind myself. No to whatever…

The rest of the band remains in the pool while Michael towels off and picks up his guitar, holding it away from his trunks.

V's eyes travel back to me.

"Have a drink," I say to her, but Patrick twists the empty pitcher in the air.

"Fetch, cabana boy."

Patrick glares at me but goes anyway.

V. works her mouth like it needs oiling.

"What?" I ask.

"I wanted to say."

Her Lucille Ball lips tremble.

"Don't."

"But I'd feel better if you'd just let me…"

"If you try to apologize, I swear I'll put a curse on you. I'll take your voice and trap it in a little jeweled box, and I will bury it in the deepest cave I can find."

Warming, I turn over and sit up. "Then I will post guards at the mouth of the cave, and anyone who comes within five miles of it will be shot on sight. Got it?"

"Why wouldn't you want…?"

I shake my head, my hair flying. I stand. I can't tell her the truth: I may need her to repeat her transgression, for Michael's sake. For the album's sake. Even the thought cements the necessity. Yes, it's the only way. My stomach tries to object, but my mind ignores it.

Before I do this, before I commit myself to this, I have to know. I don't want to ask but I have to know, even though I think I do already know.

"What exactly was it you said no to, anyway?"

My eyes will not leave hers; if I demand this, she will tell me.

She hesitates and crosses her arms over her body. Without looking up, she says, "He asked me to divorce Robert. There's no way I would ever, ever do that, Briscoe. You have to believe me."

When people say they've had the air sucked out of their lungs by something, I've always thought they were exaggerating.

I struggle, but I get it out: "I surely do." She'd be the biggest idiot ever to leave Robert, for so many reasons. I'd be the biggest idiot ever to stay with Michael.

There's only one reason Michael would want her to divorce Robert, and that's so he could marry her. Which, of course, would mean divorcing me.

Michael, that goddamned instrument. An instrument without feelings, but one that can damn sure make *you* feel.

Something on my face must worry Patrick because though his arm trembles under the burden of a fresh pitcher of margaritas, he rushes over.

"Bernita said she's bringing lunch out and that you *will* eat it."

"Pour."

After he hands me a glass, I take a huge drink from it, and then I spew red on the cement. "Where's the booze? I didn't ask for a slushy." I slam it on the table in front of me, and a corona of it lands around the glass.

"Jesus!" I pick up the pitcher and sling its contents behind me. Unfortunately, my dearly beloved house elf chooses that moment to bring out a tray of sandwiches. She puts the now-reddened sandwiches on the big table, while calmly wiping crimson from her face. "Lunch."

Though I yell at her, she refuses to remake them unless I apologize, and no way, the booze tells me, tells her. I yell some more, louder than I thought these lungs could, but she simply shrugs.

I give up.

The men flocking to the food merely push the top layer aside for the dry ones, and then eat even the stained ones, though I snap and mimic calling for a pizza.

"Way ahead of you," Patrick says, already tapping at his phone.

While we wait for better fare, Patrick and I admire the men vigorously eating the triangular sandwiches. Closely observing your average male will tell all there is to know about his, uhmm...skills.

I already know Michael's downtown technique – that's nothing new, though I shiver to see him eat so decisively. Trust me–nothin' wrong with a hungry man. The knowledge newly gained from V. me makes me momentarily determined to never experience his anything ever again.

This, too, will pass, I fear.

"There's Josh." He slowly strip-teases the crust from the triangle as the water still drips off his muscled chest, closes it back, and puts the tiniest corner in his mouth as if he's taking nothing for granted. He chews slowly, thoroughly. Patrick and I both shiver and simultaneously sigh.

Ben is a good ol' boy with a sunburned nose who shoves half of the sandwich in with one bite. Not so bad, but no finesse. He immediately picks up another half. "Poor Joy," I say to Patrick. Still, he'd get the job done.

Hoot is Hoot, and I refuse to discuss aloud my thoughts with Patrick, though Patrick has plenty to whisper to me himself about the matter.

It's not like I've ever considered what Hoot's thick curls would feel like under hand. Or wondered if the fuzz around the corners of his mouth is soft or coarse.

If you must have the complete geometric set, you peeper, he opens his mouth and takes bite after bite like a contented actor in a fast-food commercial. I fight the urge to offer him a glass of milk.

As soon as they've scarfed any salvageable food, Josh and Hoot grab a volleyball, which might explain how they can eat so much and never gain weight.

Limbs flap and flail below me. I stand to scold them for splashing me when what I hope is a misdirected volleyball hits me in the stomach and I fall forward into the water and then I'm at the bottom of the pool and my mouth asks how but it fills with water and here I am, nothing but water to breathe which makes me relax and then, dammit, my body begins floating back upwards and Hoot pulls me up by my hair and asks if I'm ok.

I fountain the water that remains in my mouth into his face in reply.

He turns his head, pounds on my back, and lets go of me once he assures himself that I'm (somewhat) standing.

Surely death's not much different than holding your breath and going from here to there. That's hardly worth fearing. I think hell was invented to frighten us into staying on this side of the soil until the choice is taken from us, which seems unfair when oblivion is as close as a deep swallow away.

Hoot pats me on the back once more and when I assure him that I really am fine, he returns to his game.

I do not thank him.

Patrick hollers that the pizza has arrived, and I climb out of the pool.

Michael watches me from where he and his guitar are well out of harm's way, his music practically inaudible over the game. I throw him a mock kiss, courtesy of alcohol brain. Bet he wishes I had drowned. I know I wish he had.

"Here." V. holds out a paper plate with a slice of pizza on it. I yank it away from her.

Michael arrives at my elbow.

"You all right?"

"I'll live."

I'm pretty sure my face tells him to go die.

He nods and turns his attention to his food, balancing it in the crook of his arm while he pretends to fingerpick with his bare hand.

V., who has been watching Michael a tad too carefully for my taste, picks up her parasol and wanders away. Somehow Michael's GPS knows she's leaving, and he swivels and follows her.

"Exit, pursued by a bear," I whisper.

Let Michael immerse himself in her music, steal every unrecorded syllable from her throat, record every high note residing in her, but it won't be enough for him.

I take a bite from the wrong end of the pizza.

It's never enough for him.

I, on the other hand, have had quite enough.

By ten the next morning, the space between the baffling on the basement walls is magically white. Not exactly exciting, but better than uninspiring block. There are streaks where someone has attempted to avoid painting the soundproofing, but anything is an improvement.

"Thank you," I say to Bernita, who has a tell-tale streak of paint in her hair, but she walks past me with a "Nada puerkita" and a smile.

It doesn't hurt my feelings when the paint fumes run us upstairs. Even though the basement is lighter, it's as confining as ever.

Once settled, Michael tunes his guitar and cocks his head,

and I know what every motion means. Maybe what we call love is nothing but sentimentalized familiarity. Intense scrutiny coupled with appreciation of what we notice. And hate (more likely, indifference) the opposite.

How often have I, when he bends over his guitar, stared at the spot in the center of his scalp where his hair is beginning to desert him? How often have I wanted to touch it, to tell him it's fine, it means nothing about him; it's just a biological fact. I have never even offered him that.

Last night, despite lying beside him with my eyes wide, I couldn't ask him why he had asked V. to divorce Robert. I couldn't bring myself to even tell him I know.

I spun every possible scenario up on the bedroom ceiling. I could make none of them mean a bright future for the two of us. You might know you can't – shouldn't – hold onto something, but you might not be ready to give it up, either.

Josh plays something bullet bright and just as fast. It zigzags through the room, and Michael grabs hold of it just as quickly. They're off.

Michael has two methods of writing: jamming and picking out a riff as he goes, or the more painful (for his writing partner) discovery session. You can't get him to tell you in advance what he wants to say…he'll play some notes, join a couple of chords, repeat them, and then toss words atop them to see if they work.

This works, too, though. He's great at jumping on a train.

Though he gives every appearance of carelessness in his songwriting, I've never bought it. The music that comes seemingly reluctantly from him is the chant of his soul rising unbidden, when he can't keep it locked in, and the words are just later in coming if, indeed, they come. Sometimes I am

214

fairly sure he finds lyrics extraneous, which is where I come in. Or did. Listeners want, need, meaningful lyrics. Instrumental music is too open to interpretation.

I walk behind him and lean down, whispering to remind him that he shouldn't allow the band to help create a song because they'd get partial writing credit, which of course means royalties. (Hey, just protecting my interests.)

He smells of sweat and metal.

He cranes his head upward, not whispering in return. "We're actually doing a run through of the songs we've already written. I asked Josh to work up the beginning earlier."

We've. It takes a moment to register: He and Velvet, "we." Velvet busies herself with retying the belt on her dress.

A dress. With a heavy collar and a belt. While writing songs in the heat of summer.

Ben pats the cushion beside him, and I take refuge. Dear Ben, so simple, so sweet, with his uniform of logo tees and too-lightly colored jeans.

I squeeze his arm, and he smiles as he pushes his fingers towards his palm to ward off carpal tunnel. The musician's curse.

Fingertips dangling the nib of his pick, Michael's voice joins his instrument, though an octave lower. He's an ancient force; he's elemental. I'm the caretaker for a precious, nonrenewable resource, complete with all of the privilege and daunting responsibilities that implies.

[A crystal-throated mockingbird has entered the chat.]

She sings like she's creating the song on the spot, sparking alive the pain that is the bedrock of country.

I count my fingernails twice. Then again.

My mother comes from nowhere, loosens Hoot's grip on

215

his brushes, takes his hand, and pulls him on his feet and away from his drums. Once clear, Hoot spins my mother and then dips her, lets her up.

They gyrate jarringly to the music, and yet it's incredibly welcome.

"Jules," he says as he lets go, bows, and returns to his makeshift percussion station, sending my mother a heated message with his eyes. Virgil barks as he intercepts the look. I knew I liked that dog.

No one seems surprised when we can't find either my mother or Hoot after lunch. Except Virgil when he wakes and growls, sniffing about the room. I feed him a treat, then, and pat him until he's calm.

****

Michael and I lounge in the living room where he caresses his guitar as I likewise caress the keys of my laptop in a rare moment when we are alone. The scent of guitar polish bats between us. How can his fingers be anything but scar tissue, the way he plays? His lightest touch elicits illicit notes. I wonder if his guitar cares for him as much as he it.

I can attest to his superior hand action.

The Mrs. Ramsay of the twisted finger is not the one who creates elaborate dinner parties and match-makes.

"Are you typing or galloping?" he asks from his chair, his sleeveless shirt showing off his guitarist's arms: not a drummer's, but still.

"So? You play like a maniac." I reread the sentence I am working on, which does away with my smile.

Mrs. Ramsay dies quietly, nearly invisibly, in the book. This unexpected killing of Mrs. Ramsay would be inexplicable if not examined through another of Woolf's lenses: that of The Angel in the House. The phrase comes from a popular poem by Coventry Patmore written in honor of his beloved (and, to his thinking it's a compliment to his) "saintly" wife in 1854.

It is impossible to read To the Lighthouse *without imagining how the lingering concept during Woolf's time informs the novel, and to see how briskly she fights against the notion.*

"Who are you raspberrying?"

He grins, leans his head to one side. I don't answer.

Woolf wrote in her speech "Professions for Women," about killing that traditional, perfect domestic woman, labeled by others as the "angel in the house." She saw her job to do away with that being in order to free herself to write and for more academic pursuits.

If Woolf admits to doing this to free herself, how much more so would she have willingly killed a fictional character to free her, Mrs. Ramsay, and the household, of the repressive notion, and to explore what would happen if Mrs. Ramsay were taken from the family?

Woolf wrote strongly about how those societal expectations plagued her.

There's so much death, so much trying to find a reason to live, in *Lighthouse*. There are scenes of rumored suicidal ideation. (Did Mrs. Ramsay's first true love kill himself?) What does this say about humans? Are you not philosophical enough if you haven't wanted to jump into the sea? That seems like contradictory logic.

Michael's fingers bruise a C chord onto his instrument after he returns to his guitar.

I recline into the stiff sofa.

Not for the first time, I wish we could go home, could be us again, before. In our house I could pretend, at least, that we

217

are okay. When we're on the road, that's not really us.

Our house is brick, with comfortable country fixins like quilts and overstuffed cushions. Wall hangings. Paintings. Lots of light. A sunporch. Original (thus worn) wooden floors scattered with latch hook kit rugs scavenged by me at garage sales and thrift shops and sewn together to make area rugs, the length of their nap the only thing matching, and yet it works. It's quirky, but it's my quirk.

Metal bed frames in every bedroom. Repurposed industrial fixtures like the one above our bed (an ornate metal porch rail with fabric draped through) have been salvaged from that great architectural salvage shop in Leiper's Fork; others have been employed as shower rods and as a surround for our outdoors shower.

I miss our house also for its bricked flower beds, its oak tree with a bench circling it, my favorite place to read. The ease of indoors flowing into outdoors via our outdoors kitchen. I am about to ask Michael if he misses it, too, when he gestures towards my mother, just visible through the doorway.

"Will Jules be leaving soon? She's distracting my band members."

"What do you mean?"

"Come on. Hoot, Josh. She's sleeping her way through them all."

"And you're next," Mother says as she walks into the room, leans over Michael, kisses his cheek.

"I'm serious. I need them when I need them; they can't be off with women at all hours."

My mother runs her hand through Michael's hair. "All you had to do is ask. Darlin', why don't we agree to acceptable rutting hours? But if we do, I think we should *all* abide by them." She says it with a breakthrough hint of her posh accent. She has such a wardrobe of accents that it's hard to keep them straight.

Michael pulls away from her, picks up the yellow square of t-shirt he's been using, and squirts brightly scented guitar polish on his instrument. He glides the cloth studiously across the blond face of his guitar. He slows to small circles, concentrating just above the pickguard. His hands move up the neck of the guitar, lift a string and run the cloth firmly along the steel, examines the shirt after each string, frowning with mock horror that I suspect is satisfaction at the grime he removes.

Carefully, purposefully, he moves the yellow between, beside, the bridge, dusting the area with his face so close that he must be fogging the guitar.

My stomach flips with his guitar as he turns it over and strokes its backside.

"Would you two like to be alone?" Mother asks.

"You can stay," I say. "I actually have a question..."

"I meant him and the guitar."

He goes after the backside of the tuning pegs, concentrating on where they dip into the wood, back and forth, back and forth. . . .

I text Patrick: Fun run!

He hates running as much as I do, but he has to go if I ask. God, I love hired people.

Chapter 14

The morning is long. I flip through a new book on Woolf and Christian culture, decide it's intriguing but not useful for my purposes, even if I do underline some passages that make fascinating connections. I read to my mother from it as if I'm picking strawberries.

Mother pulls a tablet and pen from her bag and makes notes, frowns, and mumbles before heading indoors with the book, not bothering to ask if I mind if she takes it. No matter.

The children in To the Lighthouse are both omnipresent and, as are many of the characters in the novel, symbolic to the point of being unsubstantial. That is, the children run upon the grass, gather at the table, and insist their way between their parents, but we learn little about them individually. Their fates are dealt to them casually. In fact, we are not even permitted to see the scenes in which some of the family perish.

Which is to say, the book is not about anyone. It's a brief glimpse into time, a time. Regardless, the flickering figures linger in the reader's mind. We wonder, even after finding out that Prue dies in childbirth, if her life was happy until then. We ask ourselves if Andrew wanted to go off to war or if he was pressured into it. If Cam and James are at all grateful after the trip to the lighthouse, and if it changes their relationship with their father, if it provides closure concerning their mother's death. These props for Mr. and Mrs. Ramsays' lives are but leaves on a tree, scattered with the breeze of Woolf's words. The reader simultaneously wants more, while also feeling the perfect justice and rightness of the pragmatic writing, if indeed the children are meant to be merely representational.

That our imaginations continue to inquire about the children long after they have disappeared from the stage signals that they yet live in our imagination, that she succeeded despite her aims in a way she perhaps hadn't intended, in ways it doesn't seem she could have, given what little she provides the reader. This, this is the magic that is Woolf.

Had we been given more fully developed characters, our curiosity might have been satisfied sooner, fatal for the shelf life of a novel. But questions linger. Did Nan ever slow her running? What became of Cam? And what of Lily's painting, of her leaving for the summer and, like the rest of the characters, not coming back to the cottage for a decade? Did anyone expect that Mr. Ramsay would ever bring the family back to this place surely haunted by his dead wife's memory, let alone extraneous guests?

Nevertheless, he does, and once back at the cottage, Lily awakens the following day, rising as a substitute Mrs. Ramsay, a Mrs. Ramsay resurrected in her protegee with, finally, a first name. One who still loves her family (look at the carefully meted sympathy Lily gives Mr. Ramsay, though she doesn't want to) while independently being someone she wants to be.

Lily sees both the formerly absent Mrs. Ramsay's presence and her absence, because while Lily paints, a shadow falls where her friend had formerly sat, and Lily starts crying for her. Crying for anyone is really crying for ourselves. If we see Lily as being "possessed" by Mrs. R., then it would be the former Mrs. Ramsay crying out for the life she has necessarily left behind to become an artist. She wants to be free, but when she is, she has to learn to embrace the new, learn how to give up what she was.

To take it further, the reader is really the one who becomes both Mrs. Ramsay and Lily, because they bear witness. (Plural pronoun use intentional.)

Bernita brings out a tub of obnoxiously green snap beans and plops down beside me on the glider, smelling of orange-based cleanser.

I put my laptop on sleep and reach over Bernita to put it on the table beside her.

"We going to rain," Bernita informs me as she inhales.

"No, no rain."

"Si, ci, rain."

I swipe to my weather app on my phone and scroll to where the screen reads the percentage chance of precipitation. "See? Zero percent chance."

Bernita smiles. "I will bring in the laundry before the rains."

A three-chord song sings out of the house, and my teeth grind.

Michael's hands evoke a squeak as they race across the guitar. The squeak is the equivalent of the pop and crackle of vinyl: it can't be purposely replicated, and yet its accidental addition declares and adds something at just the right moment as if it's meant to be.

I break the end of yet another bean, peel the string to the other side, and then break off the other tip before putting the de-stringed bean into the pot. My triangular ends, some studded with dark stems, join Patrick's beneath the bench. The neighbor's marauding chickens will eat them. Chickens, like fans, do not know how to honor property boundaries.

222

Bernita rescues the good beans that have missed the pot (a heaping handful and more, thanks to our less-than-careful aim) and carries them indoors.

The music struggles.

Bernita returns with another pot of green and I groan. My fingers already ache from the increase in guitar playing, the songs I've been slipping away writing in the night that I tell no one about.

Which guitar is Michael using, that an acoustic's sound carries so far? Ah, he's using an amp with it; I hear that in the way the sound ricochets off the trees and surroundings. The jazz chords are meant to seduce everyone listening.

I pat the back of my neck with a tissue from my pocket and wish handkerchiefs were still in vogue.

Brunt, brunt, brunt…the notes shimmer between pain and pleasure.

The song alerts again, something almost right in the chord progression. I hear Michael find it, so I sit back, but then he repeats instead of varying. Why? Repetition is for choruses.

I'm vaguely aware of words being uttered at my back as I find my way down the basement stairs, where I sit on the bottom one. It's just Michael and his guitar, in rare quarantine. He plays the chorus this time and then reenters the verse. He hums and sings an unintelligible word or two, hums again.

He looks down at a sheet of paper, tests a few words, rejects them.

As he sings an overly florid line, I pick up the lyrics sheet from the stool and scan the words.

"This line about winter to spring is reasonably good. But we don't need Northern stars."

We are both rigid.

His fingers trill the strings.

"What if we add 'snow to grow'? Hey, that's not bad," I say as I search for a pen. My new songs have been reopening a musical vein in me.

We revisit the words for the chorus, which are mostly fine.

In a few minutes, we run through what we have thus far, me singing V's part. V. and I have similar ranges if not tones. Fine, I can't sing as high, but who needs to sing that high? Her upper register is thinning, anyway.

V. floats down the stairs in her glitzy sun dress and wide straw hat as if summoned. We finish singing the chorus.

"What do you think of the first verse now?" I hand her the tablet.

She says nothing until it's noticeable that she's not speaking, and then: "I need my reading glasses."

Michael offers her his. I don't ask how he knows they'll work for her.

We hone the song until lunch. I have to breathe deeply more than once. I have to pretend to answer a text or two, but I survive.

The band joins us in the afternoon.

They translate the song competently, and we only make subtle tweaks. Michael decides more of this instrument, less of that one. He's not prescriptive with the band, but if he doesn't like something, he says that, too. They're interpreters, the band members. While that in itself is a creative act, it's a secondary one in the service of someone else's artistic vision. Not that anyone is complaining about that here except me.

If a child can be said to come from three parents, this song has. Never have I felt so conflicted about a tune. I'm both proud and queasy.

The sound engineer who has been coming in to help mix sound when the whole band gathers, says he will come back in on Monday to see if we are demo ready. I mean, to see if *they* are demo ready.

Another morning. The bed is empty, and that brings tons of questions, and none that I want answers to.

I rise, pull my hair back into a presentable ponytail, and wash my face, brush my teeth. I throw on yoga pants, a sports bra, and a tee, slide my feet into sandals, and take my laptop to the kitchen table. The routine is the thing.

There's something about writing an academic paper while hung over that seems apt. Seems like something I would have done had I had a normal college experience. Not that I'm complaining – everyone in school was looking for what I already had. (And I have a touch more, wouldn't you say?)

Once in the kitchen, though, I pour myself a glass of cucumber-infused water and stand in front of the fridge and contemplate making some eggs.

The scent of cinnamon coffee cake slides from under the glass dome on the counter and reaches toward me, and I think we know by now that I'm not someone to resist much of anything.

As I lift the dome, I simultaneously tell myself to stop and wonder who I should fire that it's even here, because it's not my fault that I have the self-control of...I can't even finish my thought as the sugar anoints my tongue. The cinnamon's heat makes the cake seem a tinge healthy. I mean, they say cinnamon helps regulate your blood sugar, right?

Ten minutes later, I'm in the bathroom. The problem with purging is you swap out the hugged feeling of overeating for the teary-eyed, weak-limbed, after-vomiting sensation. You hate yourself in the moment, just after, and you get to hate yourself in the mirror in the coming days. It's the gift that just keeps giving.

Patrick arrives in my bathroom wearing Minion boxers and a white tank, his hair uncombed. He sits me upright, tells me to brush my teeth and to keep the handle *away* from my throat. Shows what he knows. I don't need a toothbrush anymore.

After I'm finished, he takes my hair from its elastic and smooths it with a comb before gathering it back into a low pony. Tenderness always undoes me.

"You can't start this again," he says.

"I'm not starting anything."

We've slid this slope before: I binge, then I diet; I binge/purge, and finally I stop eating, feeling as clean as an angel the longer I resist. Blissfully empty. Pure. Then it starts all over again. It's a cycle peculiar to me, I know. ED's are all the same, though unique to the user. They just have different presenting faces. Ten pounds too thin, twenty pounds too fat, or just right for ten minutes, it's all the same, and you might have them all happen in one year.

"You texted me. I assumed that meant you wanted help," he says when I push him away.

I texted him?

"You know, if society…"

He looks at the ceiling, because he knows what's coming, this speech that rolls out of me on autopilot.

"If society didn't care about people's sizes, if food were not a hot topic, I don't think ED's would exist. Or at least they'd lose their stigma. If no one noticed anyone's weight, if it wasn't a virtue to be bigger or smaller, the urge to quit wouldn't be there and so there would be no cycle."

I get out my makeup bag and hand it to him. He picks up my eyeshadow and motions for me to close my eyes. He works in silence.

"Leave Michael," Patrick says as if he's forcing it from himself.

I collapse onto the floor, laughing, then sit up.

"Why does everyone keep suggesting that?"

"Your mom and I have talked. You'll get plenty in the divorce, won't you? I have the contact info for those other women, if needed," he whispers. "They'd testify against him."

"You're his assistant, too. You were clear about that. How are you saying this?"

He lightly punches the tiles to his left, cradles his hand with a whimper. I put it to my lips and then hold it against my chest.

"Money and status aren't everything, anyway. He's tormented you long enough. Those two are only any good together because of you. Refuse to help and their album will fall apart. Let them handle the blowback. Make them take it on," he says.

He's not wrong, but I drop his hand anyway.

My touch is the only thing melding what they write into the correct proportions, and I know it.

"You don't understand."

I bow over my thighs and put my head on the chilly floor. I turn it and raise a bit to look at him, kinda surprised at my limberness and wondering how I can notice that right now.

"But it's really not the same. This is complicated."

He tucks a leg under. "It always is. But whatever. Whatever works for you, Briscoe, my love. I'm here for the duration."

I sit up. "There are things larger than us. Like art."

I tap his arm. He flinches like I've beaten him. "Just know I'm on Team Briscoe, okay?"

I stretch back out onto the floor until Patrick pulls me up.

"I don't want you making yourself ill over a man. That's not who you are."

"People keep congratulating me on how much thinner I look. That's not nothing."

I'm down a size and a half. I'm not proud of it, and yet I am.

I rub the back of his newly clipped hair briskly. It feels like I'm playing with a puppy.

"I'm not gonna lie, you look hot, however you've managed to lose it, but you're about to reach that tipping point and fall right over into haggery."

We both stare into the bottom of the full-length mirror. I'm thinking of my mother who is thin because she ranges the mountains every day, and Velvet and all that fasting and how like a gnawed bone she looks.

"And I know how triggering this is to say, Swiss Bris, but bulimics seldom get up enough to keep thin. If you binge and purge, you're gonna be screwed–think of the health risks. And we both know you're not going to be able to go without eating long enough to develop permanent anorexia."

"That's the unhealthiest, worst advice I've ever been given. Maybe the most effective for me, but definitely the unhealthiest."

But I stand.

I have not told him that the biggest reason I haven't left Michael is how much I love Michael. It seems like the flimsiest reason, and yet, the rest of my life without him? Put me in a box and cover it with rocks, because how much emptier could life get?

Who are you calling melodramatic? I've noticed those who call people dramatic are usually the opposite – they wouldn't acknowledge a feeling if it stung them in the eye.

Patrick says that a proper diet and regular exercise are never unhealthy. Like *that's* what he was urging. He doesn't care what extreme he goes to in order to stay thin, so why would he care what it takes for me to?

He touches my shoulder. "Why don't we go buy you some smaller clothes?"

"You know I'm not going to say no to that."

Later, staring at myself in a dressing room mirror in a size six, I find I don't give a shit about a number on fabric, and I can't see that I'm any smaller at all.

This album has to get finished or I might disappear. There's only one way to be sure it successfully gets completed, but it will take more courage than I think I have.

****

My hand trails the rough rail as I descend into the basement. The paint smell has long since dissipated, and the walls look better, yet my antipathy to the place remains. The sounds that rise from it envelop me as I go lower.

Hoot's ice cream cone spills sprinkles over the bare floor. I ask him to take it outside.

"Peace," he says, heading up and out.

Michael stops, plays an Am, progresses to a D, goes back. He strums and hums, then nods when he sees me. It's just the two of us.

Drake has had Jolene calling me every few days to check on their progress.

"I really like the songs you brought off the road with you," I

229

say, the ones I have helped the final sculpting of, though we know why they sound so good.

He caresses the neck of his guitar. I tilt my head and run my hand along *my* neck.

"How does it feel," I ask, watching an ant carry a pink sprinkle on its back across the floor, "to be creating an album with her?"

The ant makes more progress with its burden than I think possible in so short a time.

His smile is cautious.

"I thought we'd create something stellar right out of the gate. But still."

When we first married, I attributed his self-absorption to the difficulties of starting a career in music, and that he was a sensitive artist. I did whatever it took to help him.

Some might call him a selfish monster. Monsters are made, not born.

I reach out and touch his hand.

"That fifth song has a promising chorus. You should be proud."

He nods.

"But it could be a little bit tighter, couldn't it? More like those songs from the road?"

I ask him to put the guitar down. After he places it onto its stand, I put my hands on either side of his face and stare into his eyes.

Virgil snuffles down the stairs and targets the ant as if he came down here for it. Before I can stop him, he's eaten it, sprinkle and all.

I follow the dog back up the stairs.

Lily describes Mr. Ramsay through his boots as "ill-tempered"

(59) yet charming. The boots are "colossal" (59), the same oversized assessment of his attire as his mind and books made by his family, who allow him to be a tyrant.

The boots are "sculptured"(59), artfully chosen by him. Often, he sets the scene for conversations by saying or doing something calculating to receive a desired response.

His boots are expressive enough to walk on their own, Lily thinks. Without Mrs. Ramsay and with his children mostly grown, he likely gets his rambles in now, but it is as if his boots go without his heart. Nothing means what it used to mean.

After his wife's death, he approaches Lily for sympathy, the same draining, taxing to herself sympathy that Mrs. Ramsay formerly gave. The artistic, early feminist Lily cannot bring herself to stoop to tending to the needs of a man rather than to the canvas before her. In the face of her resistance to helping him, Mr. Ramsay bends to tie a bootlace, which prompts Lily to comment on the splendor of his boots, the only comfort she can bring herself to give. This delights him.

Lily realizes how limited a nod she has offered him, but apparently, he does not. He asks her to show him how she knots, then tells her she doesn't know what she's doing (a male once again telling a woman she doesn't know what she's doing), and he shows her three times how to knot. He says this will keep them from coming untied, as if he doesn't realize he has just had to tie his own boot.

In another type of tying, James, who remains acrimonious towards his father, feels his father has tied him to the boat as they head towards the lighthouse, and the only way out is for James to take a knife and cut the mental rope, which is hindering his even thinking of his dead mother, even though he very much wants to.

I officially move from bingeing to being unable to force

anything but liquids down. I disguise it by playing with my food and pretending to eat. No reason to make everyone else as worried about me as I am.

Michael and Velvet huddle over lyrics. I am too much in the sun.

I pull off my clothes in plain sight outdoors just because I'm a member of the IDGAF club now, and I shimmy into my new two-piece swimsuit to combat the heat. No one even seems to notice my brief nudity, which disappoints me a little, especially since my collarbone has popped with my recent loss of five more pounds.

The house's inhabitants bask poolside with what appears to be most of the food from the house sitting on and around their chairs. Bags of chips, remnants of sandwiches, an opened package of Oreos, are strewn about the tables on the patio. My mother and Patrick hand a pungent cigarette back and forth on this Tuesday afternoon, as if that's what one does in the course of a day.

Patrick holds the joint out to me, but I ignore it as I walk to the pool and dive into the deep end.

Michael eats grapes in a chair while tapping at an iPad (he's not afraid of tech) with his right hand. He and Velvet discuss lyrics.

"Have I heard those yet?" I ask as I swim closer.

Michael glances up, his brow furrowed. "No."

I pull myself up and over, drip my way to them.

Velvet reaches into the bowl of grapes between me and Michael and picks one up, holds it up to the light as if it's a fortune teller's ball. I pluck the grape from between her fingers and contemplate all of the possibilities before attempting to hand it back to her. It hits the ground between us.

"I told you to let me see the lyrics before you actually demo anything," I say, diving in and swimming furious laps. Their songs are stronger now, sure, but they need someone to polish them. If I don't think of the probable source of the song's inspiration, it's gratifying to watch the bones pop into place. If I don't notice how automatically and frequently the traitors' bodies turn towards one another, I can think of the art alone. It's going to be a great album. Dammit.

I walk back over to the chairs, remove my swimsuit top, and lie beside Patrick. He hands me his joint, and I tug on it with my lips, though I'm not a huge fan and it does not return my appetite that has now run away with the spoon. I offer what's in my hand at a distance to Michael as he takes in my bare breasts. He shakes his head, but to which?

"I despise tan lines," I say to no one as I fling an arm over my head. But Bernita, who has come outside with a basket of wet laundry, wraps a damp sheet around me and volleys words at me. She motions towards the sky and hollers "drone" without a trace of an accent.

"Killjoy," I say as I struggle back into the upper half of the suit, turn and motion for Patrick to tie me.

I take the joint from Patrick for one more puff, but I need a clear head to write, so I pass it back right after.

"It's hot as balls out here. Why do we have a house with air conditioning if we aren't ever inside?" I huff.

No one has to tell me why: no matter how large, the house is too small. There are too many personalities, too many competing wants, to fit it all in at one time.

In the 19 chapters of The Window *section, Woolf gives us a sensuous peek into the Ramsays' bucolic world through thickly*

233

knitted shawls, a romantic seaside cottage with moldering artwork, and delectable communal suppers in this pre-war world presided over (indeed, created by) Mrs. Ramsay. Dialogue and high-flown interiority grace this section which brims with dense and florid language. For the most part, Woolf's sentences ramble in a lovely stream-of-consciousness tangle. The modern reader might ask for more plot. They would be wrong to.

My mother reads what I have so far today. It's hard to know what matters just now. And once that window section is over for good, we all know what comes next for Mrs. Ramsay.

By late afternoon, the band rehearses their newest song. Max, sound engineer extraordinaire, with his silly train cap (engineer, get it? I didn't either at first), short sleeved dress shirt, and brown hipster beard, comes and goes daily as needed. He can't be over 35, and yet his walk is weighted as if he's at least a decade older.

Sweat gleams on all of us in the basement except for V. Her arms, thinner than two a.m., wouldn't deign to perspire. I surreptitiously wipe at my face and wonder again what has compelled me to follow them down the stairs and into purgatory. Oh, right, I'm a part of this, like it or not.

I do not like so many, many things right now. I continue writing.

The secret opium eater, Augustus Carmichael, a celebrated poet, lies about, sleeping, not doing much else, as if he is through with words, with the world. The inert poet personifies the book's rejection of the construct and linear nature of time. His probable opium usage causes this stupor that enshrouds him. He reads poetry and occasionally rouses himself enough to quote it. His perpetual slumber bookends Lily's "resurrection" at the end of the second section of the novel. While some things shift, others remain the same. Action in one area is bookended with inertia in another.

Carmichael no longer writes poetry, but instead bears witness to the world. He's a sentient fixture, a rock. He doesn't give a fig for anything except his golden slumbers and maybe soup. And, as noted earlier, this desire comes into conflict with the worried-about-time Mr. Ramsay. To Mr. Ramsay, an extra helping of soup means the other guests (and he) must wait for the one having soup to finish before they can carry on. So not only is he, Ramsay, deprived of whatever the next course may be, but time is taken from him while he waits, time that is running out for him to have that all-important Eureka moment if he and his work are not to be forgotten. (News flash: they will both be, as we all will be. Why do we bother? Because we must.)

Carmichael's enjoyment of physical pleasures indicates he has already discovered what merely creeps along the periphery of Mr. Ramsay's consciousness, something he will not admit: it is already too late to be great, and nothing matters anyway. Might as well take opium, lie in the sun like a cat, and, when occasion permits, eat extra soup. Eat, drug, and be merry.

This book unsettles in its last two sections. Sensuous details, nature, a world bursting with activity and dinner parties, a world, were it truly so carefree, that any reader might like to inhabit it, sparkles in the first section on the surface. But this idyllic introduction serves as no more than a backdrop for what's coming, with plenty of ominous undertones of its own, as Lily observes.

Earbuds allow me access to both worlds so I can be available when they need me. It's not easy, but it's more bearable this way. I can check in whenever I need to. I do now, because of the impossible heat.

"Anyone call about the air?" I ask.

Michael raises his head.

"What?"

"The air can't be working down here."

He squints at me, looks at V, and away.

I search out Patrick, who goes to find Bernita to help us find the thermostat, and she says the air is off because she was asked to turn it off. Two guesses as to who requested that, with her "delicate" throat.

Once we reset it, we bring bottles of chilled water and a platter of oatmeal raisin cookies downstairs. The musicians stop long enough to snack, though Michael has that impatient air at their break that I used to find endearing.

I hand Michael a bottle and I glare at him until he drinks, takes a cookie, and bites it while asking the boys to "take it from the chorus."

Hoot leads in with a wholly inappropriate solo, crashing symbols and creating mayhem, and Michael lobs what remains of his cookie at the boy/man who picks it up off the floor and eats it.

"Delicious," he says, heading back into the song as if he hadn't stopped, though at a slower pace.

The up-tempo tune croons something about the stars and the flowers at the same hour...I call them out more than once on the lyrics that I have not approved, and any overly sentimental yet vague words that need pruning, or easy rhymes.

My pen invades Velvet's notebook. She crosses her arms. I cut anyway. I hand it back and they huddle over it. I don't care what novels say, there's no such thing as a secret shared smile.

Even on high, the air conditioning cannot keep up with the heat now that is Michael, whose entire face clenches out verse one, complete with sweat, and edges over for Velvet to enter the chorus as she winds her butterfly printed scarf numerous times around her throat.

Hearing the song, I have the feeling you have when you see a guitar you're unfamiliar with, but you know by the excellent crafting of it and its tone, it's a classic.

I text Robert about our spouses' hard work. He answers that if this album is as successful as it might be, again, more money in the bank for "us." That's the answer to my unasked question. Yes, he knows what they're up to. Or, actually, he "doesn't."

I stay until they have practiced the song enough, have tweaked it, until they are ready to demo it.

There. Another song midwifed.

Almost before it's over, another song is begun.

I notice the quick glances, the way Michael looks anywhere but at her in between songs. How he literally sniffs for her scent when she moves, and he thinks I don't see. How he's completely silent when she speaks until she's through. He certainly wasn't that reverential when he fell in love with me.

Fell in love. That sounds violent, doesn't it? Who wants to fall? Falling is the least of the damage loving him has done me.

High fives all around at the end of the song, and then a break; I promptly run outdoors and dry heave.

"Too many margaritas," I say to Patrick, who appears soon after with a wet washcloth, although I've had none.

"At least your hair was up," he says as he pushes a tendril behind my ear.

Breathing deeply, I stand in the unrelenting heat and tell it to bring it on even as I walk back around the house.

Beside me, Virgil worries an empty water bottle as if vanquishing an enemy. I tussle with him for it, and when I gain possession, I toss it into the pool. The dog whines.

"You can swim, hound. You just don't know it."

No, I don't throw him into the pool. Instead, I take my phone out of my shorts pocket and set it on a table, get in, and coax him ever closer to me. He whimpers when I reach out and take him into my arms but stills when I whirl him about above the water with my arms outstretched. We find the bottle and I try to give it to him, but by now he's pawing at his reflection. He barks. I almost let go of him, so he can try swimming, but I don't. It won't matter if he can swim if he doesn't know it.

Later, I write.

If there is a flaw in Lighthouse, it's the flitting nature of its point of view. The novel is brilliant and masterful in its scope, and its impressionistic strokes tantalize, and yet the POV doesn't settle on one character. Just as we become invested in one person, the camera shifts. Time is spent both with Mrs. Ramsay's, not her point of view exactly, so much as a close observation of her that mimics that. Then, Lily becomes the primary focus for the last third of the novel, serving as both the primary POV character and, ultimately, the family's historian via her painting.

This "bird's flight" through the book makes us long for more of each scene. Just as we settle our sight on one person and their occupations, up and away we fly.

That the story takes place in a summer home and that we never visit the Ramsays' main place of residence, also speaks of the unrealistic nature of the book that pretends to mimic reality. Doesn't the family live the majority of their lives elsewhere? A vacation is never a fair representation of life.

The crush of visitors at their vacation home alters even more the Ramsays' regular behavior and routine, so many guests that some have to be put up at local inns. Why would they invite so many when they don't have the necessary accommodations?

Possible explanations present themselves. Was Mr. Ramsay working on yet another book? We know he was constantly fretting over his theories, but was a project due? Was having all of these young minds around who so admired him meant to stimulate his thinking, an audience with which to share his thoughts, or with which to distract himself?

Was the couple merely hospitable and saw it as their duty to allow these impressionable young people and lonely older ones to visit, since the family, despite its limited finances, had a little extra to share? It certainly seems mentoring was happening between Mr. Ramsay and Tansley, between Carmichael and Andrew Ramsay.

Or were the Mr. and Mrs. afraid to be alone, afraid something might fester and explode over the summer because they were away from their routine? Did they believe the presence of others would keep them bound? What this reader wouldn't give to see the couple in their own home.

I gratefully allow Patrick to drive me to the craft store, because he gets to curse the traffic instead of me having to. In the paint aisle, I frown over YouTube videos, then half fill a cart.

What was the impetus for Lily to paint? Did she bring supplies with her to the summer home, or did she buy them on a whim? Did she already consider herself a painter? Did no one tell the insufferable Charles Tansley to shut the hell up about women not being able to paint or write because it wasn't true? Why didn't Lily tell him off?

It doesn't matter what someone's opinion is if you don't regard their opinion. That being said, you can decide you don't give a shit what someone says, but that doesn't mean it hasn't taken up residence in your mind's attic and that you don't have to drive that bat out with a broom more than once.

When we return to the house, Michael and Velvet are sitting by the far side of the pool, as perfectly paired as wine and cheese. A honeyed river of melody flows from them. Though V. shifts slightly away from him when she spots me, Michael only nods.

Patrick and I carry my purchases onto the lawn, and I motion him away as I pull the easel's legs down and lock them into place, toss a canvas onto it, and rip the seal off a number of tubes of paint. I pick up a brush and dip it into water.

You don't have to know how to paint to try to recreate Lily's painting, to attempt to get inside of her head, I tell myself. Why should I be so scared to pick up a brush?

Out of nowhere, my arms are individually thrust into the sleeves of one of Michael's dress shirts, and I stand still long enough for Patrick to button it.

"I feel like a three-year-old," I tell him, but I smile my gratitude as I pick up the brush.

I have never painted before, but how can I honestly say I have picked apart Woolf's *Lighthouse* if I haven't tried to paint Lily's painting?

Will a shadow and a line work to signify?

Signify what? What?

Because of light *here*, Lily needs darkness *there*, so she represents the couple with a purple triangle, with shadows.

240

As I rebutton Michael's shirt, I remember unbuttoning it not so long ago while he was wearing it, running my hands across his chest. The shirt has been laundered since, but there's something of his scent that can't be washed away, and I bury my nose in the right side of the collar, fingering the pointed plastic stay just beneath the cotton's surface. I lean my head further to the right onto my shoulder.

It's always been on my own shoulder.

I try not to focus on their bent-together heads, Velvet's fingers on her pen, Michael playing and singing like a troubadour. I shouldn't care; I do.

When Velvet goes inside, Michael comes to see what I've painted; I toss it face down on the grass before he gets a glimpse. He shrugs and moves away.

My mother, as she passes by right after him, picks up the painting. "Doesn't look any worse than Lily's painting must have looked," she says.

"She should have told Tansley to fuck off."

"Damn straight."

Beyond us, the pair, together again. Velvet slumps, her shoulders caving in like her body can't hold her weight, and Michael leans towards her like the two are connected by levers.

The big blank space, though, still in the middle of the canvas, a space I don't want to fill.

I capture my brush between the folds of a cloth and pull.

My mother and I have talked of all things Woolf except her end.

"Mother, why did Woolf do it? An acknowledged genius at her craft, in love, a close relationship with her sister, literary friendships, and so many, many more reasons to live. Why did she feel the need for weighted pockets?"

241

A shimmer of light leaves me and bounces onto the woman beyond us as V. laughs.

"No one owes the world, not even a writer. Woolf's life was hers to keep or not. It's the deepest of human rights, darlin.'" She puts my painting on the grass beside her, face up.

And just like that, I have a permission slip from my mother. Not that I was looking for one. Was I?

She could have pointed to the sacrificial nature of Woolf's drowning, how she sought to lighten her husband's burden.

Michael rattles a G chord, which rattles me.

Mother kneels upon the grass.

I hold my paints close to my face to see if I've got the caps on. Then I prop my head against the empty easel.

She sits, takes off her shoes, and stretches her toes.

I turn and cram paint tubes into the plastic bag they came in.

"Being married isn't like having a tattoo."

When I was six, I lost a tooth. I showed my mom and told her I couldn't wait to put it under my pillow for the tooth fairy to come.

"I never said there was a tooth fairy," she said.

So I threw my tooth away.

"Virgil, come," Mother calls.

Some tattoos can be removed.

The sun follows her as if she's called it, too. I collapse the easel's legs, slide it into its provided pouch.

Hands reach for my painting and hold it in the fading light.

Michael scrutinizes it. "Nice colors. You taking up painting now?"

"I don't know how you can claim to see in this light."

In the house, voices laugh, whoop. Something crashes.

The night tugs day's hem along to bed, and I reach for the painting. Fireflies wink.

The question slips from me: "Why did you ask V. to divorce Robert?"

"Let me carry it," he says, lifting the canvas. I pick up the paints and follow him inside. When his eyebrows ask where I want it, I gesture to the kitchen table. He places it there and leaves the room as if he didn't know he was ever in it.

A presence hovers at my shoulder. "What are we staring at?" Patrick asks. I look away from the painting with its chunky shapes. How did Lily imagine hunks of color would, could tell her anything about a marriage? That seems like a recipe for oversimplification. A painting is a photograph, *Lily*. It's one frozen *moment*.

The watercolors scrub easily off my hands. I dry them.

Patrick selects a bagel, inserts it into the toaster.

I watch the appliance's innards glow as the music starts up.

"Do you think it's situational infidelity? I mean, it could be, right?"

The bagel pops up and Patrick puts it on his plate, smears it while blowing at his fingers. He offers half to me, but I grimace.

"You know I love you. But I am full on worried for you," he says.

"I mean, if it is, then if we can just pry them apart after this album, and things will go back to the way they were, right?" Even I hear the desperation in my voice.

He bites into the thick round.

"Michael asked V. to divorce Robert."

He takes another bite and chews.

"That could only mean one thing," I say.

He swallows. "That's almost never true."

"He must want to marry her. What else could it mean?"

"What did he say about it when you asked him?"

I take his bagel from him and toss it in the trash.

I storm through the house until I find my mother. I can always speak to her as if we're already in midsentence, so I do.

"I don't think it's Tansley I should be so pissed at so much as Woolf and her reduction of a marriage to a man and a woman because first of all, that definition of marriage did not age well either. Secondly, a marriage is, is complex...it's unknowable from the outside. Lily could paint..."

They're in the basement now, and someone's counting Hoot in.

"She could paint all day every day and never..."

The room moves and I slump into a nearby chair. My heart beats along with the drums.

"Could you bring me a couple of crackers or something?" I ask before I faint.

I've had the unfortunate treat of broken sleep for the past few days, a double curse because it means that being outdoors so early today I once again encounter my mother in the buff during her morning swim. Her compact body has wigs beneath both armpits, a shine of stretch marks across her belly and thighs, and between them mostly gray hair I note, gagging. I feel no need for that knowledge about my mother or anyone else.

Feminist note: there's nothing inherently disgusting about hair color or location, except thinking makes it so, and my thinking does. I can't help it.

I attempt to write.

Because Woolf herself struggled with mental illness culminating in suicide, the finger writing Lighthouse *could be said to be twisted by madness as well.*

I make a note to reweigh the sentence because of how extreme it is.

In To the Lighthouse, *we have the surface story of a happy family with a houseful of children and guests. They have elaborate dinners and are constantly trying to make everyone as happy as they allegedly are. Yet there are moments when both Mr. and Mrs. Ramsay privately (though not verbally) express longings for another life. He imagines himself in a tiny house, all alone, so he can write. She sees his longing and imagines that he thinks he could have been more without his family relying upon him. She wishes, as already mentioned, that her children were grown so she could devote more time to philanthropy and healing societal ills.*

Lily is aware of the "twisted finger" of Mrs. Ramsay, for Mrs. Ramsay comes to her room and makes fun of the others with a "malicious twist," makes fun of the life, of the inner sanctum of men's private lives. Because she herself is not married, Lily doesn't know what to make of this dichotomy. But Lily "...had recovered her sense of her (Mrs. Ramsay) now—this was the glove's twisted finger" (26). Mrs. Ramsay appears to have manic highs and lows, moments of sadness and extremes of happiness, and times when she just wants to be alone.

The bed beside me was empty when I woke this morning. I denied myself the pile of bacon I almost wanted and snuck outside with Patrick's vape pen and a huge mug of tea, and slurped until I was a shade of full as I prepared myself to write.

Ever since I so ridiculously fainted the other day, Bernita is making sure I'm eating every few hours. Or she thinks I am.

245

I'm waiting for Mother with a towel when she comes out of the water. The sun promises everything, but I refuse to believe it. Mother takes the towel and slowly dries herself from her feet upwards. I avert my gaze.

"The towel was so you would cover yourself. Clearly you think you're still living alone."

"Clearly you still think I'm ashamed of my body. Does a bear wear a suit? We're all just animals, Briscoe."

There's no way I'm going to win this one, even though I want to quip about making a suit of bear fur for her.

"By definition, private parts are meant to be just that," I say.

"I ripped up my social contract a long time ago. Seems to me you're on your way to doing the same."

I rub my hands through the fuzzy leaves of a geranium in the nearby stone urn and raise my hand to my nose to inhale the scent reminiscent of green tomatoes. My father used to give me the red-blossomed flowers for my birthdays. I grasp a clump of dirt, squeeze it.

"Neither of the Ramsays was sleeping with others," she says, apropos of nothing.

My hand opens.

She makes a noise through her nose. "You want to know what a marriage is, what it isn't. You think Woolf can tell you? Don't you know she was even more confused than her characters were? At least she could *give* them an opinion, play with her word puppets to try to figure it out, but then she had to spread hers among them, so who knows where her true self landed? That was one conflicted lady. She loved her husband, depended upon him in every way, and yet she felt the need for Vita, to say she wasn't solely dependent on Leonard. She couldn't settle down with feelings for just him because that would make her too ordinary."

The geraniums need deadheading. I drop the dirt and I oblige them. Briskly.

"That's reductive. Of her thinking and of everyone else. No one is ordinary."

"Nonsense." The skin between her eyebrows gathers, making one brow of the generously haired two. "You mean no one wants to be ordinary, and yet nearly everyone is."

She can afford to say that — she has her name on that unordinary list, guaranteed. At least in academia.

"What's our purpose, then? Why are we here?"

"Ah, the true question behind the question. Because if our pettiness doesn't matter, maybe nothing does. I have one answer: *you're* here because your father and I had sex."

Another hunk of dirt I've taken up to pick through shatters in my hands.

I grasp at the most surface concept because the rest of her words are ones to run off into the night with and examine alone. I won't sort them with anyone, not even with my mother.

"You had unprotected sex at thirty? You, carried away by passion? It seems unlikely."

"As a matter of fact, we did not, were not. Science, in all its infinite wisdom, is not foolproof."

I don't ask why she didn't have an abortion. How much hurt would you have me heap upon myself? She'd tell me the truth, which would be something practical and not at all warm and fuzzy. Like, maybe she was too far along when she found out she was pregnant, or maybe she wanted to piss her parents off.

I hear feet on cement as Hoot dashes out in denim shorts so

247

brief the pockets hang below the fringe and cannonballs into the pool, but not before grabbing Mother's towel off her as he passes her. She stands there, naked and laughing, before leaping in after him.

I watch the two frolic (because no other word will do) until Mother climbs out of the pool. Hoot's movements are all the action verbs you can conjure. He stays in the pool, asks me to join him, but I smile a refusal as I hear the sound of Michael's haunted Martin cross the water from parts unknown.

"Want some breakfast?" Mother asks with rare, not entirely unwelcome, sympathy in her eyes as she follows my gaze, pulling the towel completely about herself for my benefit, I suppose.

My arms cross. "You cookin'?"

She is strictly a survivalist cook: sandwiches, canned food. Soup, of course. Her pantry is half full of the pouches. I almost want her to offer me chicken soup.

You'd think she was searching for a plane through fog. At night. She considers.

"Pancakes?"

"Sure."

Bisquick, milk, eggs. Oil. I gather the ingredients for her while she showers. I'm not sure how I will "offhandedly" tell her what proportions are required. I'm hoping she will know to read the box.

Mercifully, by the time she comes downstairs, Bernita has breakfast nearly finished, smoothly putting away the pancake makings one by one while asking about my morning.

Trust me, I am not offended.

My mother tucks enthusiastically into the fried potatoes,

scrambled eggs, bacon, and lightly browned toast Bernita provides. Hoot matches Mother's appetite. When offered a plate, I shake my head.

The others straggle in. What sickens me now seems to tantalize them. My senses are drying up, curling inward like leaves before rain.

"Jalapeño bacon," Bernita says, decisively putting a plate of eggs with four pieces of bacon in front of me, a pile of potatoes. She returns in a moment with toast and jam.

Eggs stolen from the chickens; flesh taken from a pig, all to give life to me that I don't really want. Potatoes grown for no good reason if someone doesn't eat them, minerals leeched from the earth. Bread baked with energy the world could have used for something else. And jam? Macerated fruit. You don't even need to know what that means to hear the violence in it.

I pick up a slice of bacon and sniff it. I nibble a corner. Okay, fine. Bacon's not the worst reason to live. Half a piece of bacon conquered, I hold up the second half to the light.

The murmuring in my head escalates as I bite into the pig flesh. I toss the bacon back onto my plate.

Bernita takes my toast and spreads jam on it. She holds it up to my mouth while she talks to Patrick about the grocery list. Before I know it, my jaws are tired.

She leaves me as she tends to another batch of eggs.

When no one's looking, I switch plates with Michael's empty one. He eats what's on mine without realizing it.

"I'll make pancakes tomorrow," my mother says quietly, touching my arm.

"Of course." I pretend I believe her. We both pretend I would have eaten them.

Who thinks she will ever make those pancakes? Though

we're not at the end of time yet, I think it's safe to issue this spoiler: she won't.

Does it really matter? Can't I buy stacks of them if I really want them? There are grudges to hold on to, and grudges to ditch, for yourself, if for no one else.

I turn my writing focus (such as my focus is) to the problem of Woolf's attitude toward her domestics, her classicism, trying to reconcile her writing of them, her insight into their plight, with her real-life treatment of them; sometimes they overlapped.

The section title for part two of Lighthouse *sounds like the directions for a play: Time Passes. It actually ends with the closing up of the rented cottage for the season before the family abandons it for a decade during the war and their resultant losses.*

The novel's biggest revelation, that Mrs. Ramsay is dead, comes here. Woolf mentions her death in brackets!

Into this narrative gap steps a group who has already been there, though nearly unnamed, and mostly unnoticed: the servants. Life at the cottage without the family, specifically, Mrs. Ramsay, has not continued the same. The sentences in this section are long and sorrowful. The verbs are woeful: "choke, scatter, dwindle," and the like. But as death overtakes the cottage, the family (minus Mrs. Ramsay and at least two of the Ramsay children who have died) announces they are returning after a decade's absence. Only one servant remains from their previous trips: Mrs. McNab. This section of the novel belongs to her. Here, we believe, Woolf will give the previously unrecognized servant her due. Then we begin to read and realize, not so much.

Bernita hands me a lidded travel mug. "Patrick say proteina shaka. Very goods for yous."

I thank her absentmindedly and sit it on the ground beside

me. She stands there until I take a sip that I pretend is a gulp, then leaves. I ease up the lid and pour the remainder into a bush.

Woolf's attitude about domestics shows in Lighthouse; she unflatteringly calls Mrs. McNab "witless" (196) and speaks of her "leering" (196) and "lurching" (197). She depicts her as an ugly, toothless, ruined woman who complains bitterly about her job and about how she is expected to ready a house that has been decaying for a decade. It's cruel to put down a woman who has likely had no option but to be a cleaning woman, an option that has broken her body in service of those who can't, or won't, do the dirty work themselves.

The language in this section is unattractive and broken, too. The sentences are long and winding, as if Mrs. McNab's lengthy tales to her helper, Mrs. Bast, are wound into the very structure of the book.

Here we get the servant's side of the glorious past. We hear of wonderfully elaborate dinner parties that, nevertheless, required washing up after midnight. We hear of Mr. Kennedy, the handsome gardener Mrs. Ramsay was so distrustful of, becoming physically unable to complete the tasks Mrs. Ramsay always kept on him to do. Mrs. Bast's son, George, fills in for him.

The house requires the domestics to bring life back to the place. Eventually, the house and yard work are completed, and the place is ready just in time for what remains of the family and their guests to return. But Woolf never lets us forget Mrs. Ramsay's absence.

Woolf is not only speaking about the role of the wife in a household. In fact, though Mrs. Ramsay is so accomplished and beloved, she takes credit for a difficult dinner, a dish her servant and not she made. It comes naturally to her to take the credit, though she only ordered it done. The servant does not complain

251

about not getting credit, but the reader protests for the servant.

We have a glimpse here of the true angels in the house, the servants. Had Mrs. Ramsay surrendered the title in full, her life might have, could have, become what she desired. Ditto, Woolf. Whereas the servants had to work or starve. Woolf's privilege is on full display here, though the problem loops back around to the problem with society, with classicism and sexism. With art vs. "real life."

No comment. Yes, comment: I think I treat Bernita better than Mrs. Ramsay treated her domestics. Don't I?

And yet, there's this: how can an author, the human being behind the words, write about something unless she realizes the injustice of it? Might we see the entire section as Woolf's very apology I am saying she owes the domestics? How can you write so cruelly about someone without realizing that you are doing exactly that? Without being able to question her directly, I'm not at all sure we can know. But we can interrogate her work for evidence of one or the other.

Truthfully, I have mixed feelings on this one. When you invite someone to be a part of your life by paying them, the money is as much for their discretion as for their service. That applies to all areas.

Around a fire, or the pool. With snacks and drinks. Riffs and humming, growing choruses, and almost-blooming verses. Most musicians want sparse demos with not much more than guitars so that the song itself can be assessed. Michael, it has been established, is not like most musicians.

Summer wars with us. One day warps into the next. I don't pay much attention to the days of the week, the weeks of the month. When you have a deadline (and I have two), you keep plugging away. You march on.

To bed late, get up, write, create music.

Feet in the pool, I tap away on my computer. I argue with Woolf's everlastingly elastic thinking on everything, while my mother does the same of me re: my essay.

Love and lust are the best and the worst influences on songwriting. But emotion alone can't shape music; you've got to have someone come along and lop the right amount of frills off while pretending to not know what they mean. (My job right now and oh so much fun. Not painful At All.)

Their fourth complete song comes in on horseback. Five limps behind, slower, but on time. Six and seven nearly twin, even though I point out that they sound similar. "They're supposed to," Michael says. "We're doing an album."

On his previous albums, Michael's had his heart broken, been in love, in lust, been broke, been drunk, been a blue-collar worker, earn-a-dollar-everyday Joe. He's a master of clever hooks, of drinking songs, of knowing what people want to hear. *Bright Lights and Bar Fights*, *Big Sh@tty City*, *My Truck or My Place*, *Beer Today, Gone Tomorrow*, *In 'Em Denim Shorts* – why go on?

As the album grows, I continue to shrink. The house shrinks, too. Claustrophobia, confinement, trouble us all. Boredom with even ice cream, something once unfathomable, with beer, with hookup apps, with watching Patrick flirt uselessly with all the men and deepen his tan except when Dustin joins him to sunbathe and swim. Boredom with each other, with the pool. With this lack of routine which has become routine.

Art may not be meant to be created by committee, but it is certainly improved by close supervision.

I sit on the side of the pool and circle a big toe in the water,

253

and my finger slips on my keyboard. Without meaning to be, I'm on the local news tab I keep open, and *On the Nash Front* tells me that the Tennessee Coneflowers are "showing up and showing off."

Long Hunter Park is the only spot within Davidson County where you can see them, the article reminds me, as if I could forget.

Though Michael and I have talked about sprinkling my father's ashes among the flowers he loved most, the day we were *this time for sure* supposed to, Michael had a song idea, and of course we couldn't go. The day after that, I was legit sick. Then he didn't bring it up for a week, and I refused to if he couldn't see how important it was to me. Finally, I mentioned it outright, but he wondered aloud if the coneflowers were still in bloom, even though I'd told him they bloom from June to August. If you miss that wide a window, you're actively attempting to, and I told him so. Then we had to go back on the road before we made it to the park.

From across the driveway, I spy arms laden with fern-like leaves sprouting delicate pink fans, rich with the aroma of peach. Mimosas. My mother peeks around her load at me. Virgil pants beside her.

I get a bowl of water for Virgil from the hose. He laps until it's gone. I refill it.

My mother speaks what she's been thinking about with no introduction.

"Nothing's really all that serious if you take the long view. Be sure to get everything you can when you divorce him. He owes you."

She pauses, puts the branches down, and attempts to retie

the bandana around her head. I come behind her and assist.

"I didn't say I was going to divorce him." A pause, then, "I know about Dad's trips to see you."

Her hands reach up and still mine.

"He didn't know I knew."

"When did you find…"

My eyes scan the trees, the sky. "The summer after you went away."

She bends, picks up the branches, and hands them to me. "Hiking was better than watching those two moon over one another and watching you moon over them mooning. It's ridiculous. Why am I here? Do you want me to say something, do something? It turned out I didn't believe in marriage, so my and your father's marriage was open, so I don't know what it's like to expect a closed one. But I can see how much it hurts you that yours has burst wide and I'll do whatever you need me to, but what exactly is that?"

I push the soft blossoms, a showgirl's feathers, to my nose and inhale. Mimosas are vacations on branches. They're my favorite, though Mother couldn't know that, could she?

This is the first (and last, I hope) we've spoken of my parents' marriage being open.

"The coneflowers are blooming," I say, running my hand down the length of the fern-like leaves. "Want to go with me to spread Dad's ashes?"

She squints at the sun until I want to tell her to stop before she goes blind. "Pass," she says. "It's time I head on home."

"I still need help with my thesis. Please." I can't say I need my mommy to stay, that I feel safer, bolder, when she's here. That I'm fading. My hands are thinner. My thighs even flirt with developing a gap. I'm worried that I might melt in the night.

She kicks with a Ked at the dirt that has gone from dry to unable to remember what water is.

"Freeing your father isn't the same as freeing yourself."

We walk through the door of the house and into the kitchen to see if I can find something large enough to stick the branches in.

"Here," Michael says in the other room as he hits a note on his guitar. He wants V. to harmonize with him, and she's not hitting the note. She tries twice, sails past it.

I swing the door open between the kitchen and the dining room and sing it dead on.

"Like that," Michael says, giving me a thumbs up.

I let go of the door and it flaps behind me.

"Mother, let's have G and T's and talk about Virginia and Vita."

If that doesn't keep her here, nothing will.

I press the keys of my laptop as Velvet passes by, and I wish my words were a spell that would cause her to turn into fog and evaporate. The musical coven joins us, and as the chairs and poolside fill, I don't stop typing. Not until I rise and have to sit again quickly. I empty the pretzels from the bag into my hand and funnel the grains of salt at the bag's bottom into my mouth, put the pretzels back into the bag.

My thesis lengthens by five, then seven, pages. I narrow the focus even more.

Woolf's letters, diaries, novels. Fiction is truth; nonfiction is truth, and yet neither are. There is no truth, only perception, and perception depends upon the perceiver.

Afraid that madness is about to strike her again, and fearful that this time she will not recover, not wanting to burden her beloved husband, Woolf drowns herself.

It's evident, then, that Woolf's finger, too, was twisted with much knitting and writing, as twisted as Mrs. Ramsay's view, the view we must not forget Woolf wrote. Just how her mental health affected her writing we can't be sure, but it certainly affected her outlook on life (and death).

Was it easier for her to take charge of her own fate because she was accustomed to making her characters do her bidding?

I realize I have typed my thoughts on the page and delete the last sentence.

The stench of chlorine, a headache from the light just behind my eyes that won't leave me alone.

Patrick claims the place on my other side, and as I stare at V., I whisper:

"Get me a gun."

"A what?"

"Mamma's going rabbit hunting."

He laughs and looks like he wants to piss himself at the same time.

"Relax. I want it for target practice."

"Is your target approximately six foot five, 220 pounds?

"Don't let Michael hear you say you think he's 220 pounds or he won't eat a thing for a month."

"I'm a gay guy in Nashville. Where would I get a gun?"

"What does that have to do with anything? Get on Craig's List, the dark web, or just go to Trinity Lane and wave some cash around."

Michael gets up and walks in my direction with this adorable expression that means he has something funny to tell me and as my face involuntarily remembers what the jackass did, he veers off and mumbles something to no one about how he'll be back.

"A gun?" Patrick asks.

He's right. What would I do with a gun? As desperate as I feel, somehow, I don't see things ending with a bang for any of us, no pun intended.

Virginia and Leonard had a suicide pact. If the Germans took over England, the couple would immolate themselves in the garage. They stored gas there for that very purpose. How difficult would it have been to go from imagining it to doing the act? Even though Virginia wrote that she couldn't see herself going through with it, of course in the end she did, though not for the reason or by the method she had agreed to, and, you know, she died alone.

The novel's third section, "To the Lighthouse," is a fulfillment of the now-dead Mrs. Ramsay's promise that if the next day isn't fair enough to go to the lighthouse, another one will be. Mr. Ramsay is taking this trip with his children, we believe, in honor of his deceased wife, though we are never told this. In this more philosophical section, Lily ruminates on her still-unfinished picture. Lily, in particular, is trying to come to terms with how she feels about Mrs. Ramsay's death — her unfinished painting is one way she tries to process the event.

Lily continues to seek to understand the Ramsays. Once she imagines Mrs. Ramsay in that chair again, knitting in that domestic role, and combines it with her sympathy for Mr. Ramsay, she is finally able to make progress with her painting.

She understands their marriage and is able to accept her own decision not to marry. Her "untwisting" their marriage is imperative. "One wanted, she thought, dipping her brush deliberately, to be on a level with ordinary experience, to feel simply that's a chair, that's a table, and yet at the same time, it's a miracle, it's an ecstasy. The problem might be solved after all" (103).

The Ramsays are an ordinary miracle, and with this realization, Lily is able to solve the paradox: "So that is marriage, Lily thought, a man and a woman looking at a girl throwing a ball" (38).

Months ago, when I realized Velvet was influencing Michael even down to his stagewear (though I was "sure" it was nothing), I mentioned it to my mother in a roundabout way in an email. She sent me a copy of *Lighthouse* as if I didn't already have two copies with different covers. I hinted again. She sent me an ornate edition of *Orlando* and suggested I concentrate on grad school. So color me surprised that *now* she's giving me advice.

Now, Mother encourages me to write; Bernita encourages me to eat. Patrick has forbidden me to diet *or* overeat, and I've told him he has to pick a lane. Michael runs his fingers over my ribs at night when he thinks I'm sleeping. He touches my spine when I turn from him. Still, he won't answer why he asked V. to divorce Robert. It's self-evident, but I want to hear him say it.

I'm literally eating fog, vaping cherry and cotton candy. You'd be surprised how full smoke can make you, how candy store flavors can convince you that you are cared for, even as they cause your lungs to ache. You can live on so much less than you think, though there are things you cannot live without. Better to have never tasted of them to begin with.

I've given up all but essential conversation with V. I don't speak to her, don't look at her, except when we're working.

V.'s velvety voice permeates the house. First the ceiling, then the walls, then the floor. Can't walk without sliding in it. Her

259

art deceives both her and nearly me. The more she sins against me, the more innocent her recorded voice sounds.

When I'm outdoors, someone or another puts sunblock on me, because I have given up doing it. I've lost all my mothering instincts, for self or others.

Nothing matters but finishing: this album. My thesis.

When I swing up my laptop's lid today, I close my ears.

I type about the aristocratic and elitist nature of Woolf not giving Mrs. Ramsay (or Mr.) a first name. How they become this universal symbol for marriage. Their marriage is uniquely theirs, though. How dare we judge it?

I check because I think I've written about it earlier in my essay, then decide I don't care if I have. The reader can just turn the page if I have already covered it.

A voice pierces the bubble. "You're making the case that their marriage is a good one?" Mother says over my shoulder.

"No. Just that it works for them."

Standing, I pace the kitchen. My mother points to the Nutter Butter in my hands. I look down, only then noticing one hand vapes, one eats, and I didn't know I was doing either. Fascinating. She is there, then she's not.

I put my vape pen on counter and throw the soggy cookie into the trash, return to the cabinet, get another cookie, and go to the fridge where I cover the sweet with whipped topping from a can. My hands shake and I'm freezing. Funny how the body can know it needs things the mind does not.

Virgil sits at my feet and eats the crumbs I drop. I root the package out of the cabinet and join him on the floor. Together, we finish every last one.

Michael comes into the room, heads to the fridge before he sees me and changes course, bending to kiss me before picking up the empty cookie sleeve and making a face.

Everything in me, even what knows better, gushes mentally towards him, makes a thousand stupid excuses for him.

"I think there are more." I try to get up, stumble, and go to the cabinet, open the doors, rummage around.

Then arms are around me and he turns me, puts his chin on my head. He moves his hands to my hips, and then to my waist.

I reach my face towards his despairing one and kiss him to keep him from asking the questions or offering the explanations that I don't want him to, not just now. He kisses me back and lifts me onto the counter. I moan and Virgil barks. Sharply.

Just past Michael, V. stands in the kitchen doorway. I wrap my legs around the unaware Michael and smirk. She flees.

But after, something wants out, and the cookies win. When Michael asks me to shower with him, I tell him I need the bathroom to myself for a moment. He asks me to leave the door open. I try to shut it; he puts his foot in the door.

The cookies are dissolving in my stomach, traveling warp speed through my blood system, plumping my fat cells, expanding my thighs. If only I can keep that from happening, maybe the tenderness in Michael's face, his concern for me, will remain. As disappointing as it is to think that love is guided by the eye, I fear it might be true.

A soft rap at our bedroom door announces Ben, who whisks Michael away to hear a new melodic bass run that he's excited about. Michael leaves with a faint apology, and I get out what I can and put on my running shoes. I don't care how hot it is out.

I only make it half a mile before slowing to a walk and

painfully plodding back, cursing my body every sluggish step of the way.

Bernita puts lunch on the picnic table, the second of the three battles I fight a day. We gather around cold cuts, croissants, deli-made salads, and a stack of red plastic cups with a jug of sacred Southern sweet tea.

As my phone rings, I swallow the miniscule bite, resenting not having been given time to savor the sweet pickle chunk I allowed myself.

"Hey, Jolene. How goes it?"

V. slaps her hands to quiet everyone.

"Give us until Thursday?" Which is only three days away.

After I hang up, Michael daisy-chains curses. V. turns her head and chides him.

"Okay, it's time to get some demos mixed down, whether they're perfect or not, Michael," I say at his grimace. "Because Drake's coming. Thursday."

"We should pray," V. says, automatically folding her hands as if her faith could ward off everything from mosquitoes to a nuclear attack.

"*You* should definitely pray," I say, pointing my fork at her.

Michael attempts to touch me in bed that night, but I manage to move just beyond his reach. I roll myself in the white top sheet.

"Three days," I mutter, and he assures me the music *will* be ready.

I switch on the lamp.

"How?"

He rubs his scalp. "We're not as far away as you might think. Maybe you haven't been paying attention."

"Attention? All I do is pay attention."

"You know…" he bows his head.

"What? What were you going to say?"

"The only thing you've been paying attention to the past few months before all of this is your precious thesis and the inner workings of *my* tour."

My eyes shoot him.

"I'm serious," he says, plumping his pillow and sitting up.

"You mean managing you, right? Because I'm way behind on my thesis."

His face makes that exaggerated "Oh really" expression.

"Besides, how would you even know with all your syco-phants?"

"Maybe I wouldn't need them if my wife could keep her freakin' nose out of dusty old books."

"You have got to be kidding me!" Technically, what he sees is me reading an e-book most days on the road.

Irrelevant.

He lowers his head. "I'm not." Then he raises it and there's the young, earnest guy I haven't seen in months. His face pulses with mesmerizing vulnerability, the kind you either want to kiss or punch.

"You go shopping during my concerts; you only criticize my music. You're right, you do manage me — all you *do* is manage me, like I'm a car to be driven from place to place. Everything I used to write used to be for you, about you. But you don't care about my music anymore."

I want to say he's wrong, of course he's wrong. Maybe he's right, but not in the way he thinks he is – I can't afford to think of the heartbreak that is his music. I can't sink down into it, enjoy it like a fan or even a human. I have a job to do that I haven't been doing very well the past weeks: manage Michael. Market Michael.

When did he become a product, even down to Mickey the cologne?

Here's where I'm supposed to reach out and poof, all is well. But I can't, because we only have three days and I need Michael to be a touch miserable because that's when he produces his best work.

Oh no, he's not a product at all.

"Why did you ask her to divorce Robert? I can only think of one reason."

His eyes glint.

"You intend to divorce me and marry her. There's no other explanation."

He beats his pillow, holds himself stiffly for the longest of times.

"Actually, I want her to divorce him so I can administer the rights to her parents' music. He has no clue what to do with them. Their greatest hits should be available on every app out there. She could create themed compilations and duets. Whatever. He's too shortsighted."

"You mean you aren't planning on divorcing me?"

He sighs. "She won't do it, anyway."

It's not about me; it's not about her. It's about the music behind her. Her family's music. I laugh and can't stop.

How much better am I, trying to market him the way I am?

"You don't want to be a cologne, do you?"

"No way."

"Eh, the sample smelled like mold and decaying hay anyway.

264

I'll see if I can get you out of your contract."

We don't discuss it, but I'm going to speak with Ben about taking over managing Michael; Ben's been saying he's ready to retire from the road. Who better? Why did I ever suppose I could, should, manage Michael?

When he falls asleep, I get up and take a shower, drink a cup of Earl Grey, plain, on the deck and watch the sun rise. Virgil wanders out the patio door I've left half open and sits beside me. I talk to him the way I used to talk to my dad while he slept. The dog licks my hand as I tell him everything in my heart.

A door opens and closes somewhere in the house. Someone sings a few jagged notes.

If only Michael could believe in his own music, he wouldn't need V's family's so much.

After dinner, Michael and V. huddle outdoors with a tablet and pen.

Michael plays his guitar quietly.

"Listen to this." She sings lyrics that are not any less syrupy than her last version, but her smooth voice nearly convinces me until I listen harder.

"Almost." I pause, struggling for a kinder way to phrase what I want to say. "You have to use supermarket words in country to show love. You're not making a gourmet dinner, though you are feeding your listeners. It has to be relatable if you want it to sell."

She bristles. "My songs have done fine in the past."

"Far in the past. Do you want to play 'Raindrops of Love' at every show for the rest of your life?"

I sit beside Velvet and read. "Listen: 'Sweet sips of summer

265

sing slowly by on angels' wings.' I think you're trying to say that nature is God's creation and that you relate to it more than you do to people, right?"

Her eyes widen.

"So how can you say that in a way that someone listening to it might want to hear it again and not flinch with embarrassment?"

Michael rubs his hands together and blows on them. It's not cold, my stare says, and he stills his hands.

"We sip summer from Mason jars?" Velvet tests.

"Better. Much better."

Velvet's shoulders relax.

"You know that country can be sentimental. That's not the issue – that's a defining characteristic of it. But it has to be grounded in the physical, with only nods to God, okay? It can't be embarrassing. Think: an edge of the everyday, right, Michael? These people actually go to the bathroom. You don't need to mention it, but you need to understand that. Your fans are people who wake up every morning and rush to work, punch a time clock. They create or ship the things you need. They are the reason you have the life you have. They listen to music to make their workday go faster. They go out on Saturday nights, maybe to the Moose, to a local bar, and they play pool and have a few beers. They play your songs when they dance. They play your songs when they make love. They play your songs when they're heartbroken. You're giving them a razor to carve at their feelings. This isn't just you making a living. It's you giving people something vital, something they need to become whole. You can help them heal."

My hands shake. My eyes leak. I love these country people, even with their stupid big trucks in every song. I love that they don't put on airs. As heady as Woolf is, country music is simple and straightforward, and I need it, too.

I close my eyes and try not to think about the problems they are working on in the industry, as they are in most: Racism. Sexism. Exclusion. Intolerance. Those Confederate flags. At least they're trying. It's so easy to point a finger at the unpretentious because they're not hiding anything.

Soon V's song swarms with trucks, jeans, bent knees and praying hands. I let it go. We'll pare it back before we record. When I hear wedding rings referenced, I call for a break. A long one.

I go indoors, not knowing what I'm searching for until I find her tossing books into her suitcase. My mother continues packing her books after she sees me.

"They're not even writing good songs," she says as she rotates a hardcover book.

"How would you know?"

"Come home with me." Her face wrinkles in concern.

I pick up a denim shirt that's sprawled on the bed and fold it.

"You're just going to sit there and take it, aren't you?"

I pick up a copy of *Flush* and fling it into the suitcase. "You don't even believe in monogamy, you hypocrite!"

She yanks the book out, fits it back in between two novels. "Darlin', I don't have to: *you* believe in monogamy. I've seen you slinking around here, trying to write it all out. Woolf has answers. But maybe she doesn't have yours. You're the only one who does."

"This is as good a time as any to tell you that I don't intend to finish my essay anyway any more than you will ever finish your book. If you were going to, you would have. So I'm thinking you're the last person I should listen to. You gave up your daughter, essentially your marriage, not to mention your parents' money, to live alone like some sea captain and your white whale is a land shark and you still can't hook it."

Her shoulders sag, but not for long.

"Don't think I don't know what *you're* doing, Briscoe. You've had your own white whale, haven't you? The minute I mentioned Woolf had attempted a novel-essay and given up on it, I knew you'd take it on. Whether you were conscious of it or not, you've never been writing an essay. At least not *just* an essay."

I sink onto the bed as her idea takes hold. I'd have to change some names, some details, for sure. I've been writing a creative response to Woolf's work. Of course I have.

"When you're done with it, send it to me. I'll see if I can get someone at the school's press to take a look at it. It would certainly have university press appeal."

I touch her arm. "I'm sorry for what I said about your book."

"No, you're right. I've always felt so guilty about leaving you for it and so unsure what I'd do after it was finished that I wouldn't let myself finish it. I just couldn't admit it."

Music puffs up the stairs, and she frowns.

"Seriously, come with me until this album is over. You're making yourself sick, literally."

When I don't answer, she disappears down the hall, lugging her suitcase. I follow with her bag. She's already whistled for Virgil.

"I can't watch you go through this. Make sure you send me that manuscript," she says, inclining her head goodbye towards the band as she takes the bag from me. "And get some help, why don't you? You're beginning to look like *her*, and that's not a compliment."

She salutes me and drops her thumb to her nose and wiggles her fingers at Michael. He doesn't even notice.

"Don't go," I holler after she's already made it back to her vehicle, loaded it. Virgil barks at me through the window.

Her Jeep swiftly disappears down the lane.

We work nonstop. My frown erases one of V.'s fluffy words after another when she asks my opinion, and when she doesn't, my pen still strikes. She humbly agrees to most suggestions.

Hoot tests his drum set like he's summoning something from another dimension.

Josh plugs his Telecaster into his amp, jostles the cord to rid it of its hum. He, at least, appreciates a crisp Tele. His energy is most evident in his leads where he exudes the perfect high-wire tension that keeps them from falling apart; he lands them, every time.

Ben raises his Fender Precision and thrums a few low notes, nods.

Hoot crisscrosses his drumsticks and hits them against one another, announcing the song's beginning: 1, 2, 3. *And now...*

Michael has reluctantly shifted to rhythm guitar in the past few years to focus on his singing. I can see his fingers itch when he's "only" playing rhythm.

Normally, the parts would all be recorded individually, even on demos as far as Michael is concerned, but there's no time. It's going to mean more takes, recording live, but that should still be faster and provide adequate demos.

This song is a duet, as most on the album are, and Michael begins singing in his guts-on-display way about unexpected love and his eyes spark. Now Velvet enters with lyrics I

269

have helped shape, and though I know what's coming as she sings about unanticipated reciprocation, it doesn't make it any easier to hear.

This album is not checklist country, not exactly, but there are elements of that, thanks to V. Summertime escapades, festivals, sweaty summer evenings, all of the things new love brings and none of its inevitable heartache. Then the heartbreaking, parting-is-such-sweet sorrow song. The album's working title is *Love's Legacy*.

Michael and V.'s voices weave impossibly tightly at the song's end.

"I'm going to Long Hunter Park," I don't mean to say. "Coming?"

"But Drake will be here in an hour," Michael says.

"I don't care."

"Tomorrow," he says, strumming his guitar.

"Michael," I ask again. But his back is to me.

"Please?" I touch his shoulder, and he turns towards me, but only partway. V. busies herself with her notebook.

My hand slowly releases Michael's shoulder.

I'm about to leave when I spin back around.

"Michael, please. Please come with me to spread my father's ashes. I need you to do this. Please?"

The others move to the opposite side of the room with made-up tasks.

My pride feels like I've just fallen off a bike in front of my entire fifth grade class, but I persist.

"You said you would when I was ready. I'm ready now."

He stares at me like I've lost it, and then seems to take in my clasped hands, how I sway towards him. Even though Velvet clears her throat and nods at him as if he should go, he doesn't take his guitar off. I hate her for imagining she has enough power over him to persuade him. I hate that neither of us do.

****

Highway 100 steadily elevates, nothing but guardrail, wild-flowers, and trees at this point. There should be a sign that warns you of the steep desolation as you pass Junction 96 until you reach Brush Creek Road. My cabin is one of the few things in between the zones.

I pull off at the cabin and retrieve the Maxwell House coffee tin my father's ashes are stored in, (because he asked me to do that, not because I'm cheap) and continue my drive.

At Long Hunter Park, in the shallow dirt of the cedar glade dozens, maybe hundreds, of Tennessee Coneflowers keep watch, their east-facing blooms thriving in heat and conditions that would kill off a less hardy plant.

The flowers, the first plant ever added to the endangered species list in the U.S., were removed from that list in 2011, just after my father died.

On my way to them, I'm interrupted by a low mist of purplish pink stars dotted with an inner halo of orange stamens that hazes the area: limestone fame flowers. I admire them thoroughly.

Beyond them, my father's beloved coneflowers. I kneel among them as they sway, gently touching a purple one, a yellow one. I smooth the jagged petals of a bloom when my phone rings.

"Where are you?" Michael asks.

"You know where I am." I hold the coffee can in the crook of my arm.

"Drake wants to know why you aren't here."

"I've done my bit for album and country. I hope the best for it, I really do. Tell Drake I said that."

"I wish I could be there with you," Michael says.

For a beat, I wonder if I'm wrong about Michael. Everything in me wants to be wrong. Just as much in me knows I'm not.

"What's stopping you?"

When he doesn't reply, I end the call and put my phone in my rear pocket.

At the glade's edge, I walk onto the limestone, take off the can's lid, and turn in a circle while telling my father goodbye. The wind blows the dust across the lichen and into a spindly stand of coneflowers at the glade's perimeter before the remainder whooshes on through and into the sky.

Back at my cabin, Bernita's green Corolla is parked on the far side of the circular drive. I make a mental note to buy her something newer to drive. I don't ask myself why she's here. Of course she's here.

I creak open the cabin's screen door with one hand as I juggle the empty coffee can and make my way inside, letting the door slam behind me to announce my arrival, as if my vehicle's tires on the gravel haven't already done so.

Bernita and Patrick are setting the bare table with napkins and plastic cutlery.

The smoky tang of barbeque rises from the white pyramid of boxes at the table's center, and I wonder idly if Mr. Ramsay wouldn't have been happier if he'd been content with an actual table and not the notional one made of his philosophy.

I put the can on the edge of the dresser, and I embrace the pair or maybe they embrace me. All I know is arms and sobs are everywhere. Patrick can't watch anybody cry without joining in, and I tell him so.

Eventually, I wash my hands.

The three of us sit at the table and hand around containers of seasoned pork and coleslaw, wide green beans and bacon, a foil bag of barbeque chips. We stare at my loaded fork silently until I bring it to my mouth and, after a time, empty it. Another forkful takes just as much effort to swallow, but I manage.

"Woolf said there should be a colony of nothing but the arts, no marrying allowed, nothing but deep contemplation of music, books, and paintings," I say. My fork nears my mouth, but I toss it onto my plate. I allow the silence to take hold for as long as I can bear it, which isn't long, believe you me.

"You know I'm going to ask for custody of you both," I say.

The gentle rain of our laughter fills the cabin.

"Hon, I have the number of a clinic," Patrick says.

I think of a thousand details I will have to work out for Ben to take over before I can leave for good, and it feels as if I'm sending my child off to camp for the first time, handing over the Michael machine. My resolve wavers, and I try to imagine I can survive on a half ration of his love supplemented by his brilliant performances. It would almost be worth it.

My phone rings. After I see who's calling, I reject the call and turn off my phone.

Bernita clears the table. Patrick and I help.

About the Author

Drēma Drudge is the award-winning author of the novels *Victorine (March 2020)* and *Southern-Fried Woolf (January 2023)*. A graduate of the Naslund-Mann Graduate School of Writing, she and her husband, musician and writer Barry Drudge, have two grown children, a granddog, and live in a picturesque town in Indiana. They also host the podcast MFA Payday. Learn more about Drēma and get a free short story at: www.dremadrudge.com.

CPSIA information can be obtained
at www.ICGtesting.com
Printed in the USA
BVHW031701270123
657316BV00005B/231